FIGMENT

The dragon seemed to rise out of the hill ahead just before Aleon reached the crest. Less than fifty paces away, it rose on its back legs to stand five times the height of both man and horse combined. A slow rumble, almost a purr, began deep in the dragon's throat quickly rising into a frightening challenge that rattled the stones at his feet. Terrified by the intense sound, Aleon's destrier reared back over his haunches.

The war-horse was trained to battle, not to endure the presence of a dragon: the horse stumbled forward and the Templar found himself facing a wall of fist-sized red scales. The horse twisted to the left and ran along one wing. Aleon let his sword arm swing free. The sword tore into the wing, cutting a shallow groove through scales and muscle.

With a squawk that would have made the Templar laugh if he hadn't still been trying desperately to stay on his frothing horse, the huge beast hastily began to rise. Aleon was astonished to see what had to be surprise and maybe even amusement in the monster's eyes. Then the wind from its massive wings sent the knight's horse speeding off in a new round of panic. By the time Aleon was able to regain control of his mount, the dragon was gone.

At least now he was certain that dragons did exist.

Dragon's Eye

Edited by

CHRISTOPHER STASHEFF

DRAGON'S EYE

Copyright © 1994 by Bill Fawcett & Associates

All rights reserved, including the right to reproduce this book or portions thereof in any form.

A Baen Books Original

Baen Publishing Enterprises
P.O. Box 1403
Riverdale, N.Y. 10471

ISBN: 0-671-87609-0

Cover art by Darrell K. Sweet

First printing, July 1994

Distributed by
Paramount
1230 Avenue of the Americas
New York, N.Y. 10020

Printed in the United States of America

TABLE OF CONTENTS

The chill bit at him, and he hurried to the warm straw and the comforting smell of horse.

It was hot. Hotter than hell, where the pagan dogs would burn forever. Karl was surprised for a moment—surprised that it was high summer and the setting sun was hot, surprised that he was young, moving without pain. Swift and fluid like an otter, his blows struck with bear strength. The knowledge that he dreamed faded.

The Saxon shieldwall was buckling. Locked together, the battle lines lurched, then moved a long step backward, back toward the great wooden temple that burned behind the enemy host. Flame birds crowed from the thatch of the roof, casting yellow light on the writhing carved figures of beasts and gods and men that covered its upswung rafters and door pillars. The dry crackling smell covered the scents of blood and dung and sweat from the thousands of men fighting and dying below. The swelling roar blurred their war shouts and the screams of the wounded.

Karl smashed his shieldboss forward into a yelling flaxen-bearded face, felt bone crunch beneath the iron. His sword hacked down into the neck of another, a dull cleaving feeling as the edge cut through a steerhide jerkin and into meat and bone. The Saxon line buckled and Karl shoved through, knocked one man sprawling with his shield and then blocked the thrust of a spear with it. The footlong head stuck in the tough leather and wood; he chopped overarm at the shaft, behind the yard of iron wire wound around it beneath the point. The wood cracked across.

His comrades and sworn men pushed through at his back, guarding him from the Saxon spears, turning to take men on either side in the flank. A champion and his thegns hurled themselves at the Frankish warriors, desperate to close the gap. Karl grinned beneath his high-peaked helm and set himself, knees bent and round shield up beneath his eyes. The Saxon wore a spangen-helm of riveted plates, with a guard of chain mail hanging like a Saracen woman's veil below his cold blue eyes; his leather jerkin was sewn with rings of iron and brass, and he bore a light axe in one hand, a small buckler in the other. It was painted with the device of a red snake, grasping its tail in its jaws.

Karl raised his sword until the hilt was above his head, the blade between his shoulders. "*Christ and the emperor!*" he shouted. "Come and be slain!"

"*Wodan, ho-la, Wodan!*" the Saxon replied.

Then there was no time for words. The axe darted for his leg. His shield moved, and the sharp pattern-welded steel head bit into leather and linden wood, hewing chips. Karl roared and cut downward with his long slash-ing sword; the Saxon moved swiftly, relaxing one knee to take him out of the way and bringing the buckler around and up. The iron banged off the slanted surface, and the buckler punched out at him. He blocked it with his shield, caught the haft of the axe on his swordblade. They skirled together, the iron bands on the axe-haft grinding over the steel of his sword.

For long moments the two men strained against each other, locked like rutting stags in the springtime, their feet churning dirt made muddy with the blood of the fallen. They were knee to knee, close enough to smell each other's sweat, close enough to see the hate and battle lust in each other's eyes.

Strong, Karl thought with surprise. Few men could stand against him so. They broke apart, heaving back-ward, and cut at each other. Metal rang on metal, banged on shields. *Fast*. The Saxon was as fast as the serpent painted on his shield. The men around them paused for an instant, panting, while the leaders fought. Then Karl's foot slipped on a patch of mud. Steel punched his side, driving the iron mail through the padding beneath and into his skin. Breath hissed out between clenched teeth, and the axe rose to kill. In desperation he thrust the point of his sword at his foeman's face. The move was utterly unexpected—swords were not spears—and the rounded tip of the weapon shot up beneath the hanging veil of chain.

The Saxon screamed, thick and bubbling. He fell backward; his thegns rushed in, some bearing him away despite his thrashings, others closing ranks to hold off the enemy and buy their lord's life with their own. Over their shoulders the Saxon leader shouted, his voice blurred by his wound and the guttural local dialect of German:

"We meet again! I eat your heart, Frank!"

Karl forced himself erect, sucked air into his lungs. His eyes scanned the ranks; the enemy were weakening everywhere. Banners moved forward, marked with the Cross.

"*Jesu Kristos!*" he bawled. "Forward!"

The Franks formed a wedge on either side of him, bristling with spears. They struck the Saxon rearguard and stabbed, cut, clubbed them to earth. The lines had given way to clumps and bands of men who fought or fled, the Saxon host ravelling away toward the trees. Frankish cavalry from either flank pursued, but Karl waved his men on towards the temple doors. Bronze covered that oak, bronze and iron and gold, but they swung open under spearbutts.

Within was a great hall, reaching upward to a maze of rafters. The floor was smooth planks, not the rushes of a nobleman's dwelling; every inch of the walls was a riot of carving and painted wood. Alone in the center of the haildom stood the great log pillar carved into the likeness of the Irminsul—son of Seax, son of Wodan, god of the mainland Saxons. Ruddy light from the burning thatch made it seem to bleed. So did the red gold all around it. The blood of the sacrifices hung from the rafters was no more crimson; they were of the three kinds, hawk and horse and man. The man wore the Romish vestments and tonsured head of a Christian priest; Karl felt his face swell with anger at the sight. From the groans and cries behind him, it was the wealth of gold that struck his followers' hearts—and there was no reason Christ's man should not grow rich. Especially when he was the most promising of the Emperor's knights. . . .

Three men stood between them and the pillar. Old men, grey and white in the beards that reached to their waists; they were richly dressed in the ancient style, caps of stiffened doghide on their heads. One bore a warhammer with a head of polished stone.

"Go," he said. "The god takes back his house in fire, and you tread on holy ground. The god honors brave men; touch nothing here and you may live."

"Apostate!" Karl said. The Saxons had surrendered to the Emperor before, made peace and agreed to pay tribute and accept the true faith. They were rebels, not foemen. "Your life is forfeit. Take them!"

His men hung back; despite the order, despite the gold, despite the increasing heat as the thatch fire spread to the dense old oak timbers above. The ruddy light swept across the haildom's interior in flame and shadow, and the carvings seemed to move, painted beasts turning their eyes on living men. It was not so very long since the Franks had followed the Old Ones. Many of his men were Thuringians and other easterners, from lands converted generations after Clovis. They feared.

Karl knew his duty; the cross about his neck was a charm more potent than any heathen idol.

"Your demon cannot stand against Christ," he said, striding near. "His priest will be avenged."

"His priest cursed our king," the guardian of the shrine said. "The blood of a magician makes a strong curse. Even now that curse comes upon him."

He smiled. Karl felt his battle fury break free once more. He roared and swung; the steel was blunted and notched, but it sank deep into the heathen priest's side. He staggered, a loop of pink gut showing through his tunic. The more surprise when he struck in his turn, the stone warhammer chopping down on Karl's undefended shoulder. Mail would turn an edge, but it was no protection from a crushing blow.

Pain, pain lancing down his arm. He dropped the sword and staggered, breast to breast with the old man. And the heathen still smiled, with blood a sheet down his side.

"I curse you," he said. "I curse your tomorrows, until the battle fought is ended twice and curse by curse is slain."

A woman screamed.

Karl combed straw out of his grey-streaked beard, shaking off the dream—the same dream as always, haunting him like a night hag. The woman was probably no business of his. Then she screamed again—words, this time, and in a Frankish accent. A man cried out in pain as well. He came up out of the straw, snatching at his round shield as he did. The stable door banged open onto a dawn that held sunlight, weak and watery with autumn, but sunlight none the less.

A gang of youths was grouped around the woman; they'd pulled her off her palfrey, which was snorting and backing. One of them was clutching a slashed arm, dancing about and howling threats; as he watched a staff knock the knife out of the woman's hand.

They'd also pulled down her bodice, and obviously had more in mind, grabbing at her legs beneath her skirts despite her blows and curses. The woman was young but no girl, with black hair and green eyes, well-favored but not a noblewoman; Karl thought she might be a house servant, from the silver collar about her neck.

"Halt, swine hounds," he grated in a voice like millstones, and drew his sword despite the twinge in his shoulder.

His bones felt stiff and sore this morning, and the weak fall sun was not enough to warm them. He lumbered. That simply made him look more dangerous, like an illtempered bear prodded out of his den untimely and turning to rend the hunters.

"Stand off, Frank; this is no affair of yours."

The young Saxon's words were bold, but the grip on his cudgel was white-knuckled, and he looked right and left for the reassurance of his pack. None of them bore a sword or spear, although most had the *seax*, the long single-edged knife of their tribe, thrust under their belts.

Karl grinned and kept walking; the others backed out of his way. The leader cursed as he passed, and lashed out with the club. *The old boar knows*, Karl thought; he'd twitched his shield into the way before the younger man even started to move. You lost speed as you aged, but experience could compensate, if you had the wits. He slammed the hilt of his sword into the young Saxon's mouth and he went down like an oxen in the shambles, crawling in the grey slick mud of the laneway and spitting blood and teeth. Behind Karl's back came a shrill bugling, and the sound of crashing wood. A tall Ardennes stallion came trotting out into the street between the rows of huts half-sunken into the ground. He was sixteen hands at the shoulder and shaggy-massive; his eye rolled as he came up behind his master, and he chopped eagerly at the mud, throwing up huge clods with his platter hooves.

The Frank still smiled, showing the gaps in his teeth, and let the heavy broadsword swing negligently back and forth. "I am the Emperor's man," he said mildly.

Implying that the local count would send soldiers if he disappeared; no longer strictly accurate, but he'd said the same thing often enough over the years when it *was* the truth for the words to carry conviction. Two of the village louts took their friend under the armpits and helped him away; the rest scattered.

The knight turned back to the woman; she'd pulled and pinned her dress back together, which was a pity—a fine pair of breasts they'd been.

"Thank you, my lord," she said.

Frankish right enough, he thought—from the Rhinelands, at a guess. Those from further west had a whistling accent, when they hadn't abandoned the old tongue altogether for Roman speech. Karl thought that foolish; old ways were best, and had made the Franks masters of lands broader than Rome had ever commanded. Although he himself could speak Latin—the spoken tongue—well enough to be understood anywhere in Gaul and to give simple commands in Hispania or Italy. Writing and the pure ancient language of the Caesars were for priests, of course.

"What are you doing here unescorted, wench?" he asked. Her horse was good, and the saddle well-made; her clothes were fine-woven wool, dyed saffron and blue. She looked him boldly in the eye, which he liked, as she retrieved her knife and sheathed it.

"On my mistress' business, my lord," she said, "which could not wait."

Karl nodded. "Come. Best we go." Best not to give those young dogs time to think; think of a spear thrust from behind a bush on a forest road, for instance.

With that in mind he saddled his war-horse and put the pack frame on the ordinary mount he kept for travel; his helm went on his head, and the long lance with the crossbar below the point rested in his right hand with its butt on the stirrup iron. The war-horse snorted again and sidled as the woman came up at his side. Perhaps it was her moonblood time; that disturbed stallions. They cantered out of the village and through its fields, stubble hidden in the last of the morning mist. She produced bread and hard cheese from her saddlebags, and a skin of real wine; he drank with relish, belching and smacking his lips. Once he'd drunk good wine daily, at the table of the Emperor, but that was long years ago.

"My name is Ermenagarde, lord," the woman said. "What brings so brave a warrior to these lands?"

It was a goodly while since a pretty, well-spoken young woman had looked at him so. "I am Karl von Obersberg, the emperor's knight," Karl replied. "The old emperor, Karl the Great. Most recently I fought the heathen Danes in the north, for the margrave of the North Mark. I travel to Franconia to take up my lands."

Her look was demure, but he knew she saw the shabbiness of his harness—his weapons and armor were good, and well kept, but the rest of his gear was not. And he had no servants .... *And the fief in Franconia is barely more than three peasant farms,* Karl thought sourly. Once he'd have given as much to a huntsman who served him well. He shook his head. Where had the years gone? The years when he'd been the strongest of the emperor's paladins, the bravest, one whose voice was listened to in council. There was no time he could point to and say: *Here I failed.* It had crept up on him, like the gray hair and the pain in his bones. *Enough.*

"What of you, wench?" he said roughly.

"My mistress is taken prisoner, as she rode to her wedding," she said, not calmly, but with fear well kept. "Her dowry with her, a great treasure, and all her escort slain or fled. She is of high birth, and her father's only child. I ride to bring her kinsmen; for vengeance, or to pay ransom."

Karl grunted and looked around. They had ridden out of the ryefields, into deep oak forest. That thinned, oaks gave way to pines, pine to naked heath knee-tall on the horses; the damp floral scent filled his nostrils. This was good country for bandits, and the new emperor did not keep them down as his mighty father had. Landloupers in the woods, Dane raiders on the seas—things were not as they had been in the great days.

"These are evil times," he agreed; the bride's father would have to pay a second dowry to get her free, and the bridegroom wouldn't be getting a virgin. "The count's castle is near," he said. "Why didn't you ride there, if masterless men overfell you?"

Ermenagarde hesitated. A suspicion narrowed Karl's eyes; bandits would find a knight's gear very useful indeed. But if she were a decoy, what of the struggle at the village? That slash she gave one of the louts was real enough; it might kill the man if it mortified, and wounds often did.

"Lord," she said slowly, "I fear if I tell you, you will think me crazed or demon-ridden. Come first to the count's fortress, and then I will tell you—and then you will believe."

"We can't reach the castle today," Karl said. Not without pushing the horses to exhaustion, which he would not do. A man with winded horses was no better than a man on foot, if he had to fight or run.

"Then, lord, I promise that I will tell you at the count's fort, but not before. And my word will be true, as God is my witness."

He nodded shortly. They spoke little after that, stopping a few times to let the horses drink or graze or roll. They made camp beneath an ash tree, tall and great, still with most of its leaves. When they'd eaten, Ermenagarde came to his blankets with a smile and no false modesty; he was glad of that, although of course it was the due of his rank. It would be a short ride to the count's in the morning, and he could demand hospitality—demand men to hunt down these bandits, if it came to that. He was feeling kindly inclined.

"Christ have mercy, God have mercy," Karl said, crossing himself again and again.

The count's castle was built in the familiar pattern the old emperor had built to stake down his conquests—a rectangle of great upright logs on an earthen mound, with a three-story tower on another mound in the center, also of logs, laid horizontally, notched and squared. On the inner side of the fortress wall would be quarters for soldiers and servants, a smithy, storehouses, a well— whatever was needful. This was an isolated outpost, and so there was little in the way of a village outside the fort.

Now there was much less of everything. The thatch and wattle buildings were knocked flat, scorchmarks and mud to mark their passing. The huge oak timbers of the fortress wall were scattered like twigs. Many lay tumbled, the thick rawhide bindings which had laced them together snapped like single hairs. Others were frayed into splinters, as if they had exploded; still others were scorched and charred, though that might have happened afterwards, when thatch fell on cookfires and braziers. Fires often started so, in a burg that had been stormed.

"Catapults might have done this," he murmured to himself, drawing his sword and dismounting.

It was more for reassurance than otherwise. The emperor had catapults at Aachen, from the Greeks, or the Saracen caliph at Baghdad, gifts like the elephant that had shivered through a few winters in the north. Nobody would be building Roman war engines here, in this desolation of backwardness. This stank of magic.

What was inside was worse. Men—and women— clawed and torn, as if by some great beast, and burned by a fire like that of the Greeks. The count himself lay by the ruined gate of the inner tower. His face was still intact, locked in a grimace of despair; the helm had rolled free, and his bare pate was wet and shiny. The rest of him was charred. Karl prodded with the point of his sword, and found the expensive mailshirt the man had worn was now soldered together into a rigid cage of welded iron rings. The sword by his hand was melted like a wax candle. The charred scraps of a nightshirt beneath the armor proclaimed that the attack had come in the dark and by surprise. The knight imagined it: peace, the sleepy rounds of the sentries on the walls. Then flame arching across blackness, screams and terror, the great scaled shape descending . . . .

He shook himself and looked around. The bodies had been looted; no surprise, peasants would have done that in the week or so they'd lain, whoever did the slaying. There were fewer bodies than he'd have awaited, in a place like this. No livestock, and many of the humans were mere fragments, a limb or a head. That brought unpleasant thoughts.

"Who did this?" he turned to Ermenagarde fiercely. "The margrave, the duke, perhaps even the emperor himself—they should know of it."

Ermenagarde made a sign against evil, one he recognized. "They could do nothing. What can soldiers do against the Wurm?"

Karl signed himself, sheathed his sword, and sat on a timber; he ran his right hand through his beard, the hairs sticking and catching on the thick cracked calluses on his palm and fingers. Trolls and night hags, drows and wurms . . . all more often heard of than seen. Yet they did haunt more often here, where the Old Ones lingered, than in lands long Christian. He himself had seen the whirling dust demons that the Saracens had brought with them from their deserts to Spain when they overthrew the Goths. He moved about, searching, and found the tracks of great three-toed clawed feet in the dirt, one baked to brick by the flames. The span was broad as his paired hands, larger than the largest bear he'd ever seen. From the spacing, it took strides near the length of a tall man's body.

"The margrave could send priests to exorcise a thing of evil," he rumbled, deep in his chest.

Ermenagarde pointed silently to the ruins of a chapel. Not even the body of the priest remained. Perhaps a bishop with holy relics might prove more effective; perhaps not.

Karl went on: "Then what could your mistress' kinsmen do?"

"Pay, my lord," she said bluntly. "Remember the story of Sigurd Fafnirsbane. Ever did the breed of the great Wurms long for gold; and many of them are not just beasts, but creatures who speak and think as men do. This one—"

"You have seen it?"

"With my own eyes; may I be stricken blind if I lie. This one longs greatly for more gold, though it lies on a bed of treasure. Only gold, or some great champion, may free my mistress. And the Wurm hungers for the flesh of maidens also, so it had best be soon. Its fear for its hoard is what keeps it penned close to its lair. Otherwise all the lands about would have been ravaged long ago."

Temptation seized Karl von Obersberg between one breath and the next. *I was the emperor's champion.* Now he was just an old man with many scars, shamed by the niggard generosity of the old emperor's son. In Franconia he'd sit and wait to die, with only his sister's daughters left alive of his kin. Somehow the time to marry had never come, the right match never presented itself; so he had no sons as yet, and no inheritance to give them. No bard would make a song of Karl von Obersberg's deeds; after the Saxon wars he'd seen fighting in plenty, but never where the greatest glory fell. Good useful work, but out of the eye of the great—he'd even missed the disaster where the rearguard was caught by the Basques when the emperor came back from fighting the Saracens in Spain. The pass *he'd* been sent to secure *was* secured, and used . . . but it was the men who'd died at Roncesvalles who'd gotten the gift of undying fame.

Like Sigurd. Though he'd been only a heathen, men still knew Sigurd's name centuries later. And there was a horde of gold, too. With gold and the head of a great

Wurm, his fame and might would run from Brittany to the Slav marches. Beyond, even into the lands of Danes and Greeks. Part of the wealth he could spend to buy the favor of the Franconian lords he knew, favor that would bring him a real fief. Noble fathers would fight to give him their daughters' hands; he had good seed in him yet to breed sons. He might even take this noblewoman whom the Wurm held captive—she'd still be virgin, having been hostage to a beast rather than men, and her father would be grateful.

You go to your death. Karl had fought and wandered for twenty years and more, and learned to calculate the odds. What of it? Better a chance at glory than the certainty of his last years crouching by a niggard hearth, biting the coals and dreaming of when he was a man.

"I'll free your mistress," he said abruptly, standing and looking around once more. The dead should be given burial, or at lest dragged into shelter against beasts. He could hear a wolf pack now. They would be in among the ruins, when the Wurm's scent washed away. "It would be a knightly deed, to rescue a noblewoman from so foul a thing. And a Christian one."

She knelt, bowing her head. "Thank you, my lord!" Her voice was trembling. "I feared ... I feared it would be too late when I came to my mistress' father's house. The beast is cunning, but it hungers for the flesh of maidens only less than it craves gold."

"Come," he said to Ermenagarde. She was watching him with awe; yet with a hint of calculation in her green eyes. No doubt thinking of her prospects if he did the thing; they would be no worse than now if he died. "Tell me of this Wurm."

The cave was in a low hillside, tunneled into sand and clay. Scorchmarks showed about it, the very earth fused into glass about the mouth. Outside was a broad flat area of dirt pounded to the consistency of rock where the

Wurm wallowed and basked. Trees had been pushed aside or snapped off or burned for half a league about, except for a few huge oaks; the damage was long enough ago that saplings sprouted fifteen feet from some of the stumps. Karl von Obersberg frowned at them thoughtfully, noting the lay of the land, snuffing at the wind— from the cave area, thankfully. The songs didn't say if Wurms had a good nose for scent, but he was going to act as if they were as keen as slothounds until it was proved otherwise. He could smell *it*, a stale rank serpent's stink.

Beside the cavemouth was a thick pillar driven into the ground, ancient oak cracked and mossy. Karl's eyes were no longer keen at short distances, but as if to compensate for that loss they'd grown better at distance. Across half a league he could see the form of the woman chained to it, her hands high above her head. A young woman, he thought, richly dressed, with jewels sparkling at throat and belt. Her golden hair hung to her knees, hiding her face, but that was no matter. If she was beautiful, all the better; the bards would make her so, regardless, in their songs, once he'd slain the Wurm. From what Ermenagarde said, the family was rich, Saxon nobles who'd stood by the emperor in the wars, and been rewarded well for it.

"How will you slay the Wurm?" the serving woman asked. She sounded as if curiosity devoured her like wolves; all through the day while he patiently quartered the area, he'd said nothing.

Karl grinned tautly. "In knightly fashion, with the lance," he said. "It's the only weapon likely to harm so large a beast, in any case. Get you gone over there"— he pointed to a dense thicket—"and hide in safety. I will make ready."

Ermenagarde licked her lips, tasting the salt sweat of fear. This Karl was a mighty warrior, that was plain to see, and a wise one. Still . . .

What is he doing? He'd been gone long enough for the shadows to move a hand's breadth. Then he trotted out of the woods again, onto the open ground. His cloak clung to him, and the horse—the horse was sopping wet. Her lips moved silently. *Clever.* Very clever indeed, but he seemed to have left his lance behind. Instead he lifted the aurochs' horn from its sling by his side and sounded it, a ripping blat that echoed back from woods and hill. Again and again he sounded it, until the clearing rang. Between blasts he roared a challenge.

The Wurm came forth. Four times longer than a man, low slung on feet like an eagle's, with legs that jutted up beside its ridged backbone in high-elbowed tension. Its body was much like a crocodile's, but the neck was much longer and the head narrow. Red eyes peered out from beneath a shelf of bone; when the mouth gaped, teeth showed like daggers of yellow ivory.

Ermenagarde caught her lip between her teeth. The Wurm gathered itself to leap . . . and Karl von Obersberg turned tail and ran, as fast as his horse could gallop. That was quickly, since he rode his trail horse, not the heavy war steed.

The woman watched for a second, open-mouthed. *A coward? He is a coward?* There was not a strand of grey in her black hair, but she was no girl in her judgement of men, and she knew Karl better than *that.*

The Wurm pursued, in a hunching, bounding run. Sunlight shone on scales like enameled metal. Flame bloomed forth from the jaws, setting the scrub alight; when the bulk of the charging monster struck the trees, even the whippy saplings were crushed to splinters. Trees broke. Flame billowed up again amid a scream of rage vaster than hills.

Then there was another shriek, of pain this time, and a billow of fog. Ermenagarde's eyes widened; she ran for the cavemouth with her skirts hitched up in her hands and her knees flashing.

"Quickly, Lady Gudrun!" she gasped, fumbling with the other woman's manacles. Then she darted into the cave, came out with two hunting bows and quivers. "We have little time. Something is wrong."

They kirted their skirts through their belts and dashed out along the trail of the monster.

The cold wetness of the cloak and the sudden padding under his mail hauled at Karl as he rode out into the clearing; no colder than the knot of fear beneath his breastbone. Only a lad new to battle thought he could not die. Wrong then—he'd seen so many perish with their bright swords unblooded—and a greater error here, where he fought something not of this world. That was good; it was his revenge on the world itself. He raised the horn to his lips and sounded it, slitting his eyes until the drops caught in his eyelashes sparkled like jewels against the morning sun.

"Come forth!" he called, between blasts. "A Christian knight calls you forth to die, monster! Spawn of Sathanas, come forth!"

He'd thought himself prepared. When the Wurm came forth, he felt his bowls loosen and stopped them just in time. Five times the weight of a bear, he decided, and teeth the length of daggers, and a hide like an elf-lord's armor in a ballad, fitted jewels that shone in the sunlight. And it breathed fire.

I COME, CHRISTIAN. The voice rang between his ears without going through them, soundless. It was huge, and very weary.

Karl's horse tried to buck, turn and flinch all at the same time. He controlled it with a brutal jerk of the reins and pulled its head about. Once the beast realized what he was trying to do, it stopped fighting him, put its head down, and ran. He doubled the reins in his fists, bracing his feet to keep some control, and steered the berserk animal down the path he'd selected.

Fire exploded at his back. The wet cloak sizzled, and he could smell singed wet horsehair. The horse screamed in pain and ran faster; the Wurm was snake swift itself, but too huge to pass down the narrow trail without crushing the undergrowth, and that slowed it. Karl whooped like a boy as he ducked and wove to avoid the branches that might have swept him from the saddle. Another blast of fire—hot enough to singe his hair where it escaped under the edge of his helm, hot enough to dry the last water out of his cloak and set the padded gambeson beneath his hauberk steaming. Yet it was not as large and did not reach as far as the first blast. *Praise be to God,* Karl thought. He would have spurred the horse, except that it could run no faster. The last section of trail was straight and broad. He could hear the earthshaking beat of the Wurm's feet behind him.

Now. The trial and the ground vanished beneath the horse's feet. It did not jump, simply ran out into empty space. That was enough to take them two lengths out into the river; Karl parted company with the saddle in midair. By luck he landed clear of the thrashing hooves, although he lost his helmet to the waters. They were deep enough for him to claw fingers into the mud and be well hidden. Even through the water he could see the shadow of the Wurm as it tumbled into the steep riverbank. Too heavy to jump, as he'd thought. And—

A scream, loud even through the waters. Steam exploded off their surface as the stricken monster crashed down; around him the river went from ice chill to warm in an instant. When Karl surged up through the surface, the mist still boiled, but only a trickle of flame came from the Wurm's jaws as it thrashed. The stub of his lance protruded from its side, driven in to the very crossbar by the Wurm's own weight. Only such force could have pierced that armored hide, which was why he'd braced it beneath the riverbank where the Wurm must come, if it followed him.

"Haro! Haro!" Karl shouted—half wheezed—as he drew his sword and darted in.

Beyond expectation, his war–horse came to the call. The huge beast reared and chopped down at the crippled Wurm. Ironshod hooves struck bone, and one clawed leg dangled limp. The Wurm tried to breath fire again, but only a trickle came forth, enough to burn his eyebrows dry and no more. Two-handed, he swung. Sparks rang, but the fanged head juddered to the shock. There was an old scar along the left side of the face, ending in a ruined eye; his blow reopened that old wound, and blood spattered out to hiss and steam on the wet rocks of the riverbed. Karl roared his triumph and stepped close, raising his sword above his head to drive it into the eye socket and the brain beneath.

"Die, beast!" he shouted. The long years fell away; he was the emperor's paladin, young and strong and victorious, the future open before him in blood and fire and gold.

Blackness struck.

Ermenagarde lowered her bow. The range was close, no more than twenty paces, but she'd never expected to strike so well. Karl von Obersberg stood like a statue with his sword raised and the arrow quivering in the base of his skull. His victory shout was still echoing as he toppled forward rigid as a tree and splashed down on the stones. His sword rang and sparked on river stones.

"Father!" Gudrun called, running forward and kneeling by the Wurm's head. "Father! Are you all right?"

The huge scaly muzzled moved feebly, and one fore-limb pawed the air.

More practical, Ermenagarde looked around for the warhorse. Trained war steeds were the most valuable part of a knight's plunder, if the most difficult to sell, and Lord Widukind had a deplorable tendency to devour them if not reminded. The beast had retreated a hundred paces or so; she advanced slowly, with soothing words. The horse had had time to grow used to her voice, and to the taint of magic that hung about her. She got within arm's reach, took up the reins, and looped them firmly about an oak limb.

Gudrun's scream brought her about. Her eyes widened as she dashed to the other woman's side. The Wurm—Lord Widukind—was . . .

Molting, she thought in amazement.

The armor of brazen scales dropped from his sides like rain, plashing into the water like rain or tinkling on the rocks, then dissolving into dust. Steel bone and stony flesh melted, like sand in the purling water. Wriggling out of the mass, like a snake out of last year's skin, came . . . a man. A man she had not seen since she was an infant; not since the night they fled from a burning hold and the swords of the Franks.

"Father," Gudrun wept. "Father."

Lord Widukind, last overlord of the Saxons, staggered to his feet and stood with the water rippling around his bare knees. He was tall and fair-haired, with the massive scarred body of a fighting man of seven-and-thirty years. One arm hung limp, and a wound gouged up the side of his face to take his left eye, but he smiled—grinned and shouted for joy:

"The curse is broken!" He embraced his daughter with his good arm. "And Gudrun—I see you with a man's eyes, a father's eyes." He looked around in wonder. "How different the world is . . ." Down at himself. "I'm older. Well-a-day, that comes to us all."

Ermenagarde slung her bow and knelt, heedless of the water. "My lord," she said, breathless. "My lord."

Widukind raised her. With one hand he parted the silver collar about her neck. "Keep this as a gift," he said, handing it to her. "For your loyalty."

He looked down and pulled the dead knight onto his back. The face held no pain, only a look of transcendent happiness. "I know this man," he said slowly. "Not his name or his deeds, but I know him. Somewhere—"

"His name was Karl von Obersberg," Ermenagarde said.

Widukind shook his head. "*I curse you until the circle is broken,*" he quoted softly. "So the priest said. Hengst said the magic could be turned on itself, but only when the two were one. He was the one I taught at the last battle, when the temple burned."

The three looked down on the body. Widukind spoke at last. "Come. We will give him burial; he was a brave man, and a great warrior. And we will splint this arm, and rest before we go north."

"North?" Gudrun asked, wiping at the tears of joy on her cheeks.

"To the Dane king's court," Widukind said, wincing. The pain of his wounds was returning. "We won't lack for a welcome, with the gifts we bring."

Ermenagarde trudged through the water to retrieve the fallen knight's sword. *Twenty-seven swords*, she thought. Mostly with full sets of armor to accompany them, and other gear besides—a fair number of knights had passed by over the years, and few had been able to resist her story of Gudrun's looks.

"I'll cut the splint," she said, and headed for the woods.

TO KILL A DRAGON

by Teresa Patterson

There was a dragon terrorizing the barony of Bryngallad. The best archers and fighters in all the barony had
tried to kill it, and had failed to even drive it away.
The foul creature was burning crops, destroying villages,
slaughtering livestock, and wreaking general havoc upon
the land. Faced with the failure of his own forces, Baron
Alemandus was forced to admit that defeating a rampag-
ing dragon was well beyond the scope of his abilities. He
finally sent a messenger to the king for help.

When the messenger returned, heralding the arrival of
the requested aid, His Excellency Baron Alemandus of
Cambrea rushed to don his best finery. Arrayed in his
favorite gold brocade surcoat, with an ornate jeweled coronet adorning his salt-and-pepper mane, Alemandus
entered the tapestry-covered expanse of the audience hall
prepared to greet at least a full company of knights and
royal archers. Instead he found himself facing a young,
slightly travel-worn knight and his squire.

"You are to be my dragonslayer?" Alemandus could

not keep the contempt and disappointment from his voice as he surveyed the slender dark-haired knight. "But you are only one knight."

"Forgive me, Your Excellency, but it was my understanding that there was only one dragon." The young man answered smoothly, the hint of a smile on his lips. He was used to people underestimating him. "His majesty would not have sent me if he did not believe me well able to serve you."

"You honestly believe you can take on this dragon when all the baronial forces have failed?"

The knight bowed low before the baron, moving with a muscular grace which belied his bedraggled appearance. "I am Sir Cedric de Chavoney, Knight of the Order of the Ruby, holder of the King's Gauntlet, from his Majesty's personal guard." Cedric kissed the baronial ruby signet ring, determined to maintain some semblance of proper courtesy, even if his superior did not. "And I do not truly know whether I can defeat your dragon, as I have never had cause to fight one. But I do know that I am sworn to serve you as I would my liege . . ." his dark eyes raised to meet the Baron's, pinning him with their intensity, "or die in the attempt."

Alemandus' eyebrows rose at the mention of the Order of the Ruby, the most prestigious of the knightly disciplines. King Inman had indeed sent him one of his best, even if the handsome man before him looked far too young to have garnered such honors. "Well, my boy, for all our sakes I hope it does not come to that. In the name of the king I accept your service." The knight bowed his acknowledgement, then stood, futilely brushing at the trail dust that stained his deerskin jerkin. "But for now, let me show you the legendary hospitality of Bryngallad. My steward will show you to your chambers. Then you will join us at the feast table."

Bathed and dressed in a clean tunic and green velvet surcoat, Cedric looked and felt much more the image of a proper courtly knight. He found the supper of beef, dark bread, and cheese to be quite filling, though not as elaborate as most baronial feasts. Still, the ale was superb and hinted at a quality well beyond that of the simple repast. And the baron, in his glittering finery, was just as pompous and arrogant as Inman had warned.

"I must beg your pardon for the meager quality of our feast these days." The baron spoke in between healthy draughts of ale from his jeweled flagon. "The dragon has left us little fresh meat and even less grain. I do not wish to think on the state of affairs if our larders had not been well stocked before this rampage."

"How many people have you lost?"

"No deaths so far. Providence has at least smiled on us in that regard. But far too many have been sorely wounded trying to bring that foul creature down. Whole villages have been burned by its scorching breath. It is only a matter of time before our luck runs out and the deaths begin. As it is, the winter will go very hard on the entire barony with so little food and shelter. Unless, of course, you can destroy the beast."

Cedric nodded absently, a frown creasing his brow. This creature was not the only dragon in the kingdom, to be sure, but he had never before heard of a dragon actually attacking a village, much less making war on an entire barony. Even the studies he had done before undertaking this quest had indicated that most dragons preferred to keep to themselves unless harassed or attacked. Some scholars even believed them to be quite intelligent. Cedric had doubts about that, but he wondered what would make a dragon go berserk.

"Forgive me, Excellency, but do you have any idea what might have caused the dragon to begin these attacks?"

"Cause? What cause does it need? It's a dragon, by God!" Alemandus slammed his goblet on the table for emphasis, drawing the immediate attention of the other lords and ladies of his house.

The baroness, silent till now, glared at her husband. "Mandus, how do you expect this brave young man to succeed if you do not warn him about the dark sorcery?"

"Sorcery?" Cedric's goblet froze midway to his face. His dark eyes locked with the baron's grey ones. "There was no mention of sorcery in your message."

Dropping his eyes, Alemandus seemed to visibly deflate. The matronly baroness patted him on the arm reassuringly, a silvered curl escaping from her veil. "He still finds it difficult to talk about." she began. "Years ago an evil mage ensorcelled our daughter. We have reason to think that that same mage may be responsible for the attacks from the dragon . . . ."

" . . . But we have no proof." the baron finished, recovering his composure.

Cedric's stomach knotted at the thought of facing magic, especially that powerful enough to coerce a dragon. He had given his word of honor to his king, but what good was a strong sword arm against magic? "What else did you neglect to put in your message, your Excellency?" He made the title a frozen curse.

Any answer was drowned by the blare of mighty war horns.

"It's the dragon!" the baroness cried, her rosy face gone pale.

The steward and several men at arms burst into the hall. "Excellency, it's in the courtyard!"

"It's after the cattle! We put them there to keep them safe. To arms! At once!" The baron raced out of the hall with Cedric close on his heels. Cedric's squire met them in the entry hall carrying bow, sword, and shield.

"Shall I get your armor?"

"No, Jason. There is no time." Cedric hurriedly strung his bow. If the dragon was here, perhaps he could dispose of it quickly. Alemandus cautiously opened the large carved wooden doors.

In the courtyard all was bedlam. Terrorized cattle charged blindly through the confined space, trampling anything that got in their way. At first Cedric could see little but dust and frightened animals. A man, racing to escape the melee, stumbled and fell just short of the doorway. Cedric grabbed him and pulled him to safety, barely missing being trampled himself. He choked on the thick dust as he helped the man to his feet.

"Open the gates! Let the cattle out before they trample us all!" Someone understood enough to start the huge portcullis moving upward.

The war horns sounded again, but were drowned out by an unearthly wail. A shadow loomed over the yard, followed by a plummeting shape as something large swooped from the sky. Cedric watched in amazement as the creature flashed earthward. It struck a bellowing bull with force enough to snap its spine. With this prize clutched beneath its claws, the creature turned to face them, screaming in triumph, its cry echoing off the stone walls of the yard. Cedric's breathing stilled as it unfurled gleaming wings, arching a graceful neck to glare with seeming insolence at the helpless armsmen. It was definitely a dragon. And it was magnificent!

Iridescent blue-green scales glittered over rippling muscles as it tore into the dead bull. Deep green eyes glowed like jewels on a wide-browed face tapering to an elegant, deadly jaw. Cedric imagined that those jewel eyes were gazing directly at him, pulling him into their depths.

"We can't get at it past the cattle. Use your bow!" Alemandus was shaking him excitedly. "You'll never get a better shot than this!" The blood smell had crazed the remaining cattle. They battered themselves against the stone struggling to force their way through the gate.

Belatedly, Cedric remembered the war bow he held.

Shaking himself free of the dragon's spell he quickly chose a barbed broadhead from his quiver and nocked it. As he drew the powerful bow and sighted, he felt a moment's regret for the destruction of such a creature. But he was a knight sworn to his duty. He released the arrow.

The shaft streaked true towards its mark, but the dragon was no longer there. Puzzled, Cedric nocked another arrow, aiming more carefully. Again the arrow sped towards its mark, but the dragon was faster still; moving like quicksilver it avoided the deadly barbs. Cedric tried a third and fourth arrow, with the same result.

An eerie, almost human cry issued from the dragon as it tossed its head, negligently snapping at the last of the cattle as they struggled to leave the yard. Cedric imagined it was laughing at him.

"Jason, my sword."

"But your armor!" The red-haired youth gestured at Cedric's courtly dress in dismay.

"There's no time." Cedric took his sword and shield and joined the ranks of mail-clad armsmen converging on the feasting dragon. "On my signal. We'll all go in together. It's our only chance!" The armsmen nodded and spread out, careful to stay clear of dragon teeth and claws. Cedric waited until it lowered its head to feed, then signaled.

Moving as one, the armsmen converged on the dragon, only to be met by fiery breath and slashing claws. Cedric deflected a gout of flame with his shield. Cringing under the intense heat and the acrid smell of his own singed hair, he struggled to get close enough to use his sword. Sunlight sparkled off something fastened around the dragon's neck, drawing his notice. A jewel? A collar? What would a dragon need with such a thing?

The man to his right struck at the creature's face in an attempt to blind it. One sinuous movement of the elegant head easily deflected the blow. Snapping jaws and a second motion disarmed the man and sent him sprawling. Cedric used the momentary distraction as an opening. He drove forward with his sword, his attack focused on the jewel suspended around its vulnerable throat.

Before he could strike, something slammed into him. There was only a blur of shining blue-scaled tail; then he was flying through the air to slam head first into the stonework like a rag doll.

He awakened in his room to see the baroness and several lovely young ladies hovering over him. For a moment, he thought that such a pleasant sight might even be worth a few bruises. Then he made an attempt to sit and was forced to revise that idea. Sore ribs, a dizzy, throbbing head, and bruised muscles all clamored for equal attention. Even his stomach threatened to revolt from the abuse. With a groan he gave up and collapsed back onto the bed, closing his eyes against the jig his room seemed determined to perform. His hands groped towards his aching skull to find it swathed in bandages. Somewhere beneath those bandages a blacksmith with a very large hammer was trying to reshape his brain.

"Perhaps next time, my lord, you will not be so hasty to rush into battle without your armor."

With effort, Cedric opened his eyes to find the source of the familiar voice. He finally spotted his squire at the foot of the bed, a smug look on his face and a lady on each arm.

"And what are you so cheerful about?"

"I'm just glad you didn't get your fool head completely removed."

"The way it's throbbing I'm not completely certain it wasn't removed." The ladies laughed, pleased that their handsome charge appeared to be recovering at least his sense of humor.

"You know, if you had worn your armor you probably would not be hurt at all."

"Are you determined to rub it in? Perhaps I should be your squire, 'Sir Jason.'" The young man grinned mischievously back at him.

"Besides, look what lovely nursemaids I would have missed." Another set of delighted giggles issued from the ladies. He forced a brilliant smile for their benefit as his squire escorted the lot of them to the outer chamber.

The fake smile dissolved into a sigh of relief as Jason returned. He enjoyed the ladies as much as the next man, but only in small doses. "Speaking of casualties—how many?"

"Six dead and twelve wounded."

"All by the dragon?"

"No. All the dead were trampled by the livestock. Yours was the worst of the wounds actually inflicted by the dragon. No one else tried to bounce their skull off the castle wall. Most of the other injuries were bruises, broken bones, and a few burns."

Cedric's brow creased in a thoughtful frown. "And yet the creature could have killed us as easily as it broke that bull."

"All jests aside, my lord, you very nearly were killed. The chirurgeon is quite concerned with the hole in your head, although I did assure him that it was the most impervious part of your body, and has said that you will require at least a fortnight's rest."

"Devil take the chirurgeon! Jason, find my clothes, I must see the baron."

At Jason's call, the ladies scurried back into the room to restrain their wounded knight. Between the pounding in his head and the insistence of the ladies, Cedric grudgingly allowed himself to be convinced to remain abed while the baron was summoned. Carefully propped up with soft furs, he felt very foolish giving audience to a noble of higher rank. Fortunately the baron, perching himself on a bedside stool, did not seem to mind.

"So, my lad, how are you feeling?"

Cedric winced. The difference in years between himself and Alemandus was far fewer than the baron seemed to think. "Quite well, Excellency, for someone who has lost a fight with a dragon."

"Well, it was to be expected. After all, you are only one man." The baron's condescending smile grated. "Perhaps now the king will send more knights. At least your quest has ended."

"I . . ." Cedric tried to control the edge in his voice, "have barely begun my quest. But you could begin by telling me about the sorcery you almost forgot to mention. Perhaps then I will know why a wild dragon wears a jeweled pendant about its neck? And why that same dragon easily kills livestock, but does little damage to its human attackers? If there is magic involved, I need to know everything."

"All I want is someone to put an end to that dragon."

"And if you had told me everything from the beginning I might have had a chance to do that. I have no more patience for games."

The baron arose with a glare, unused to such insubordinate treatment. Heaving an exasperated sigh, Cedric tried again. "I have sworn to my king on my honor to serve you. If you want me to have any hope of ending this siege I must understand what has happened here. Who is this wizard and why do you believe him to be consorting with dragons?"

The glare faded as Alemandus sank onto his seat, removing his coronet with a sigh. "One man cannot end it. It has been going on for far too long. But you have earned the right to hear the tale." He stared into the baronial leaves of his coronet, seeming to seek inspiration.

"Years ago the evil mage, Gwydion, came to live in the barony. He gave the appearance of a peaceful scholar by day, but by night he secretly despoiled our lands and livestock. I believe he went so far as to consort with demons. He used his black powers to ensorcel my only daughter, then abduct her for his own foul purpose. Over the years my men and I made many attempts to rescue her. We even managed to corner Gwydion once. But his young apprentice intervened, allowing the mage to escape. He took refuge in the depths of the Veldtar forest. We eventually killed the boy and left his body in the forest, hoping his death would deter his master. Instead Gwydion swore vengeance, conjuring a dragon to drive us from his forest. I am certain it is his worm that now assails us."

"Then you know where this dark wizard hides?"

Slowly the baron's eyes rose to meet Cedric's. "We believe he lives in the Drachen valley, but we cannot be certain. All who attempt to enter the area are driven back by the beasts he has corrupted. And the dragon itself guards the valley."

Cedric paused to consider. He knew he could not defeat the dragon in single combat. But the mage was the key to the dragon. If he could defeat this Gwydion, the dragon would have no master. The thought of going up against dark magic terrified him. It was small consolation that magicians were notoriously poor fighters once bereft of their magic.

"I must go to the heart of the matter. Tomorrow I will ride to the Drachen valley."

Alemandus nodded agreement, a spark of hope alight in his face.

It was actually two days before Cedric finally managed to convince the chirurgeon to free him from his bed. But on the third day, head still bandaged, he, his squire, and ten armsmen set out at dawn for the Drachen valley.

It took half a day's easy ride over rolling countryside to reach the edge of the Veldtar forest, the largest single forest in the kingdom. Another halfday was spent wending through its imposing depths. Tall trees stood to either side and shaded the trail while scenting the air with the fragrant aroma of sap and warm leaves. Just before nightfall they reached the grassy clearing that marked the edge of the Drachen valley. Cedric dismounted and studied the area, deciding it would be a good location for a base camp. The forest bordered them on two sides. To the west there was a stone pillar rising above their camp like a castle tower that had been roughly carved by giants. It was part of a ridge that made up the west wall of the valley, giving one side the appearance of a canyon. Just east of the pillar, at the edge of the clearing, the grass sloped gently downward towards the valley floor. A dim trail followed the slope downward, disappearing in the foliage draped shadows below.

Gazing across the width of the thickly forested valley, Cedric wondered how he would find one wizard amid all that greenery. Especially one that probably did not want to be found. As he eased his aching body onto the grass near his squire's cook fire, he glumly considered that facing the dragon may have been the easier task.

A commotion in the camp caught his attention. Several of the men were yelling and pointing at the sky. Others were hastily stringing bows. He looked up to see a great winged shape silhouetted in the red glow of the sunset. The dragon lightly touched down on the stonework tower portion of the ridge, furling its wings and emitting a lonely cry that sent chills up his spine. The bowmen fired. It sidestepped the arrows as easily as it had avoided his days before.

"Wait! Don't waste your arrows!" The firing ceased. Everyone was still, waiting for the dragon to make a counterattack. But the beast held its place. It seemed content just to watch. Gradually everyone returned to their tasks, sending occasional nervous glances towards the shadow lurking above them, illuminated by the failing moon. Cedric positioned his sleeping furs carefully, determined to keep an eye on their visitor.

He awakened the next morning, partially healed ribs sore from a night on the hard ground, to discover the dragon had flown with the sunrise. He was angry with himself for falling asleep. He was even more angry when the men refused to enter the cursed valley until and unless he found the wizard's lair. They were not afraid of a military confrontation, even with a mage, but they wanted no part of the enchantments this valley was said to possess.

So it was that Cedric and Jason rode down the trail into the shaded maw of the valley unescorted. Cedric's temper did not improve as the winding trail separated into a tangle of lesser paths, bending and weaving amid a gradually thickening mass of trees and brush. Thick foliage draped the trees, occasionally obscuring the trail completely. The whole thing was a maze. The pungent odor of rotting vegetation permeated the air, making it thick and hard to breathe. Creatures skittered through the vegetation just out of sight, causing the horses to become nervous and difficult. Things seemed to be watching them from the shadows. Even Jason gave up his usual light banter to concentrate on calming his mount. Cedric tightened his leg and rein to steady his own horse, but continued to press on. Until there was a direct attack he would not allow fear to rule him. Perhaps fear was the mage's chief weapon. That and a seemingly endless maze of looping trails.

Eventually, approaching sunset and the threat of full darkness forced a return to camp. Tired and disgusted, neither man even considered spending the night in the valley.

At sunset the dragon returned to its perch.

The next day Cedric suggested they split up in the

hopes of covering more ground. "This valley must have a river or creek at its base. I plan to find that watercourse and follow it. If the mage is in that valley, his home is probably somewhere near the water. You take the path near the ridge and try to work your way around the western edge."

"Do you really think we'll find this mage?"

"Probably not, but if he thinks we are serious and that we do not intend to leave, he may well find us!"

Jason looked grim at this less than reassuring plan, checking his sword and dagger before obediently spurring his big bay towards the ridge. Cedric smiled at his squire's courage, then mounted his grey gelding.

On re-entering the valley, Cedric concentrated on following only paths that sloped towards the valley floor. He refused to think about the increasing darkness as the canopy thickened overhead, shutting out the sun, or the shapes that rustled and flitted to either side. Several times he thought he heard the sound of rushing water, only to have the trail veer sharply away from what he was sure was the stream he was seeking.

Finally, in frustration, he decided to make his own path. The water sounded so close he was sure he could reach it. On Cedric's command the powerful war-horse plunged into the lush undergrowth, snorting his displeasure as thorns and brambles cut at his hide. Vines caught at them, slowing their progress. Cedric ducked low on the gelding's neck to protect his face from sharp branches. He could hear the gelding's breathing become labored as he fought against the unyielding foliage, feel his growing fear. But the knight continued to encourage the struggling animal forward. The stream he heard should be just ahead.

Something burst from the brush in front of them. A flash of moving fur and shadow. His startled horse shied and tried to bolt, only to become tangled in the vines that entwined his legs up to the knee. Off-balance, the horse went down, taking his rider with him. Something—a tree?—struck Cedric's head as they fell. Dazed, he could barely force himself to roll clear of the panicked animal's thrashing hooves.

Once relieved of his rider's weight, the horse managed to kick itself free of the entrapping vines and lurch to its feet. Cedric had one glimpse of his mount's terrified white-rimmed eyes before it bolted into the forest.

For a moment, he could only lie amid the brambles and dirt, gasping for breath as he waited for his head to clear. Perhaps the chirurgeon had been right, he should have stayed abed another week or two, maybe a month. Or perhaps he should never have become a knight at all. If only he hadn't given his word, he could walk away from all this right now. With a groan he sat up, wincing as his ribs complained. Of course, he knew that was a foolish wish. It was that dedication to honor that gave his life meaning. Without it he was nothing. Better to endure a horrible death than live without honor. But for now, better to find that blasted stream. He needed cool water to rinse his aching head. Then he would find his horse and continue this hopeless quest. Climbing slowly to his feet, careful not to jar his head, he stumbled towards the sound of gurgling water.

A few yards later, as he forced himself through the tenacious grip of vines and branches, another sound caught his attention. A faint ringing melody trembled on the air. At first he thought it an illusion, created by his reinjured head, but as he followed the sound, it grew stronger. Someone was singing! It was a woman's voice. Sweet and clear as silvered harp strings, the music soared in gentle counterpoint to the water's burbling voice. The language was unknown to Cedric, but strangely compelling. Entranced, he drew nearer until he found himself on the edge of a small glade. Careful to stay hidden, he peeked through the leaves.

Within the glade a raven-haired girl sat singing to herself as she rinsed her hair in the waterfall. Dressed in a clinging gown of green velvet pulled low about milk white shoulders, the girl arched her back to hold her long dark hair under the falling water. Cedric almost forgot the pounding in his head as he watched and listened to her haunting melody. He had never seen such a creature. Surely she put all the ladies at court to shame. Still singing, the girl stood to twist the water from her hair. An ornate golden girdle and belt pouch clung to her hips as she moved, accentuating the graceful lines of her figure. She reseated herself on a nearby stone, still singing, and began to comb her thick tresses, revealing her delicately sculpted face and brow to her hidden admirer. The crimson hue of her full lips accentuated her pale skin and dark eyes. Cedric thought he might be content to spend all eternity watching her.

At the end of her song she laid aside her comb and turned to gaze directly at the knight's hiding place. He knew he had made no movement or sound, yet she looked right at him. Laughing, she rose, a movement like flowing water, and glided towards him. His breath caught in his throat as he met her eyes, deep pools of sky reflecting wisdom well beyond her apparent years. Had he stumbled upon one of the fairy folk? Or perhaps he was still unconscious from his wound.

She smiled, a dazzling sight that challenged the sun, and held out her hand to him. "You need not hide from me, good sir. Come forth and name yourself."

Embarrassed, Cedric stepped from his hiding place, stammering an introduction as he tried to brush the leaves and dirt from his jerkin. She calmly took his hand, her skin the softness of flower petals, and led him to a sitting stone by the brook. Dizziness assailed him as he gazed at her.

"So, you are the dragonslayer. I have heard of you." Her voice was musical, even when speaking. "I am allowed so few visitors. You must stay a while and talk with me."

He meant to ask her name, and where she came from. And what she might know of the mage. But when he looked at her, everything save her beauty evaporated from his mind.

"I have never heard a song like that. It sounds like something the fairy folk would sing."

She laughed delightedly and pirouetted before him. "Do you think so? I would love to meet one of the fairy folk." She enlarged her pirouette into a dance and began to accompany it with a song that hinted of lofty heights and mystic places.

As she whirled about him, Cedric marveled at her movements, all quicksilver and sunlight. A blur seemed to envelope her dancing form as his temples joined the rhythm. Her song and the waterfall's gurgle echoed louder and louder in his ears. She smiled and beckoned him to join her. He stood, reaching out to her through the growing haze . . . .

And abruptly collapsed.

With a cry the girl was beside him, touching his brow in a featherlight caress. She gently lifted his head—and gasped as her hand came away covered in blood.

"You are injured!"

"I must have reopened the wound in the fall." Somehow it didn't matter so long as she held him.

"How did this happen?"

"I lost a fight with a dragon."

"The dragon did this?" She looked stricken, as if the identity of the perpetrator was more horrible than the wound.

"I'll be fine." he lied, unwilling to upset her. "Just let me rest for a while."

"No, you need a healer." She seemed to consider for a moment. "I will take you to Gwydion. He will help you. He must."

As consciousness dimmed, he marvelled at the irony of the situation. He was going to meet the dread mage after all. He sincerely hoped the man did not want to fight. He was not quite up to it just now.

Somehow the girl managed to catch his horse and help him to mount. Cedric was only vaguely aware of the process. "I don't even know your name to thank you," he gasped, slumping against the grey's powerful neck.

She smiled back at him and began to lead the gelding down an all but invisible trail. "They call me Aurora."

At first he struggled to remain awake enough to watch their route, knowing that this might be his only chance to learn the way to the mage's secret lair, but all the twisting and turning began to blend together in his pain-fogged brain. If only there was a way to mark the trail! His unfocused eyes settled on a blur of color. It was his brightly fletched arrows. He could leave a trail of feathers!

Carefully he peeled the feathers from the arrows, trying not to alert Aurora, or jar his head, and dropped them at every turning of the path. Fortunately his guide never noticed.

He was almost out of feathers when the trail widened into a clearing. At first, there appeared to be nothing there. All he could see was a large expanse of grass, broken only by the stream running through it and the stone ridge that made up the valley wall. As they crossed the gently flowing stream and approached the wall, the stone of the wall seemed to change. Cedric thought it a trick of his delirium as its features began to blur and shift, revealing the shadows of what seemed to be towers and windows. As they drew nearer, the shadows gradually solidified into the crenelated walls and towers of a small castle. It was built into the ridge wall, fashioned of matching stone. So clever was the masonry work that the castle was indistinguishable from the cliff at a distance.

After slowly dismounting and releasing the horse into

the care of stableboys, Aurora helped Cedric climb the wide stone stairs to the massive, carved wooden doors that made up the entrance to the keep. He noticed that the wood was painted stone grey to match the surrounding construct. A portly woman in peasant clothes met them at the door. She seemed quite agitated to see Cedric, as she escorted them to a modestly furnished antechamber, then disappeared, leaving Aurora to help Cedric recline on a low padded couch near the center of the room. The cloying odor of incense filled the candle-lit chamber. Intricately carved wooden furniture was scattered throughout its length, while two large tapestries hung on opposite sides of a great carved thronelike chair. A large iron brazier stood to one side of the chair and a table cluttered with parchment and candles perched beside it.

Cedric was trying to force his eyes to focus on the candles when a very dignified older man strode into the room. Silver haired, with a close-trimmed beard and sharp chiseled features, the immaculately robed man projected tightly controlled power. He signaled the girl to attend him, ignoring the young knight. Anger seemed evident in his brisk gestures and sharp tones as he spoke to Aurora. Cedric tried to hear what they were saying, but was finding it increasingly difficult to concentrate. He could only catch brief snatches of their conversation.

" . . . know who he is, yet you brought him here?"

"He is badly hurt. He needs your help. You were a healer once."

"That was a long time ago. Before . . . ."

"But you must help him. It was the dragon that injured him!"

Something in her desperate tone of voice must have touched the mage, for he fell silent for a long moment. Then he touched her cheek and sighed heavily, as one who is preparing to reshoulder a great burden. "Very well. I will see what can be done. Ask Giselle to bring my potions."

"Thank you!"

"And then see to your duties. I do not have to remind you that you are still bound to serve me."

"Never, my lord."

Cedric tried to thank her as she glided past him, but found his voice would no longer responded to his will. His body felt very cold and far away. He watched with disengaged interest as a statuesque woman with straw colored hair bound up at the nape of her neck entered the room. She was dressed in riding leathers and carried an array of odd-sized bowls and flagons and a hand-sized jewellike stone. The mage carefully took the containers form her and set them on the table, casually brushing the parchment aside, then moved with her to hover over Cedric.

"She brought him in just in time, eh Giselle."

"It will take the last of your medicants to heal this one. Are you certain you have the strength?" The woman's voice was clear and strong.

"There is still some power in me, and the potions will help."

"But are you certain it is wise?"

He did not answer her, but moved to light the brazier. Then he picked up the faceted stone from the table and began a low, musical chant, holding the stone out before him. After a moment, the woman joined him, adding her lilting contralto to his baritone as she placed her hands over the stone in his. As Cedric watched, they slowly pulled their hands apart, leaving blue fire glowing in the air between them. Cedric felt his old fear of magic surface, urging escape. But his body would not respond. The pair moved so that each stood at one end of the couch, and lowered their hands until the blue fire surrounded Cedric. He wanted to scream, but no sound came. The blue fire brought with it a tingling sensation that gradually stole his fear away, then lulled him into comforting darkness.

He awoke to find the straw-haired woman smiling at him from beside the couch. He touched his head experimentally and discovered there were no bandages. His expression must have shown his amazement for Giselle laughed, the movement crinkling the skin around her soft hazel eyes.

"Gwydion is a marvelous healer when he chooses to be. You are very lucky."

"I would thank him."

"I am right here." Cedric had missed him, sitting so quietly in his great wooden chair, the table beside him littered with empty containers and a burned and blackened stone. The young knight scrambled to sit up and face the mage. "Not too fast, boy. Even an eldritch healing takes time and rest."

The woman smiled and left the room, gently touching Gwydion's shoulder as she passed him.

"So, you are the knight who would be a dragonslayer?" The mage's slate-blue eyes bore into him.

"I have sworn to stop the dragon's rampage. I am prepared to do whatever it takes."

"Even kill me, no doubt, since I control the dragon. Despite the fact that I have just saved your life."

"If I must." Cedric did not like the direction this discussion was taking. "My liege has charged me to put an end to the destruction."

Gwydion glared at him. "So there will be more bloodshed in the name of false honor."

"I am a knight, not a fool. Battle is only a last resort. The people of the barony want only to be left in peace. As one reasonable man to another, I beg you to rein in your pet."

"The people of the barony deserve what they get. I have no peace. There can be none for them."

"Then you are an evil man."

"I am evil?" Gwydion erupted from his chair, clenched knuckles white with fury as he advanced on Cedric, who stood unsteadily to meet him. "And what are those who destroyed and defiled the sacred groves? What of their evil? Do you even know the meaning of the word? Those same fools who sent you to destroy me are responsible for blighting earth magic that has stood since the time of man. Is that not evil? They have killed people for no reason other than their own fear and lack of understanding. They drove me from my home, from my land, forced me to turn outlaw. And when I tried to fight back, they cut down my only son in cold blood!" The mage's hands were shaking. "Can you not understand the honor demanded by love? No price is too high for such a crime. I will not recall my dragon!"

"But you ensorcelled the baron's daughter!"

"Do not presume that which you cannot understand! My war is with the baron and his people, not you. Do not make the mistake of standing between us, or, by the Goddess, I will have your life!"

"Then kill me now, for I am sworn to stop you." Cedric hoped he sounded more convincing then he felt.

"I will not take the life which I have so recently given. You will be escorted back to your own men. If you ever return, however, I will make good on my promise." So saying he whirled and stalked from the room, his robe billowing like storm clouds about him.

Cedric sank back down upon the couch, trying to still his own shaking hands. Military encounters were so much cleaner, somehow. There was no doubt, no time to consider right or wrong, only the swift justice of the blade.

Some little time later Giselle came for him. As they left the keep, Cedric looked for Aurora, but there was no sign of her. Giselle wasted no time mounting her horse and trotting into the forest, forcing Cedric to give up his surreptitious search and follow lest he be left behind.

Evening shadows all but obscured the path so that Cedric would have been completely lost without a guide. At least he no longer felt any malevolence from the surrounding forest. He maintained a companionable silence, half afraid that any conversation might distract the blond woman enough to lose the path. Eventually he sighted the ember glow of the camp's cook fires. Turning to thank his guide, he discovered she was gone.

That night Cedric dreamed of Aurora, while the dragon again watched from the ridge.

The next day he rode into the valley alone. Somehow he managed to locate the waterfall glade. Perhaps it was easier because he no longer feared the forest. He tethered his horse to a stout tree and entered the glade, afraid it would be empty. But she was there, waiting, seated on a rock. Her beauty was even more radiant than before.

"I was afraid you might not come after what Gwydion said to you."

"Dear lady, I could not stay away."

She stood to greet him, hesitantly, as if unsure of how to proceed. He looked into the depths of her blue-green eyes . . . and was lost. Before he was quite aware of moving he gathered her into his arms, savoring her sweet suppleness against him, and kissed her. She did not resist, but looked at him in wonder as he released her. Tentatively, she reached out to touch his lips, as if amazed at their texture.

"I'm sorry. I should not have presumed so, my lady." Embarrassed, he stepped back. How could he assume that she would share his feelings?

"No, my brave knight, there is no need for forgiveness." She lithely closed the space he had placed between them and initiated an embrace of her own. He joyously returned it, breathing in the honeysuckle scent of her hair as he swept her off her feet to lay her gently on the grass.

They spent the day together, sometimes in each other's arms—she seemed to find each embrace wondrous and new—sometimes talking or playing in the waterfall. She wanted to know everything about him. What it was like being a knight. All about court, all about his life. Cedric delighted in telling her. Never had he had such an attentive audience. Only once when he tried to turn the subject back to her, did she withdraw. But as soon as the topic returned to other subjects, she was her joyous self again.

Even looking at her, touching her, he could not quite believe she was real. He wanted to memorize each nuance of expression and movement. At last he understood why the court minstrels went to such lengths to sing the praises of love. Everything he had known before was but a pale imitation of this moment.

All too soon the shadows began to lengthen. Aurora suddenly pulled away from him. "It grows late, I must go."

"But you're coming with me, back to camp."

"I can't go with you. I'm sorry."

Cedric could not believe he had heard correctly. "What are you saying? Have I done something wrong?"

"Oh no, beloved knight, but my place is here. I am bound here."

"Is it Gwydion? Does he have some kind of spell on you?"

She avoided meeting his eyes. "You would not understand." Just then a distant horn sounded, a long, low, mournful sound echoing across the valley.

"Oh no! I must go. Now!"

"But why?"

"He calls. They know I am gone. He must not find me with you. He will kill you if he finds you here." She turned to leave, but he grabbed her arm and spun her back to face him.

"I will protect you from him. Do you not love me? Do you not trust me?"

A look of profound sadness covered her face. "Oh, dearest one, I do love you, more than you can know. And I do trust you to protect me, so far as you are able. But you do not understand. I must never see you again. I am bound to him!" She leaned forward, kissed him passionately, then turned to flee into the darkening wood. He tried to follow, but soon lost her in the shadows. As he gave up and began his lonely return to camp, he noticed a brightly colored arrow feather lying on the path. Perhaps there was still hope.

"So do you think she is the baron's daughter?" Jason asked that night as Cedric dispatched a man to ride for the baron.

"I do not know for certain. She avoided the subject completely. Whoever she is, the sorcery that binds her is very powerful."

Jason's eyes widened. "It must be if even love could not break it."

Cedric looked shocked. He had told his squire nothing of the day's events.

"It's all over your face. You've fallen for her! The knight who could not be moved by any of the pretty faces at court has fallen for a mystery woman!" The red-haired youth could not keep the edge of glee from his voice.

"She is unlike any woman I have ever known. And she is in trouble. I must find a way to rescue her."

"And defeat the dragon."

"And defeat the dragon. But Gwydion is the key to both; either way I will have to face him." He glanced over at the stone pillar. The dragon was not there. "Tomorrow we will attack in force. With luck, and a fleet horse, the baron will be here in time to see our success."

Dawn found the armsmen clad in mail and riding single file into the valley. Though still leery of the dark magic they believed infested the area, they followed Cedric because he had been to the wizard's lair and returned. Their idle chatter faded away to silence in the thickening shadow of the wood.

Cedric led the way directly to the glade, hoping that she might be there. But the glade was empty. He led them through it, trying to hide his disappointment. The horses' many sharp hooves tore the sod, defacing the soft grass where he had loved. Guiding them to the trail of arrow feathers that marked the way, he prayed it was not an omen. Not even Jason had been told of the threat the mage had made to him.

After an uneventful trek they reached the clearing. Cedric heard the men gasp and saw his squire cross himself as the castle "appeared" before them. Guiding his horse across the stream, Cedric saw a familiar form running towards them from the castle steps. "Aurora!" He spurred his horse towards her, vaulting from the saddle to take her in his arms.

"You must leave here at once, Cedric." Worry lines creased her smooth brow.

"Because of Gwydion's threat?" He gently smoothed the frown from her face. "I am not afraid."

"You should be! He intends to see you die. Please, beloved, for my sake, leave these woods."

"Only if you will come with me."

"I cannot! Do not ask that which I cannot give!" The anguish in her voice tore at him.

"Then I must free you so that you can!" He signaled Jason. "Take her to safety." Remounting his horse he rode up to the silent castle.

"You cannot free me! You do not understand!" She wrenched free of Jason's hold and ran to place herself between Cedric and the castle steps.

At that moment the great doors opened to reveal Gwydion, cloaked in crackling blue fire. "Stand aside, girl." His voice reverberated with authority. "I warned this knight of his fate and he has come seeking it." Sparks flashed in his hands. Several armsmen drew their bows at the sight.

"No! It is my place. I will deal with him!" Standing tall, the girl faced Cedric, her voice carefully controlled. "I begged you to leave in the name of love, now I beg you in the name of honor. Leave this place, or I will not be responsible for your fate."

"It is because of honor that I cannot leave. I am a knight. My sworn quest can only end with his death," he pointed at Gwydion, "or the death of the dragon."

"Then by my honor, I am sworn to stop you." There were tears in her eyes as she pulled a large pendant from her belt pouch and put it on.

"Do your duty, then!" Gwydion called to the girl as he advanced on the young knight. "Or I will end this myself."

"Step aside, Aurora." Cedric glared at the mage beyond, sword raised to signal the attack.

"NOOOoo!" Grasping the pendant, Aurora threw back her head and screamed in anguish. A strange green glow enveloped her, emanating from the pendant. Reining back his startled mount, Cedric looked on in amazement as Aurora's body melted and flowed, coalescing into the form of a great dragon. Her human cry ended in an inhuman scream.

Cedric's horse tried to bolt as the dragon spread wings and launched herself skyward. He quickly dismounted and released the terrified animal, to stand gaping as the great dragon disappeared into the clouds above. For a moment, no one moved save to scan the empty sky.

"My lord! Behind you!"

Cedric spun around to see the great dragon streaking towards him, claws outstretched. He could see fire flaring from her nostrils as she drew near. Quickly he threw up his shield, remembering this creature had broken a full-grown bull.

She struck the shield with claws extended, gouging through the metal and knocking Cedric off his feet with the force of the blow. He rolled and brought his shield up as she came after him, spitting fire. Could this creature really be Aurora? She dove for him. He rolled away at the last moment, coming up beneath her belly.

She screamed in frustration and reared up on her hind legs, leaving her vulnerable underside open to Cedric's sword.

And he could not strike. Dragon or girl, he could not kill the one he had loved. He lowered his sword, diving behind his shield as a burst of fire singed him. Claws raked at him once more as she lifted back into the sky.

Crawling out from behind his ruined shield, Cedric wondered that he still lived. Jason ran to his side to help him to his feet, both men scanning the sky for her next attack. The swordsmen and archers were drawn up in formation, anxiously watching the sky, bows at the ready.

A blood-chilling scream heralded her approach as she broke through the clouds to plummet towards them. Cedric saw the archers sight and draw as she approached.

"No! Hold! Do not shoot!"

It was too late. Cedric saw the arrows fly towards their mark. Time slowed for him as he breathlessly waited for the dragon to make that amazing quicksilver evasion he had seen so often . . . .

But she never altered her course. The arrows struck true. They slammed into gleaming flesh, eliciting a scream of agony from the wounded dragon. For a moment, she hovered gently on the wind. Then the great wings sagged and fell slack, leaving the gleaming creature to tumble limply to earth. She landed at the steps of the castle she had protected.

Cedric raced towards the fallen dragon, ignoring the gasps of the men as the dragon's body slowly melted into that of a young woman. He gently scooped her into his arms, trying not to jar the bloody shafts protruding from her flesh. She looked up at him with pain-filled eyes, and smiled.

"Why?" he gasped through his tears.

"I had no choice." she gasped. "I had to fight to preserve my honor, but I chose death to preserve my love."

"What honor? I don't understand!" He felt a presence beside him and turned to see the mage standing over him, bereft of blue flame, looking very old as he gazed at the dying girl.

"Just as you were honor bound by your king, she was bound to me to serve myself and my people at any cost. You see, she was a lonely dragon who wanted nothing more than to be human. And I was a bitter man who had just lost his son and wanted nothing more than revenge. When I used my waning power to grant her wish and swear her to my service, I never dreamed she would be so human as to become trapped between love and honor. You see, dragons take honor very seriously. She has chosen death rather than betray her lover, or her liege." Gwydion choked on the last word.

"Then you must save her. She kept her word! She faced death to protect you!"

"I cannot save her. I no longer have the power!"

"But you're a healer—you healed me! Do not betray her like this!"

"Do you think I would let her die if there were any choice?" The mage's voice cracked. "I have already seen one child sacrificed in my name! Do you think I want to discover a daughter only to lose her?" He turned his back to hide his tears.

The straw-haired woman, now wearing a flowing gown of blue, stepped from the castle and ran to the mage's side. Taking his hand she turned to Cedric. "He used the last of his focusing gems and potions to heal you! Even that was a near thing. Yet your wound was not so grievous as this. With the destruction of the sacred groves the old magic is waning, and even Gwydion no longer has the strength to compensate for its loss."

A sudden bellow of war horns broke the moment as the baron and his men burst from the trees to thunder into the clearing. The baron rode directly to the steps, dismounting as he shouted excitedly. "They said you shot the dragon! They saw it fall . . . ."

He stopped when he saw the girl, pierced with arrows, in Cedric's arms.

"Yes, Father, the dragon is dying. Your sworn man carried out his duty." An icy feminine voice snapped from the top of the steps.

Alemandus turned in shock to the blond woman glaring at him. "Giselle!"

"She dies by your command, just as my son died, two years ago."

"Your son?" His face went white as he stumbled back against his horse. "My God! My grandson!"

"Giselle is your daughter?" Cedric did not try to cover his own shock. "Just how long has this feud been going on?"

"Seventeen years ago I ran away to marry Gwydion." Giselle answered, "Our son was born the following year."

"I didn't know!" Alemandus pleaded.

"You didn't want to know! Nothing mattered but your politics and your stupid war. You could not believe that I would choose to be with Gwydion rather than be the baron's daughter. Now there is another death upon your head!"

"Perhaps not!" Gwydion approached the fallen girl to kneel at her side. "There may yet be a way to save her." He touched the small stone still hanging from its thong on Aurora's neck. "But it will require the aid of all assembled." Standing, he looked directly at Alemandus. "It will require that you join with me in a healing circle."

"You must be mad! I cannot join you in your heathen rituals! Find someone else to share in your evil!"

"Then you would condemn this girl to death, just as you did your own grandson?" His words lashed the baron.

"But you have said this girl is the product of sorcery. I will not risk my soul to save a creature that has none!"

"Enough!" Carefully handing Aurora to Jason, Cedric stood, sparks in his eyes. "This was has already gone on far too long. While you bicker, a girl is dying! Your hatred has already cost you a child that was blood kin and heir to both of you. Must it also take the life of one whose only crime was that she would not be foresworn? Do you value honor so little that you will let her sacrifice so much? You have a choice. Let this hatred continue to drag you to ruin, or put aside your grievances and regain some of the honor you have lost."

Alemandus looked at the girl, lying so still on the steps, and thought of the grandson he never knew. Raising his eyes he met the unflinching gaze of his daughter. He would win her, or lose her forever with his choice.

"Very well. Let no man say that Alemandus is a coward. I will join you, as will my men."

Gwydion inclined his head in solemn acknowledgement, and led the way to the sanctuary deep within his castle.

Hours later the great hall looked like a war zone. Exhausted men sat or sprawled throughout its length, drained from the healing they had aided. Drudges moved among them offering food or mead. Gwydion slumped in his great wooden chair, forehead resting on one hand. He had not moved since they had left the sanctuary.

Cedric himself sat wearily on the rush-covered floor, too tired to even find an empty bench, his back braced against the stone wall. For all he could tell, the ritual had been a success. Of course it would be a matter of time before anything was certain. Gratefully he took a cup of mead from the drudge who offered it. He noticed that the mage took nothing. But the baron was drinking his third glass.

Finishing his mead, the baron stood and approached Gwydion's chair. The mage slowly raised his head to regard him warily.

"I cannot forgive you for who and what you are, and I will never understand you . . ." the baron began.

Gwydion's eyes narrowed.

". . . but even I must give honor where it is due. What you wrought this eve," he gestured towards the sanctuary doors, "was well done! I have gained honor in the sharing of it." Alemandus held out his hand.

For a moment, Gwydion just stared at him. Then, slowly, he raised his own hand to clasp the Baron's.

"I would also like" the Baron continued, "to propose a treaty that I think will be mutually agreeable. I would grant you the Veldtar forest, in fief for me, of course, to protect and preserve. With the understanding that the people of the barony be allowed to pass through it unmolested. In return, you will cease your war upon the barony. You will also confine any sorcery and magical solicitations to the forest, and avoid troubling my people with your heathen practices."

A flash of anger lit Gwydion's eyes at the last, but he quelled it. "This will not end what is between us, but for now, it is enough."

The moment was interrupted as Giselle entered the room. "She is awake."

Cedric spilled his mead in his haste to get to the sanctuary. He entered to see Aurora, eyes closed, lying on a pile of sleeping furs in the center of the a great circle, surrounded by guttering candles. He knelt by her side, frightened by how fragile she looked. Her eyes opened. As she saw him she smiled and reached out for him. Suddenly nothing else mattered.

THE STUFF OF LEGENDS

by Jody Lynn Nye

" ... Then Verrol and Liaya challenged the Dark Queen herself," old Mikal said, drawing light from the hearthfire into pictures to illustrate his tale. Minute figures in jewel colors sprang into being, moving and reacting as if they were true beings. "Armed with the sacred Spear they could not fail, but they were sore afeared. On the battlefield, Red Nachriia turned her three faces toward them, all eyes glittering. They moved together . . . ."

Out of the corner of his eye, Duffy noticed something else glittering, something that looked familiar, in the hands of the Wanderer female who'd been sitting beside him when the old mage began his storytelling. He felt the sheath on his belt. His dagger was gone. The wretched creature had stolen it!

"Give that back," Duffy said, standing over the Wanderer with his hands on his hips. The rest of the folks in the tavern stopped to watch. Mikal fell silent.

"I was only just looking at it," the Wanderer said, blinking up at him winsomely. She held out the dragon's-head dagger she had taken off his belt. He hadn't felt a thing, which was part of what was making him furious. Teeth bared, he snatched the dagger back and put it securely into his belt. "Pretty, isn't it? I saw one like it these fifty years back, oh, where was it?"

"We don't like thieves in our town," Perog, the landlord, said, coming up to add his bulk. The child-sized creature nearly disappeared in the shadows cast by the two big men.

"Oh, I didn't steal it. I just picked it up," said the Wanderer, imperturbably. All wanderers were unflappable.

"And I suppose it wouldn't have gone into the pack with this collection of junk?" Perog said, picking up the Wanderer's knapsack and shaking it. It clattered noisily, and the landlord looked inside. "Them's my wife's candlesticks! Put her out, boy," he growled.

"With pleasure," Duffy said. He picked up the offender by the ragged collar at the nape of her neck in one hand and the sack in the other.

"I've done no harm! Put me down!"

Duffy paid no attention to her protests. He'd been interrupted in the middle of hearing his favorite legend— just as they were getting to the battle. The pleasant rapture of imagination was broken, as thoroughly as if he'd had a bucket of water dashed in his face. At the very least, Duffy wanted the source of his discomfiture out and gone. One of the other patrons of the pub opened the door for them, and he carried the kicking Wanderer out into the moonlit night.

"The road's that way," Duffy started to say. "The r—"

He swallowed and tried again.

"The r—"

"That's a dragon, isn't it?" the Wanderer asked brightly, swinging from his right hand. "My, a well-grown specimen it is too. Its tail goes clear around the building and comes back again. I didn't know dragons slept like that, did you? Oof!"

Duffy dropped the gnome-creature on the ground and scrambled back into the pub.

"There's a dragon out there!" he bawled. The pub's twelve patrons crowded around the single small window, and the publican, with the greatest of care and a broomstick, urged the casement open. Moonlight shone into the smoky room.

"There's nothing outside but that dratted Wanderer," Perog said, shaking his head.

"I tell you, I saw it," Duffy said, goggling. "Big, shiny dragon, curled around your pub like a cat on a hearth."

"No more for you tonight," Perog said, grinning and shaking his head. "Go on home, Duffy. Sleep it off."

"I'll start again for you on the evening,' Mikal promised, with a wink and a finger laid aside his nose. "See you tomorrow, lad."

The others, relieved to find out the alarm was a false one, called out their good nights and went back to their pints and jokes. Duffy, disgusted, slammed out into the warm night.

"I saw it, I did," he said.

"We saw it," the Wanderer corrected him, falling into step. "And then it was just gone—blink! Like that." She flicked her dainty fingers outward.

"Get lost," Duffy said, opening his stride. The small woman, barely waist high to him, hurried to catch up.

"Can't," she said cheerfully. "I've been about everywhere. This town used to be bigger once. I know it. Back along, oh, thirty years it was. Is this your house? What a fine place!"

Duffy growled a little under his breath. He didn't need the sympathy of gnomelings. He knew what the great house looked like, with the burnt husk of one wing indifferently cleared away, and holes in the wall patched with

white plaster because the man who'd made the original
blue wash had been killed by the last raid of Voern's
Minions passing through here. If he'd been more than a
fourteen-year-old stripling back then, he'd have shown
those misbegotten, overgrown lizardfolk what he thought
of their destroying his home. But, he thought with a sigh,
his strength lay in the future, and his family's glory was
fast receding into the past. Like everyone else, the gentry
needed to work to survive.

A single candle in the upper storey showed his mother
must still be awake, then he realized it wasn't even
moonset yet. The Dragon's eggs be blessed, but why did
a vision of one of Her offspring have to interrupt a nice
evening's drinking and tale-swapping? He unlocked the
latch with his key, and glanced over his shoulder. The
Wanderer hung back on the path, gazing up at him hope-
fully. He realized she probably had nowhere to go, might
even have been thinking of staying at the pub, until she
was caught stealing.

"You can sleep in the barn," Duffy said, pointing past
the shell of the west wing. "There's straw, and a horse
blanket or two. But don't talk my cows' ears off, will
you?"

"Not a word," she promised, beaming, clutching her
small hands over the strap of her carryall. "Thank you
most kindly for your hospitality. Good night. Sleep well—"

Duffy fled inside and shut the door on her chatter.

"There's a lizard outside," Gillea, Duffy's six-year-old
sister, said from the doorway. "I went to let out the cows,
and it *looked* at me."

Duffy lifted his head out of the pillow, his eyes only
half focusing. The sun was no more than a red streak at
the horizon. "Oh, aye?"

"The cows won't go out. And there's a Wanderer in
the barn. She's only as little as me, fancy!" The girl's
blue eyes were round as eggs.

Duffy sat up, fully awake, the events of the night before registering. "So it's not a dream," he said, pulling on his tunic.

"Your dragon's back," the Wanderer said happily. She sat on a stone in the sun, sorting the contents of her bag. There were bits of colored stone and glass, a short length of bright chain, and a few interesting twists of metal. Duffy heard the distressed mooing and shuffling hoofsteps of his herd inside the barn.

"It's not mine," he said heatedly. "You brought it, didn't you?"

"I?" The Wanderer wasn't interested. "Oh, no. If I had a dragon I'd talk to it myself. It's yours."

"This way. It's back here now." Gillea tugged on Duffy's tunic hem, and guided him around the side of the building.

They peeped around the corner. Beyond should have been the fields, with the hundred or so head of cattle that belonged to the village grazing placidly. Instead, the green was empty, but for one dragon. Not even birds sang in the trees. A few farmers huddled on the common concealed from sight of the thing talking in low voices.

Duffy eyed the great beast. No doubt about it, it was the dragon he'd seen the night before, silvery white and immense. The creature had to be a good fifty feet long. It opened its eyes and looked directly at Duffy. Then it disappeared.

The village elders at once called a meeting to discuss the dragon. By virtue of his family's position, and his late father's office as a knight of the Dallen, Duffy was titular headman of Greenton, but the seniors talked over his head, oblivious of the blow to his seventeen-year-old feelings.

"Just poof, vanished!" Farmer Orack declared, raising his hands to witness the truth of his statement. "But my cows are scared that witless they still won't go out. I'm having to feed them in the very barn!"

"Mine dropped a calf early out of fear," Farmer Eise said. "Praise be to Her on high, and to Mikal's skill," he nodded to the old hedge-magician, "that we could save it."

"What's it *doing* here?" Miller Varney, the tallest man in the village, asked. He didn't mean the calf.

No one had a clue.

"This daughter of the Silver One has to go," the blacksmith declared, folding his massive arms. Sandor was short and dark, not unlike the dwarfish mountain folk.

"Why? It's giving no offense," Mikal said mildly.

Orack stared at him. "The milk turned—none of my cows escaped it. I've got vats of sour milk—what are you going to do about that?"

"It looked at *him*," Eise said, pointing at Duffy.

"Then you're responsible for it," Varney said. The elders, as one, turned toward Duffy. The youth stared at them.

"Aye, Duffy," the others agreed.

"What am I supposed to do about a dragon?" he asked, incredulously.

"You're the headman, right?" Orack only remembered that when it was convenient, or when there was an unpleasant job to do, as now. "Kill it?"

"Kill a daughter of the Protector Liaya?" Varney sputtered. "Do you want to bring the wrath of the elder gods down on us? Send it away."

"Find out what it wants," Mikal suggested.

After an hour's bickering, the group still couldn't come to a consensus on what they wanted done with the dragon, but they all agreed it was Duffy's responsibility to do it. After another hour's persuasion, Duffy agreed to try and find out why there was a silver dragon in Greenton.

The dragon turned up only where and when it had

wanted to. Duffy decided that the logical thing to do was start out where it had last been seen. Feeling like a fool, he walked around and around the empty common. Gillea and the Wanderer went out with him.

"Should I call it?" he asked, pausing in mid-stride after pacing out the circumference three times. "What do you do to attract a dragon's attention?"

"Let's sit down," the Wanderer said, grabbing his hand. "Not for me, you understand, I could walk forever, but this lass is about to fall over. She's only about as tall as your legs, and there's two of them."

Gillea was trailing behind them. She wore a game expression, trying to show she was tough enough to keep up, but her strength was flagging. Duffy walked back and scooped her up. "Sorry, gillyflower, I'm not thinking too well."

"I'm all right," Gillea said, but she wound her arms around his neck.

With the Wanderer running alongside chattering soothing talk at the child, he carried her over to a big flat stone on the edge of the field that lay against the boles of a semicircle of oak trees that had grown up around it. It was a favorite place for children to sit on hot days. Gillea pried herself loose and claimed the coolest hollow at the rear of the stone. Duffy sat at the fore with his feet dangling off the edge. The Wanderer sat companionably beside him.

"How do I find out what a dragon wants with us?"

"With you," the Wanderer corrected him. "Why not talk to it?"

"Talk to it? A dragon?"

"I do speak," a voice said behind them. Duffy jumped. A dragon head the size of his whole body poked through the tree trunks. For a moment he couldn't see Gillea.

"Where's my sister?" he demanded.

"Here," said a very small, scared voice. The child scrambled out on hands and knees from under the great neck, and hid her head in Duffy's lap. The great head turned, and one huge, jewel-like eye studied him.

"You have questions, ask." The voice came from within the dragon, not from its mouth and tongue.

"Ask," the Wanderer said, eagerly. "Ask her. Shall I ask her for you? I think I've seen this lady before. Now, when did I see her? Fine and beautiful, but that's all silver dragons. But I'm sure this is the same lady."

"Shush! Uh, honored dragon person . . . ." His voice died in an embarrassing squeak. Duffy's mouth kept moving, but no sound came out.

"I have a name," the dragon interrupted. "Shortened for use by you humans, it is Soraya."

"I'm Fernli," the Wanderer said. "I'm pleased to meet you. Or is it re-encounter? I don't remember if we were introduced, back along."

Duffy realized he hadn't ever thought to ask the Wanderer's name. "What are you doing in our village, er, Soraya?" he asked, pitching his voice over the Wanderer's incessant chatter. "A silver dragon, well, I'd think you'd be in one of the great cities, or out in the mountains of the south. It's small, I mean our town."

The vibrations of the great voice made his chest throb. "I am here to fulfill a pledge made to Sir Karal Zovali. He marched under my banner in the last war. That is his symbol, is it not?" The head tilted toward the silvertopped dagger in Duffy's belt.

"Uh, yes," Duffy said, wiggling his bottom as close to the edge of the rock as he could. If the dragon made a wrong move, he was going to grab Gillea and run for his life. "It belonged to my grandfather, then it passed to my father. One of his companions brought it home to us over a year ago."

The dragon inclined her great head. "Then you are the one I seek. Karal saved my life, and in so doing, lost his. His last wish to me was that I protect his son and see that he receives teaching to become a knight. His

efforts were in vain—I perished later on that same day—
but I honor his bravery, and my word." Its pupil opened
up to consume most of the glittering iris, and Duffy was
drawn toward it. He saw a man lying braced in the curve
of a huge silver claw, gasping for breath. A great wound
split the armor covering his chest. Duffy caught a horrific
glance of sundered bone and flesh through the welling
blood. He swallowed, and the vision faded. The dragon's
eye returned to normal.

"You say you perished later?" Duffy asked, glancing
down the great neck. It was sticking through the tree
boles, not between them. *Through*. "That makes you a
g—a gh—"

"A ghost?" the Wanderer finished for him, now intent
on the shiny scales of the dragon. She appeared to be
counting them.

"But a ghost of a servant of Good. A vow of honor
supersedes even death. As a knight of the sword your
father understood that." The dragon looked into the distance as if seeing visions of the past. "He would have
been raised to the Order of the Heart, had he lived. He
had similar hopes for you."

Duffy was awed.

"But my father died three years ago. Why are you here
now?"

"It was not necessary to protect you before this," the
dragon said simply.

"You mean I'm in danger?" Duffy asked.

"Ooh," Gillea said, picking her head up and staring
wide-eyed at the dragon. "What's going to happen to
Duffy?"

"I am but a dragon, not an oracle," Soraya said, baring
her huge, pointed teeth. "It is time for you to become
the leader your father knew you could be. You need to
muster your village. Time is short."

*　　*　　*

"Muster? For what?" Varney asked. He grunted as he bent to pick up a sack of grain half his own size.

"An attack!" Duffy said, following the miller up the stone steps to the storeroom. "Soraya didn't say what, but she knows it's coming soon! You can't ignore the warning of a ghost, and a dragon ghost at that, now can you?"

Varney dumped the sack on the floor and blew chaff out of his graying mustache. "I suppose not, but what if she is an illusion sent by the evil ones? What they couldn't do with armies, they'll do by frightening us into tearing our own village apart?" He shook his head heavily. "Save them the effort. No, if there's trouble, we may as well surrender or flee. There's nothing left in this place but children, women, and old men."

"And me," Duffy said, stung. He drew himself up to his full height, which put the top of his head just underneath the miller's white-daubed nose.

"And thee," Varney agreed, kindly. "And a ghost, for all the good that does us. Some are saying it's unlucky that it's come here. Orack thinks it means death for all of us."

"Well, it won't," Duffy said, wishing his voice wouldn't crack when he was under stress. "I swear it, by my father's name."

"Lad, if you don't have more in you than your father's name, all is lost," Varney said. "I'll help. But you'll have more trouble convincing the others."

As Varney had predicted, the men were skeptical of the dragon's warning but promised to cooperate just the same. The Hearthstone Tavern became headquarters for the defense of Greenton. The adults, men and women alike, clustered together to plan for the coming attack. It was difficult to make plans without knowing what for.

Barata, Orack's wife, stood up.

"What are we doing, mustering for war?" she asked.

"Old folks and children! If only some of our fighters had survived, if only Sir Karal lived, this exercise would be reasonable. I say to stop the nonsense right now."

"Unless we defend ourselves, we'll have to flee," Duffy said from the foot of the table. "Evil things are marching this way. Soraya wouldn't lie. Silver dragons are the children of the One who protects us."

"Now, don't you quote your lessons at me!" Barata said furiously, leveling a finger at him.

Duffy's mother stood up.

"I offer the shields and spears which hang in my family's hall," she said quietly. "They are old, but there is still some virtue in them."

Duffy was proud of her upright carriage and dignity. He remembered that before their fortunes fell and Sir Karal died, she had been a court lady, trained to the sword and shield.

After such a generous beginning by the highest lady in the town, the others put up their donations.

"Strawing hooks!" "Cooking knives!" "Any of my hammers ye can wield!" "The millstone!"

Miller Varney looked around in satisfaction. "And the rest of you can offer your two good hands," he said. He glanced up at Duffy. "I'll start organizing this lot, with your permission, General, laddie. You take the rest." Gratefully, Duffy nodded.

"The rest" consisted mainly of the village children.

"Since we're without weapons or magic," Duffy said, leading his band of youngsters along the forest path toward the main road, "we have to outthink our attackers."

"When will we learn to fight?" one boy asked loudly, and was hushed by the others.

"Never, I hope," Duffy replied, wondering if blatant honesty helped in being a general. "You're going to set traps and act as spies."

"My mother doesn't want me out in the forest by

myself," complained Dirk, the small son of Eise. Some of the others made fun of him, but their eyes were worried, too.

"We'll work in teams," Duffy said, looking back over his shoulder at all of them. "Everybody will have a partner, and I'll go around between all of you to make sure nothing is going wrong. You're all being very brave. Between us we'll keep the village safe."

Soraya, glimmering like a star, flew through the tree boles across their path, her claws stretched out, and came to a perfect landing before Duffy.

"Time is short!" she cried, her great voice booming. "Ogres! Ogres from Voern's Minions are coming. The foe is within hours' march of here!"

Some of the children screamed. Orack's daughter snatched up her younger brother and sister and fled back toward the village. Her threshing footsteps resounded in the quiet forest, scaring small animals and birds into flight. The rest of the children remained, huddled together, staring at Soraya.

"Ogres," Duffy said, his eyes wide as saucers. "Then we're lost. We'll have to get everyone together and hide them in the caves along the rivercourse."

"No, we will fight them," Soraya said. Her eyes gleamed with a formidable inner fire that surprised Duffy into taking a step backward.

"How?" he asked helplessly.

The light in Soraya's eyes flared. "First, you must set your traps. Then we must make plans."

With difficulty, Duffy persuaded his small force to continue with their tasks. With coils of rope and sinew, they set snares at intervals where a foot might fall. Thanking the gods for the copious rain that Greenton had had recently, Duffy helped a group of boys deepen pits in the roadway and plant sharpened spikes in each. Carefully, an elder girl in hide gloves up to her elbows painted the stakes with brownish goo from a lidded pail. Very small girls and boys filled up the pits with debris to disguise the trap. The Wanderer was here, there, and everywhere, offering advice to the children, and telling them merry stories of her many years of travel. A few were distracted by the gnomeling's silly talk, but most of the children couldn't forget that what they were doing was no longer a game. All of them had been brought up in wartime, and knew that those who fell in battle never came back.

Gillea comforted her best friend, who dashed the back of her hand at weeping eyes and nose even as she tied triplines around the boles of trees.

"I don't want to die," Loie said.

"Duffy won't let you," Gillea assured her, dabbing her friend's face with the edge of her own increasingly dirty apron. "If he did, Mother would kill him."

Duffy, a few yards away, helping another boy tie back a springy tree branch with a length of rope, hurried what he was doing and sought out Soraya. The silver specter hovered a man-height above the ground, watching each pair of children in turn. She settled disconcertingly through the undergrowth as the agitated boy approached.

"I'm responsible for the protection of all these children—in fact, all the people in the village," he burst out, guiltily. "What am I doing? We can't outfight ogres, or even outrun them. Varney was right. There are no warriors left in Greenton. What can a bunch of children and old people past their prime . . ."

"And a dragon," Soraya interjected calmly.

"Well . . . and a *ghost* dragon do to stop a force of ogres? You can't breathe on them or claw them or even stand in their way." Duffy put his hand out, passing it without obstruction into Soraya's muzzle. "There's nothing that will keep ogres from marching upon Greenton and tearing us to pieces."

"We've got you," Gillea said, coming up and tucking

her hand into his. "The one shining hero who will save everyone, like in all the stories."

"Sounds familiar," the Wanderer said, intent on her bits and pieces of broken glass again. She seemed to like tumbling them over and over in her fingers. Duffy wondered in some irritation if she liked them so well to be interested in nothing else, why had she spent the fifty years she'd claimed wandering all the lands of the Dallen? "Sounds like the tale the old man was telling in the tavern t'other night."

"The story of Verrol and Liaya?" Duffy said. He turned to Soraya, whose giant eye grew even brighter.

"That is the answer," Soraya said.

"What?" Duffy demanded. The image that grew in the dragon's eye was such an obvious solution that it made the young man laugh out loud.

"What is it? What is it?" Gillea demanded, jumping up. Duffy caught her in his arms and swung her so she could see the dragon's face.

"Soraya is a spirit," Duffy said. "The enemy can fire arrows or swing clubs but they can't hit her. Anyone who sees her with a rider will think that he's a ghost, too. We'll be the ghosts of Verrol and Liaya. Ogres are terrifying warriors, but they're as superstitious as sailors."

Soraya blinked her approval, and turned her eye toward Gillea, so the child could see in it the image of a young man, all in white, a-dragonback and wielding a great spear. The children abandoned their tasks and gathered around the huge dragon's head, chattering excitedly. They all knew the tale by heart. Duffy himself had heard it several times a year since he was a baby.

"But you can't ride a ghost dragon," Gillea said, practically, pitching her shrill voice over the hubbub. Duffy's heart sank in dismay. He turned to the dragon.

"Leave that to me," Soraya said. "For now, we need what magic we may muster, and the disguise."

Duffy ran all the way back to the Hearthstone, and

burst in through the door. The elders were holding their own worried conference over the hearthfire.

"Is it true, boy?" Perog asked. "Ogres are coming?"

"It is. Varney," Duffy panted, as the miller turned to stare at him. "I need a bag of flour, at once!"

"A what?" Varney asked. "Have you gone mad, son? We've things to do before the force gets here."

"It'll save our homes!" Duffy insisted. "A bag of flour. A small one. Please, Varney. Mikal," he said, catching his breath, "we need you, too."

The old mage rose to his feet and squared his shoulders proudly. "With pleasure, General Duffy. Lead the way."

Soraya stood by, enjoining them to hurry, while Mikal and the women of the village made Duffy up as the ghost of Verrol the hero. Eager to help, everyone donated something to the effort.

"Thank the gods for something to do," Cara the Weaver said.

She quickly stitched together a pair of breeches out of freshly bleached cloth and tied the waist shut around Duffy's middle. Barata brought out the white tunic Orack had worn when he married her. His own mother sacrificed a fine, snow-white tablecloth to make him a cloak. With a small kiss on the cheek for bravery, she tied the cloth around his neck and left him, to go help with the preparations for defense. For luck, Duffy tucked his father's silverheaded dagger into his belt.

"And the flour to make you a ghostly color," Mikal said, pressing it to Duffy's skin. By virtue of some cantrip the old hedge-wizard recited, the stuff adhered to Duffy's face and hands, leaving them looking chalky and dead.

Gillea sputtered with laughter. "You look like you got into a fight in the kitchen." Her brother made a face at her, which made her giggle more.

"It won't look so in the forest," her mother admonished

her. "Have we time?" she asked the spirit, who was
wavering around the edges in impatience.

"They are near. Four ogres and a handful of takkin,"
Soraya said. She vanished, and reappeared almost
instantly. "They are a half-hour's march, no more!"

"Well, I'm ready," Duffy said, brandishing a washing
pole that Cara had donated. The whitewash painted on
it was still damp, but that tackiness would keep the makeshift lance from falling out of his hand.

"Wait, wait!" The Wanderer rushed up and planted
something in his other hand. "It's only a loan, mind. I
want it back, but it'll help you, I'm sure."

"What is it?" Duffy turned over the contraption of
wires surrounding two round bits of glass.

"A gnomish invention," the Wanderer said. "Useless.
Pretty, though. I liked it, and no one seemed to mind
me taking it. Had it a long, long time. Thought I lost it
once, but here it is again! Put it on. Over your eyes. It'll
make them look like spirit eyes."

With the Wanderer's help, Duffy slid the half loop
between the glass lenses over the bridge of his nose and
hooked the loose pieces of wire over his ears.

The gnomish device must have retained some magical
aura, because suddenly Duffy could see more clearly.
Every object took on a deeper dimensionality than he
had ever known.

"Why, thank you, Fernli," Duffy said, looking around
in awe. He glanced down at his feet, shod in white riding
boots saved from the bequest of someone's grandmother.
They seemed very far away. He took a step and staggered
because the ground was not where he expected it to be.

"Ooh, scary!" Gillea said, with delight. "You look like
a week-dead fish."

"One more thing," the dragon said, her deep voice a
murmur. "Find you a feather."

With difficulty, Duffy tottered toward the farmhouses,
aiming unsteadily for Orack's goose pen. In a short while,

he returned, clutching between his fingers the largest goose feather he could obtain, culled at great personal peril from the threshing wing of one of Orack's highly territorial geese. Soraya looked at it disappointedly.

"It is small but it'll have to do."

"Small?" Duffy exclaimed, measuring the feather. It was easily a foot long. "Compared with what?"

"A roc feather, an eagle feather," she said, trying to make him understand. When Duffy continued to look blankly at her, she brought forth images in her great eye of huge birds, perching next to a knight. Whereas the head of Orack's goose came up to Duffy's waist, the head of the man in the image barely touched the breast of the crouching roc.

"Uh," Duffy said, somewhat inadequately.

"Put the feather in the small of your back. Yes, under your clothes. There. You are ready," the deep voice said.

Duffy disliked the way the feather tickled, and the point dug into his spine like a guilty reminder. But he held himself upright, and walked into the town center proudly. Gillea, claiming the honor of serving as a squire, tagged along behind him. The fascinated Wanderer followed.

The villagers had bare moments to snatch up the elderly or makeshift weapons they possessed and get into their hiding places before Soraya's ghost swept through, warning them the enemy was upon them.

Duffy, hidden in the heart of a hollow tree at the edge of the village common, heard the force from the Red Horde before he saw them. The tramping of their feet sounded like a fire burning down the forest. In his mind's eye, he saw them coming nearer and nearer. The front line must be almost on top of the buried stakes—now!

Angry bellows ripped through the air. Some of the fell warriors at least had stepped into the hidden pits. More howling and yelling resounded as the rest of the enemy stomped by their wounded members, and stepped into more of the concealed traps. Pretty soon, those who had trodden on the stakes would be ailing, maybe dying, when the rodent poison took effect.

Not all the evil force stepped into the pits. Threshing footsteps grew closer. The foreline would be getting closer to the snares. Some of the triplines were set high, some low. Even if by chance, a few of them *had* to close on prey! Duffy clenched his hands closed against the damp, shreddy interior of the tree, and hoped.

Twang! Twang! A couple of the line traps went off before there was an outcry alerting others to the danger, followed by harsh orders from the enemy. Duffy heard the unmistakable clash of steel on steel as swords were drawn. Whistling and chopping noises followed, as the point guard slashed through the remaining snares. Duffy wondered how many had died, and how many remained. Soraya, who could have told him, was remaining concealed until the last moment.

The next obstacle was the most dangerous, but not for the ogres. Old Mikal, liberally daubed with flour, waited in a clump of bushes, to try and scare the warriors off— or at least put the fear of the unknown into them. He'd argued in conference that he was the only logical person for the job, being old and mostly expendable. Varney and Eise had shouted him down, insisting that one of them be the one to show his face. In the end, Mikal bluntly refused to enchant anyone else for the job. He was doing it, or no one was. Duffy could just see him flit out of his hiding place and take to the air.

"Bewarrrre!" the old mage cried, waving his arms, and then he floated out of Duffy's view. "Bewarrrre! Tuu-urrrrn baaack! Tuuurrrrn baaack lest the spirits of this place consuuuume you!"

The heavy footsteps halted, and Duffy heard muttering in the ranks. He fancied he could count at least eight voices, but only half were the ogrish grunt. The rest were a sibilant hissing that he remembered from his early childhood, and his insides turned to water.

"Tuurrrn baaack!" Mikal cried again. Then he screamed sharply and fell silent. There was harsh laughter. One of the bolder warriors must have called the seeming ghost's bluff. Duffy prayed that Mikal hadn't been killed.

"Be ready!" Soraya's voice hissed. One huge eye opened up inside his hiding place. Duffy gulped. "They come! Now!"

Summoning all his courage, Duffy stepped out of the tree trunk. Soraya manifested only her face so he could see where she was. The dragon's voice hissed out a rhyme in an ancient tongue that tasted of power.

"What do I do now—whoooaaa!" he cried, as he was lifted, scruff first, ten feet into the air.

"Don't lose your lance!" Soraya's voice warned. "Now, hold your legs apart—no one will care about proper riding form—and keep them that way."

His cloak flapping, Duffy hovered above the long silver back, trying to make it look like he was riding the dragon. He fought nervousness to keep hold of the washing pole, now glowing with the same light as Soraya's scales. To his surprise, the light also issued from his borrowed clothes and his flour-covered hands.

"Here we go," the dragon said.

The effect was impressive even though he knew what was happening. A little at a time, the dragon emerged out of invisibility and glided smoothly into the open common. First the head, then the horns and ears, then the snakelike neck, then the gleaming scales of the breast, and finally the back apparently bearing Duffy issued smoothly into the sunlight. By the time the long tail emerged from shadow, the whole green was silent.

"Stop, foul spawn of Nachriia!" Soraya's melodious voice commanded.

"Go back, evil warriors! You are not welcome here!"

a deep man's voice cried out. Duffy was astonished to realize it was his own. He straightened his back and proudly held the washing pole on high.

For the first time, he could see the Minion horde.

In the front hulked four ogres. He had heard stories of the ogres that served the usurper Voern, but had never seen one alive. Mikal's stories did not do them justice. The manlike giants were more fearsome and uglier and more evil than any illusion the herb-mage had drawn on the hearthstone. Easily seven feet tall, the monsters' massive arms and chests were clothed in leather armor covered in scales each the size of a man's hand. Their faces were studded with knobby bones that parodied the contours of human visage. Teeth bared, they ignored bleeding wounds in their feet and slashes from the whiplike strands of the snares, intent on their task of destruction.

Behind the ogres came two files of scaly beings with doglike faces—takkin. Those Duffy had seen before. The usurper sent a force through Greenton the first time, forcing his father and the other young men of the village to fight for their homes and families when Duffy was only a boy. These dragonchildren were canny warriors, much smarter and subtler than the ogres, and as evil as any creature created by the Queen of Darkness, the Red Dragon Nachriia.

For the first time, the Horde force could see Duffy and Soraya.

They were paralyzed, staring. Suddenly, an ogre burst out laughing, and raised an axe with a head the size of Duffy's chest. The beast-man flung the weapon. Spinning head over haft, it arced toward the silver apparition, and went through without touching anything. Duffy felt the breeze it caused as it passed harmlessly inches from his leg. The axe head buried itself deeply in the ground. The ogre stared from his missile to the dragon and back again. His mouth fell open.

"Fools!" Soraya boomed. "Ye cannot touch us, for we

are the spirits of Liaya and Verrol! We bear the Spear of Truth! We defend this place with its light. Flee, or die!"

Gibbering in fear, some of the takkin turned lithely and dashed down the path into the woods, never to return. The rest stood and stared defiantly at Soraya and her rider.

"Ready your spear, Verrol," Soraya announced loudly. Duffy couched the washing pole against his side, and hoped fervently whatever spell was holding him up wouldn't run out of virtue. As he watched, the homely rod became a lance, sharp pointed and beautiful in proportion. It gleamed with righteous silver light. Duffy let out a war cry. Together, man and dragon swooped in toward the horde.

No being, however stupid or stubborn, would stand still while one of the most fearsome weapons in the land was charging toward it on the back of an angry dragon, let alone in the hands of a legendary ghost rider. The files of takkin and ogres broke apart, and each warrior fled in a different direction.

That was the moment the other villagers had been awaiting. With a wild cry, Sandor the dwarf blacksmith jumped out of a tree onto the head of an ogre. He pounded on its helmet with his largest hammer while the manbeast whirled around, blindly clutching at his passenger. The clanging sounds of hammer on helm alternated with the ogre's cries for help. Sandor, grinning like a skull, locked his short legs around the ogre's neck. In a moment, he knocked the evil warrior's hands out of the way and managed to undo the fastening on the helmet. The next hammer blow lacked the mellifluous clang of metal upon metal, but it was far more effective. The ogre staggered and toppled. Nimbly, Sandor rolled off before his victim hit the ground, and looked around for another tree to climb.

"We go this way, Duffy!" Soraya warned him.

The invisible hand clutching the back of his clothes shifted him sideways, and Duffy found himself charging toward a cluster of takkin. From nowhere, the besieged lizard men were pelted with stones ranging from pebbles to handsized rocks. Duffy caught a glimpse of Gillea and her friends standing on the roof of the smithy with a large heap of ammunition. As the takkin ran away from the legendary ghost, the children followed, leaping from roof to roof, tossing stones, garbage, old birds' nests, and whatever came to hand.

"This way!" Varney cried. "Drive 'em this way!" The old miller beckoned from the narrow alley that led between the mill and the house next door. The takkin saw what Duffy intended, but were unwilling to dive underneath Soraya's feet to escape. It might be safer to risk fighting humans than the ghost. One daring lizardling tried to slip around Soraya's wingtip. Duffy swept the mock Spear of Truth down and caught the beast in the chest. Suddenly, fire ran down the rod's length, and the takkin's armor burst into flames. Screaming, the lizard man dropped to the ground. Duffy was so startled he almost dropped the pole.

"Hold on," Soraya said. Duffy swept his "spear" around in an arc, urging the takkin into the trap.

The lizard men were canny warriors, but the villagers were prepared and on their own ground. Experienced swordsmanship was no match for the anger of the besieged farmers. As Duffy herded his prisoners toward Varney and his cohorts, he heard screams and splashes from the other side of the wall. The men were throwing or forcing the takkin into the millrace. The powerful current of the river could drag a cart horse under the inexorably turning paddlewheel. The takkin emitted desperate cries as their heavy armor weighted them down. Women with straw forks and hooks jabbed at any hand or head that showed itself above the water's edge. Varney and two of the old men armed with ancient polearms held off two more takkin who had eluded the trap. Duffy gasped as one lizard man whisked his sword in an arc and swiped off the axe head from one farmer's weapon. The old man jabbed his attacker in the face with the stub, and got the sword blade in his ribs for his trouble. Duffy gasped.

Soraya roared, and an insubstantial looking silver arrow appeared transfixed through the lizard's eye. The warrior toppled to the ground beside its victim. By anger and main strength rather than skill, Varney took care of the other takkin.

The dragon's great head swiveled bonelessly over its shoulder.

"We are needed elsewhere," she said. She turned in her own length in the narrow gap, nearly brushing Duffy into a wall. He clapped his legs together so they disappeared into her body, and opened them out again as soon as she was back on the green.

Soraya lifted her feet off the ground. The spell keeping Duffy aloft raised him, too, and the two of them glided swiftly into the forest toward the sound of screaming and fighting.

An ogre lay in a clearing nearest the path. He reached up to grab weakly at Soraya's legs as they flew over him, then collapsed, as if the effort took too much strength. The rodent poison had begun to do its job. Two down, and two more to go.

The three children minding the snares and branch slings were clinging for their lives high in the branches of a tree. Below them, a third ogre was shaking the trunk to make them fall out. The invisible hand keeping Duffy in the air lifted him straight up to where the children huddled. He held out his arms to them. The smallest, a little girl, started to lean away from the bole towards him.

A dagger whisked between them and buried itself, humming, in the bark. Soraya, left on the ground, stalked the ogre, growling at it and manifesting terrible images of the heroes of Good. The ogre continued shaking the tree, unafraid of a ghost. Duffy was scared. They needed a distraction for him to free the children.

"Yoo hoo!" the Wanderer called out. "Hello there!"

The ogre stopped and looked back and forth. Fernli appeared standing on a rock only two paces away from the manbeast. She waved at it. It dove for her, but she was no longer there.

"Oh, I'm so sorry," she said, turning up beside him, her hands busy at his waist. "And what a pretty belt buckle that is. Mind if I have a look at it?"

The ogre roared and reached for her with both arms. Fernli backed up. The ogre took two steps, and fell over his great feet as his sword belt slid down around his knees.

"Oh, thank you so kindly," the Wanderer said, again standing on her rock. She had the buckle in her hands, and was examining it with care. "This is very old, did you know that? I bet this is something from your grandda, or could it be your great-grandda?"

The ogre threw aside its belt and went after Fernli with its axe.

Nimbly, the Wanderer skipped along from branch to stone to clod of earth with the ogre in heavy pursuit. Not wanting to waste the opportunity, Duffy clasped the children in his arms, and called out to be lowered to the ground. The two small girls were weeping, but the boy was game for more adventure. His eyes were shining.

As he set them upright and took his place once more astride the ghost dragon, he heard a shout and a *splat!* followed by roared obscenities. Soraya turned her head back toward him, her eyes glistening.

"The Wanderer is resourceful," she said.

"I recognized it," Duffy said, grinning. "She led him into the midden pit."

*   *   *

The fourth ogre, commander of the force sent to level Greenton, found himself almost alone in the midst of the village. The takkin had fled or were being trounced by a ragged, disorganized troop of peasants. His own men were nowhere to be seen. That left him alone to fulfill the task on which Lord Voern had sent them. Fire was the quickest tool for destroying houses and killing trapped villagers. From his pouch he took a red-gold amulet in the shape of a dragon's head. If only Liaya and Verrol did not come back too soon . . . .

As he approached the houses, tiny arrows rained down on him from the rooftops. All but one of the missiles bounced harmlessly off his armor, and the dart that penetrated was as weak as an insect bite. He peered upward to see who'd fired them. Verrolnspawn, nothing more. The ugly little creatures would roast to death when he set this place alight. With an act of will he ignited the small device and held it to the eaves of the nearest house.

Duffy smelled smoke and cast about to find where it was coming from.

"The green," he called. Soraya's long, sinuous neck arched in comprehension. She lifted her legs, and they flew toward the common.

Smoke was pouring from several rooftops when they arrived. None had burst into flame yet, thanks to the soaking they'd received from the fresh spring rains, but if the fire was of magical origin, it wouldn't remain quiescent long. Cries alerted the guardians to a corner of the common area, where a cluster of children on top of a house were throwing rocks and shooting arrows at a single ogre holding something up under the edge of the roof.

Shrugging off the defenders' missiles, the ogre tramped from house to house. Led by Gillea, the children followed, leaping from roof to roof, screaming defiance at him. They were running out of ammunition, and

Duffy could see flames beginning among the shingles atop the first houses the ogre had set alight.

The children had to stop on the roof at the end of the row. There was a gap of a hundred feet between the last low cottage and the manor house, set back among its gardens and outbuildings at the end of the open square. Duffy recalled suddenly how his house had been fired by the last army to march through, and how helpless the child he'd been was to stop the evil army then. This time, he had a dragon on his side, and he was no longer a babe.

"After him!" he yelled at Soraya, leveling the washing pole lance at his side. The silver dragon had but to open her great wings, and they were on top of the manbeast.

The ogre saw the dragon poke its head out of the woods and come sailing down toward him. The spirit of Verrol couched the Spear of Truth in attack position. His pale face was grim.

The commander knew that the warrior and his mount were only ghosts. Praying for protection from the Dark Queen of All Evil, he ran toward the last house in the row, the big mansion. He would finish his task, no matter what. Hopping the low garden wall, he ran toward the house, his amulet at the ready to apply to the wooden rafters of the roof.

Quick as thought, the ghost of Liaya closed the distance, and suddenly the ghost of Verrol leaped out of the saddle toward the ogre commander and cannoned into him.

Not expecting a solid warrior, the ogre was taken by surprise, and toppled over onto the ground. He struggled valiantly against the spirit of the mighty warrior, expecting a divine force and iron muscles. He found his hands were around the neck of a mere stripling, a young humanspawn covered with white powder. Dropping the lance with a clatter, the boy pulled a dagger from a

sheath and tried to plunge it into the ogre's chest. Effort-
lessly, the ogre flipped the humanspawn onto its back
and sat on its chest. The boy gasped. The ogre commander chortled.

"Fool me pretending to be a spirit, will you? Well,
now you'll be a real ghost! Hope you haunt your own
town for the rest of eternity!"

With a horrible grin, the ogre put out two huge hands
and squeezed his neck. Struggling for every breath, Duffy
forced his foot outward, feeling for the red amulet. He
knew it was only inches away from him. Get it away or
the village will burn, his brain sang, even as his lungs
threatened to tear apart struggling for oxygen. Catching
it with the tip of his toe, he kicked it as far away from
the ogre as he could. Then he fainted.

He awoke as something cold and wet slopped into his
face. Sputtering to clear his mouth and nose, Duffy sat
up.

"The High Ones' blessings on you, you're alive," Cara
said, on her knees beside him. "That was the bravest and
most foolhardy thing I've ever seen a man do in my life.
I thought we'd be burying you in my last good bit of
bleaching."

"The ogre!" Duffy tried to shout, but his words were
only an unintelligible croak. He touched his throat.

"Your would-be assassin," Cara said, moving to one
side so he could see past her. Duffy peered at the lump
on the village green. It had arms and legs, all right, but
the rest looked like a millstone.

"How . . .?" he whispered, levering himself upright.
The fires on the roofs were out, and people were going
up and back between the row of houses and rubbish
heap with baskets of burnt shingles and scorched wood.

A little ways apart from him, a row of bodies were laid
out on the ground. One of them had its face covered by
a cloth, but the rest were alive and groaning as healers

worked to ease wounds and burns. Most of them were children.

"It was Mikal," Varney said, coming over and helping Duffy to his feet with an assist from a massive arm. "He raised my millstone right out of its frame, across the green, and dropped it right on the ogre's head. It was a wonder it didn't kill the both of you."

Mikal himself lay propped up against the sitting stone, a gash in his side being tended by Duffy's mother.

"I aimed it better than that, Varney," the old man said weakly. Duffy's mother hushed the herb mage gently, and bound a herbal compress in place over his ribs.

"Sure you did," Varney said, cheerfully. "Nicely placed, truly. Crushed the evil bastard like corn in quern. But you'll have to move yon stone back again as soon as you're well. You borry things in this town, you right well bring them back!"

"Right, and I'll be wanting my gnomish invention back as well," said a little voice. With effort, Duffy turned to see the Wanderer standing beside him. She put out her little hand. He scrabbled at his face, and pried loose the wire and glass contraption. She cradled it happily, and put it back in her pack.

"Many thanks, and glad to lend it. I never saw anything so brave as what you did, except for once," the Wanderer continued reminiscently. "Back around fifty years it was, in the great war. A man with a similar looking dagger as you've got there in your belt—can I see it to make sure?" She fixed the little knife with a hopeful eye.

Automatically, Duffy said, "No." He swallowed. It hurt to talk. The Wanderer shrugged.

"Likewise, I'm sure it was the same one." She peered up at him. "Looked like you, too. Probably your grandda, Duffy. A brave man, like you'll be one day. I'll look forward to telling the story of your fighting here today. Out of your weight class, I thought, but no, you downed the big fellow without trouble. The stuff of legends, you are. Ah, but I've got a couple of nice things today. See, a belt buckle, courtesy of the big fellow there under the stone, won't need it any more, and see here, a pretty gold thing to make fires." Clasping her treasures, she smiled up at the humans and Soraya. "I'll never be cold again nights with this to hand, no, indeed."

Gillea appeared with the rest of the force of children who weren't having their burns dressed. She brandished her birding bow and a handful of the short arrows that went with it.

"We have to go after the takkin!" she exclaimed. "Lots of them got away. We're all ready, Duffy. Will you and Soraya be leading us?"

Having scented blood and come away from their first adventure unscathed, the children wanted another taste of action. Duffy was fit enough to go if he had to, but he didn't want to. He glanced at the dragon for direction. Soraya shook her great head.

"You need not. Those dragonspawn will tell the commanders this place is under the protection of Verrol and the Spear, and they'll never come back again, not without the full horde behind them."

"Oh, no!" Duffy croaked.

"Ah, but by then you will have a militia. The town will be organized into a garrison for its own defense."

"And who's going to lead this?" Duffy asked. "You?"

"No," the dragon said mildly, "you."

"Oh, no. Not me." Duffy raised his hands in protest. Soraya turned a huge, glittering eye toward him.

"Remember your father, to whom I still owe a great debt. It was his wish that you train to be a Knight of the Heart, if your talents and honor are sufficient to the task. I will lead you to my riches once Greenton is ready to carry on in your absence, and that will pay for armor and teacher both."

Duffy found that he was genuinely tempted by the twin thoughts of riches and honor. "Really?" he asked.

"A silver dragon doesn't prevaricate."

"But where does your fortune lie?" Duffy asked curiously.

He noted the amused glint in Soraya's eye. "Are you ready so soon for your second quest?"

Duffy remembered abruptly that he had just ridden a ghost dragon, been instrumental in the defeat of a handful of takkin, and had jumped an ogre in full armor. In reflection, he wondered what in the world he must have thought he was doing. He wasn't a mighty warrior, he was a boy *pretending* to be a mighty warrior. Hastily he stooped and began to pick up pieces of the debris scattered on the ground, including the borrowed washing pole, now smudged with grass stain and soot.

"There sure is a lot to do here," he said, forcing the words out of his wounded throat. "It could be a long time before this town is ready to defend itself. Years, maybe."

Soraya lowered her head to peer into his eyes, and he felt himself blush.

"Just long enough for you to grow up, perhaps," she said. "I can wait. A ghost has all the time in the world."

THROUGH THE DRAGON'S EYES

by Bill Fawcett

Far above the green valleys just below the clouds, the great dragon soared. When it bothered to glance down at all it was to search for one of the great herds of grass eaters that long before had roamed the plains, though it had no great enthusiasm for the task. Hundreds of years ago the herds had dotted the wide spaces between the few clusters of twig-and-leaf huts. Five dragons had shared the valleys. Then the strangers had come marching in tight formation, and filled the air with arrows. The earlier men had called him a god and left offerings. Those newcomers had brought only death. After two of his fellows had been killed, the memory was still bitter; he had chosen to travel to the less hospitable but empty lands to the north. Three days before he had returned, older, stronger, and determined to reclaim the mountains in which his ancestors had dwelled before men had learned about fire. If the wild herds were gone, so he would eat the villagers' fat cattle.

Briefly, but without interest, the great beast noticed as figures scurried in the center of one of the villages below. It swept on, the humans too wrapped up in their own struggles even to notice its majestic passage.

It was a cool day, but the hilt of the rune-covered sword held by the white-and-red mantled knight felt almost warm in his grasp. Twice now he had barely deflected powerful swings from his opponent's heavier longsword. That Tartar's longer weapon had also effectively nullified the advantage a man fighting from horseback had against a man afoot. Seconds before he had turned his attacker's blade, the longsword's point had been deflected so that it tore a shallow cut in the unprotected side of his horse. Frightened and stung by the long wound, the war-horse was becoming difficult to control. The rider had barely regained control when the short, dark-haired horse nomad began another sweeping strike.

Rather than meeting the blow, Aleon forced his mount to back away. The momentum of the heavy sword forced the nomad off balance and he spun slightly off guard. As the man struggled to recover, the knight leaned forward and drove the point of his own blade into his enemy's chest.

The blade cut through the horse nomad's poorly patched chain coat, meeting with little resistance, and continued through the wiry body until it jammed against the man's rib cage. Turning a surprised and accusing stare at Aleon, the nomad collapsed, nearly dragging the sword from the young knight's grip. He folded to the ground with a gurgling gasp.

The newly mantled knight was unprepared for the satisfaction he felt when his blade tore through his opponent's armor. This was his first real battle. He'd contemplated many times how he might react. Most of his thoughts had concerned whether or not he would be courageous. But in the urgent moment of battle, that hadn't been important. He hadn't even thought about it when he spurred to attack the raiders. Now something else worried him even more. He'd studied the Bible and knew that Jesus was a merciful lord. Since his first days the brothers had told him to emulate the apostles and saints. Those were merciful men who worried for their souls and the souls of others. The entire process of killing should have sickened a holy knight, but it didn't. It had been kill or die, and he had prevailed. Instead of remorse, he felt a rightness about it that left no room for mercy. Even now he had no concern for the fact that he had just guaranteed eternal damnation for the man he'd killed. That lack worried the young Templar. Was this what he had spent years of prayer and fasting to become? Was he now more a killer than a Christian? A poor Christian knight in title only? Had he ever not been?

Ignoring the danger posed by the Tartar's few remaining companions, the youthful Sir Aleon de Couveour, newly invested companion of the Knight Guardians of the Temple of Jerusalem, dismounted and stood over his fallen enemy. The nomad wasn't dead yet, though he was breathing only in painful gasps. Hypnotized by what he had done, Aleon stared at the face of his enemy. The raider appeared to be about his age, no more than twenty years; it was hard to tell from his dark skin and squint-eyed face. Since the man wore chainmail Aleon concluded that he must have been a minor noble or the son of a lesser khan.

The body convulsed, arching its back and twisting until the knight wondered if someone so badly wounded might still try to attack him. He was about to back away when he noticed the haunted look in the dying man's eyes. Aleon had seen that look before, in other men who saw death approaching to claim them. The fallen nomad calmed, his muscles relaxed and only his dark eyes still showed fear. Then the eyes were empty, life gone from them. He was the first man Aleon had ever killed. Aleon had to resist the urge to kneel and offer passage prayers for the man. Any prayer learned in the Cathedral would hardly be welcomed by a pagan of the steppes, nor did Aleon feel his prayers would be sincere.

Concern over his lack of remorse mixed with a grim satisfaction. He had arrived in this distant corner of this valley two months earlier. He had entered that first village proud and self-important in his new role of defender of the region. The Templars were a small order, founded less than a decade earlier. Even so, they already had a reputation for the effectiveness with which they defended the kingdom's borders. The villagers, themselves newly settled in the former wasteland, had cheered his arrival. They had expected a guardian and were happy to receive a Templar. The more cynical among them observed that much of the valley's richer residents' joy was due to the fact that, having forsworn all personal wealth, a Knight Templar asked only food and shelter from those he protected, and would be unlikely to threaten their fortunes with importunate demands for monetary rewards.

The wind increased, as if it had been holding its breath during the duel. Aleon's white mantle emblazoned with its red cross slapped against the young knight's leg in mock punishment for the guilt he didn't feel. The Templar raised his head and looked into the eyes of the nearest remaining Tartar. Ranged in a wide arc in front of the lone knight were five more raiders. While less dangerous singly than their leader, fighting five attackers meant that Aleon would most likely die. The horsemen chattered among themselves in their heathen language, spreading out while staying beyond the reach of his sword. Occasionally one would glance at the horses they had staked at the edge of the village. Aleon worried that the five had been sworn to the fallen noble. They might have no choice but to attack, yet he couldn't tell a thing from their gibberish. The young knight strained to remember what he had been taught but couldn't recall whether a Tartar's bodyguard's duties included revenge for his death.

In the two months he had been the guardian of this most distant outpost of the Kingdom of Worzcraw, Aleon had arrived on the scene again and again only after the Tartars had already fled with their booty. Chided by those he was sworn to protect, he had scurried these last weeks from village to village, hoping to be at the right spot to intercept the valley's tormentors, but always arriving too late. The village he had first been cheered in upon his arrival was now a smoking ruin, and its inhabitants dead or prisoners marched off to the steppes and the pens of Saracen slave traders.

Finally Aleon's frantic pursuit of his foe had brought him to this newly founded village close to the forest's edge just when he was needed. Half the houses were already burning when he arrived, but the nomads had not yet fled with their loot. He'd ridden straight to the center of the village, ready to fight and almost expecting to gain quickly an honorable death that would erase his failures and guarantee his place in Heaven. One nomad had run at him with a levelled spear. Using his shield to brush aside the iron-tipped weapon, Aleon had swung his sword across the saddle and felt the blade hit home. The man stumbled into the forest with his shoulder welling blood and one arm dangling limply. There'd been no time to react to that victory. His horse continued its gallop and stopped only after it had carried him into the midst of the dismounted raiders.

Within seconds he'd engaged and struck another Tartar. The man's small shield had shattered, and with a shriek of pain he'd run away between the burning huts. At his cries the rest of the squat raiders had dropped their loot and scurried away from the heavily armored knight. Only the nomad's chain-clad leader had kept his head and called for his followers to join him as he rushed at the Templar, sword at the ready. But before the others could regroup Aleon had won their brief duel and slain him.

One of those followers now hefted his spear and Aleon's muscles tensed, guarding. Those who remained were a ragged lot, only one even wearing any semblance of leather armor. Two men carried small axes, one a spear, and the last two rusty short swords. The Templar took a single step toward them and raised his sword and shield to the ready. This pose was too much for men who'd just seen their leader, presumably their best warrior, die after only a brief instant of combat. All five began to edge toward their mounts and, when far enough to feel safe, turned to scramble onto them and flee into the woods.

Aleon knew he should follow them, but didn't. Reluctantly, the knight moved instead to where one of the peasants lay sprawled. The man was still alive, but the blood flowing copiously from the wound in his side gave him little hope for his survival. A scythe lay nearby, attesting to the farmer's courage in defending his home even with such poor weapons. There was little the Templar could do to aid him. Using strips of the man's tunic, Aleon bound the wound as well as he could while mumbling a prayer, and moved on to the Tartar's next victim. A short time later those villagers who had fled during the attack returned and began to care for the fallen and mourn their dead. By this time the first farmer had died. Cries of despair rose from his widow and children whenever the armored youth passed nearby, as if blaming him for the Tartar attack. To escape their wailing, Aleon stalked to the edge of the forest and made sure that the bandits had not turned back or hidden themselves but continued to run.

One farm lad tended to Aleon's horse. The young

knight was gratified to learn that in spite of the blood, the animal was not seriously injured. Five dead peasants had been gathered in the village and were laid near the man Aleon had killed. Some women spat on the corpse. Afraid they would take unholy revenge on the body, the Templar insisted two youths bury it unmolested in the forest, and leave the grave unmarked.

As Aleon rode out of the village an old woman took hold of his leg.

"My son's one of those there lying dead! He died to give us a chance to escape those bastards. Why didn't you come sooner?" she lamented. She dashed tears off her cheek with a filthy, soot-stained sleeve.

"I came as soon as I could, good woman," Aleon said.

"God should not take ones so young," the old woman said brokenly.

All sense of victory lost, the young knight brushed her off with a murmured prayer, and spurred on with tears in his own eyes as well. The tears were, he told himself during the long ride home, only due to his passing through the smoke still belching from the green grass roofs on three burning huts.

For years Aleon had trained to do what he had just done: kill a man. His family, minor gentry back in Normandy, had nearly impoverished themselves to buy his equippage and secure him a position as a squire. It seemed to him a glorious future lay ahead of him, and he entered into his training with outward humility but a high heart. When he took his oath he had not fully realized that to defend some people, he would have to kill others. The young Templar recalled the emptiness in the eyes of the man he'd just killed, he lost control of his stomach and had to lean over the side of the horse as he lost the meager remains of the distant morning's breakfast. After that he tried not to think at all.

*　　*　　*

Sagging with exhaustion, Aleon was most of the way back to the dormitory of the small temple in which he lived when he saw a delegation hurrying toward him. At its head was the local Patriarch. The head of the local Greek Orthodox church came from a noble family, and ruled over this area in both a secular and spiritual sense. This high cleric was Aleon's host and a source of constant annoyance. He had resented *his* district being sent a newly invested and unproven knight. Worse yet, the Templar, sent as part of a gesture by the Grand Master, was in his eyes almost a heretic, a Roman Catholic and Papist. The darkly-robed priest had harassed Aleon almost from his first day, constantly criticizing the knight's inability to defend every inch of the shire, ignoring the reality of geography and the limits of human strength.

A tall, heavy man with white hair and age-spotted skin, the Patriarch tended to avoid all physically strenuous activity, so Aleon was dumbfounded to see the old cleric was virtually running toward him. Behind the Patriarch, Aleon could now distinguish several more shop owners and the head men of three nearby villages. Since there was no way they could already know he had slain the Tartar noble, Aleon braced himself for more criticism as they approached.

"Thank ... the Almighty ... you've returned," the Patriarch began most uncharacteristically as he hung onto the barding of Aleon's horse, panting. Aleon noticed that his black and gold surplice was moist across the back and his face was dark red from more than the exertion of his hasty approach. Something had to be very seriously wrong.

"I met the Tartars and slew their leader," Aleon informed the cleric while the man tried to regain his breath. He'd meant the news to be reassuring but it felt awkward. For a moment the image of the young nomad breathing his last returned and his stomach twisted.

Seeing the announcement had no effect, the Templar asked, "Sir, what brings you in such a hurry?"

". . . over by Creshski's village . . . cattle . . . dragon," the holy man's words were lost amid the clamor of other voices and the knight realized everyone was suddenly yelling at once. Aleon let them babble for a few breaths, then bellowed in a voice loud enough to carry.

"What dragon?"

Another burst of senseless noise arose as everyone tried to answer at once. Aleon waved his arms for silence. They ignored them.

"Patriarch!" Aleon demanded over the din. "What is everyone talking about?"

"It is a dragon!" the elder insisted.

Aleon could only sit and gape at that reply. "Dragons are the stuff of stories that the old men and women tell in my native Normandy, my lord. They are a myth."

The Patriarch showed his annoyance. Finally, he managed a few words between gasps for breath.

"This . . . is here . . . not Frankland."

Aleon tried not to smile. Dragons were legendary, tales used by peasants to frighten children. Dragons were symbols, representing power and evil, and a way to teach young squires about courage and sacrifice. A few peasants must have seen a large bird and the tale had grown in the telling. He was almost annoyed that this rumor was overshadowing his triumph against the Tartars.

When his breathing returned to normal, the old cleric raised his arms.

"Silence, all!" He turned to confront Aleon, who hastily wiped the traces of amusement from the corners of his mouth. "You, boy, you don't know. We have received a messenger, who tells the tale of this so-called-by-you legend. Two weeks ago, in the westernmost part of this shire, cattle began to disappear at night from the byres."

"Thieves," Aleon shrugged, unconcerned.

"No! It could not be. The village folk suspected the

Tartars, but they steal whole herds. Yet these stories concerned only one cow or bullock at a time. There were no cattle tracks, not a trace of how they left."

"No prints? So the thieves were sweeping the ground behind them with branches. On my father's land . . . ."

"I did not say there were no prints," the elder informed him sternly. "My messenger brought me the tracing of the single print that was discovered in the field from which a cow was stolen." He thrust parchment at Aleon, who unrolled it. On the sheet made of the entire hide of a sheep was the tracing of a single beclawed footprint.

"An invention," Aleon suggested.

"No, sir knight," a man said. Aleon recognized him as an experienced woodsman who had often guided him through the forests. "Three days later the dragon itself was seen. It bore no rider, no livery. It was carrying a whole deer in its talons. I and another hunter saw it pass within bowshot overhead."

"And neither one of them shot at it," the Patriarch said severely. The crowd around him laughed nervously, and the woodsman grew redfaced.

Aleon shook his head, trying to keep his voice from sounding partronizing. "There is little a hunting bow could do to the thick scales of a dragon, my lord. They would have risked their lives in vain to alert it to their presence." At his words, the woodsman bestowed a worshiping gaze.

"So you do believe in this *legend*?" the Patriarch asked with emphasis.

"I . . . I am less certain that what I am hearing is a mere rumor," Aleon said carefully. The woodsman had been there, and he was widely respected for his integrity. He was not likely to invent a hysterical vision of a dragon. Though it was hard for the knight to accept what he said, everyone else listened in nervous silence. "Tell me about it, friend," he asked the woodsman.

The dragon was a large one. Even discounting the hunter's exaggeration, whatever he had seen was not just an oversized bird or lizard. It had been a clear bright day when they'd seen it no more than a league away and just taking flight with a still live deer in its claws. It had been huge and the flapping wings thunderous. "The monster had to be easily half an arrow's flight across, my lord!"

The man sounded so sure, so sincere. Aleon, while still skeptical, had to accept that the woodsman believed what he was saying. Even the town's well-travelled and thoroughly jaded merchants crossed themselves and glanced nervously at the sky as the hunter went on to describe arm-length claws and man-tall fangs. As he and his companion watched from beneath a bush, it had flown northeast into the mountains.

Aleon felt the stirrings of adventure within him. In a way he was relieved that such a deed needed to be done. He'd spent weeks chasing Tartars, and only today, almost by accident, met with some success. If nothing had interrupted this assignment, he foresaw many more months of frustration. He had been raised from infancy on the ancient tales of brave knights slaying massive winged monsters. Should a dragon actually exist, and Aleon managed to defeat it, he could leave this dismal kingdom and return to the Commandery in glory. So for now he would assume, perhaps even hope, that the dragon existed. Aleon addressed the Patriarch, who had recovered his strength, and was now standing at a haughty arm's distance from Aleon and his steed.

"Your grace, as I said when you met me, I have finished my present task. The Tartar band who were harassing your northern villages has been routed. With your permission, I am now free to pursue this new threat."

All the villagers, merchant and peasant alike, cheered his announcement. The Patriarch nodded regally.

"Defeat this monster, and you will have our gratitude, Sir Aleon," he said.

Aleon found it difficult to sleep that night. He suspected that in reality one single man, however gorgeously armored, however swift his horse, was no match for a full-grown dragon, but at least it would be an enemy who would stand and fight. The thought reassured him strangely. While there was a better than even chance he could be killed, in his present mood the thought of fighting a dragon held more appeal than continuing his fruitless chase of the elusive Tartars for an ungrateful Patriarch who would send him away in disgrace when the whim suited him. Death, glorious death, was better than such dishonor.

The Patriarch was in fine form two days later as he invoked a blessing over Aleon. He made such an enthusiastic speech about how courageous the Templar was that everyone cheered quite loudly as the young knight rode out. It wasn't until the village was beyond sight that Aleon realized part of the Patriarch's good mood was partially because if Aleon died his valley could be assigned a new, and likely more experienced, guardian the churchman felt befitted his own lofty station.

Twisting against the high pommel of his saddle the knight searched the sky. He was forcing himself to believe that there really was a dragon, though he would still take some convincing. Leaving the forest for the bare hillsides beyond had made Aleon more than nervous. Under the thick cover offered by the trees, he had a chance to see the dragon before it saw him, and maybe hide once he saw it. In these low hills, there was no way to hide from anything that flew. Most of the ground was barren and the few bushes that grew on the stony slopes rose barely to his stirrup. Even though he was wearing his chain surcoat and thick breastplate, the Templar felt naked and exposed.

* * *

After days of riding through the scrub-covered foothills, Aleon no longer cared if he encountered a dragon or the devil himself. His heavy mail surcoat and iron cuirass were meant to be put on only minutes before entering combat. Since the dragon could appear and battle begin any instant, Aleon had felt constrained to wear his constantly for all three grueling, sweaty, miserable days. He was now too uncomfortable to worry, as he had the first day, about death, and each of his horse's steps provoked a new spasm in the muscles of his lower back.

The sun was past high and the spring day cloudless. Aleon found it surprisingly hot for being at the foot of a major mountain chain and kept hoping for a stray breeze to roll down from the snow-covered peaks to his right. None did. With the sun baking the outside of his cuirass to a roasting temperature he'd debated removing some of his armor. Sweat dripped inside his chain and made his leather gloves feel as if they had been dipped in a stream. The drenching sweat added to his annoyance by causing his leather britches to chafe as he moved in the saddle. Finally he compromised by removing the heavy cuirass and retaining the chain surcoat.

All during the long days of discomfort and frustration, Aleon worried the nomads might have returned to raid in his absence. And he dreamed alternately that he was standing over the man he had killed or that a dragon stood in the same way over his own mangled body. He knew he should have felt remorse at even a Tartar's death. The fact that he didn't ate at him, even as he tried very hard not to think about it. His conscience pricked him for his lack of conscience.

The cloudless heat continued. Halfway from high sun to sunset on the fourth day Aleon began to feel that even facing a dragon would be preferable to his increasing misery.

Half awake and dazed by the sun, the knight was concentrating on the exquisite pain caused by the clinging gray dust that rose with each step his horse took and was working its way into his joints. The tired horse slipped on the gravel that covered this side of the steep hill. There was a moment of intense activity while the knight fought to remain in the saddle and force his mount to continue upward. Then they resumed plodding up the pebble-strewn slope. Aleon sat unthinking, sure that the result of all of his recent effort would be to ride equally uncomfortably down the hill's other side.

He was wrong.

The dragon seemed to rise out of the hill ahead just before Aleon reached the crest. Less than fifty paces away, it rose on its back legs to stand five times the height of both man and horse combined. The wings, spread wide and flapping gently, filled his vision with a wall of red scales and claws. What began as a slow rumble, almost a purr, deep in the dragon's throat, quickly rose into a frightening challenge that rattled the stones at his feet. Terrified by the intense sound, Aleon's destrier reared back over his haunches.

Aleon fought to stay on and regain control of the frightened horse. He pulled hard on the reins, spinning the panicky mount until it settled upright and began to run—directly toward the dragon. For the first instant the Templar was sure he was doomed. The giant dragon had only to fall over upon him and he would be crushed. He expected a claw to sweep him from the saddle at any moment, or a stream of fiery breath to meet him. But the dragon did nothing. It just stood there, wings extended, watching as he was carried toward it.

In the instant he had before reaching the monster, the knight decided that if he was going to be carried straight at it, however reluctantly, then he might as well make use of the charge. There wasn't enough time to free and set his lance. It was all he could manage to draw his sword and stay in the saddle.

The war-horse reared. It was trained to battle, not to

endure the presence of a dragon. The image of being squashed by a scaled foot inspired Aleon to grip the sides of the horse with his knees until his leg muscles hurt. Even as he considered discarding his sword and holding on with both hands, his mount stumbled forward and the Templar found himself facing a wall of fist-sized red scales. Its escape blocked by the dragon, the horse twisted to the left and ran along one wing. Holding onto both the reins and pommel with his other hand, Aleon let his sword arm swing free. Driven by the force of the turn, the sword tore into the wing. The edge cut a shallow groove through the scales and muscle.

With a comical squawk that would have made the Templar laugh if he hadn't still been trying desperately to merely stay on his frothing horse, the huge beast hastily began to rise. In a swift glance at the monster as he passed, Aleon was astonished to see what had to be surprise and maybe even amusement in the monster's eyes. Then the wind from its massive wings sent the knight's horse speeding off in a new round of panic. By the time Aleon was able to regain control of his now exhausted mount, the dragon was gone.

At least now he was certain that dragons did exist.

Later, as he sat in the feeble shade of a bush watching his horse drink muddy water out of a puddle, Aleon began to shake. He ought to be dead. He wasn't and he didn't know why. The masters of the sword and the spear never taught you how to kill a dragon. They weren't concerned that one might someday encounter a legendary beast and need to slay it.

The sheer hopelessness of his quest pressed down on the young man. He was three days' hard ride from any help. His strongest sword blow had barely scratched a tiny portion of one enormous wing. And he couldn't allow himself to admit defeat. There was only one possible outcome to the whole situation: he was going to die.

With this realization his breathing, having just calmed, came again in short, jagged bursts and the young Templar watched the darkness begin to narrow his vision. The horse, concerned for its master, stuck its muzzle in his face and blew muddy drops on him.

Lying back, Aleon closed his eyes and forced himself to breathe deeply and slowly. His heart pounded so loudly that he was sure the dragon could have bellowed another challenge and he would not have heard. It beat even faster as he thought of the dragon. Finally, after long minutes, he was able to sit up again.

Like the knight's clothes, his horse was covered with sweat. Aleon forced himself to brush down the destrier. He was thorough, but not really gentle. The knight was hardly happy with his mount, though he soon realized his anger was not at his horse's panic, but his own. Still, the animal found the familiar act soothing, and soon Aleon was able to persuade it to let him ride gain. He set out in search of, not the dragon, but a clean stream in which he could bathe and clean his clothing.

Aleon didn't want to admit even to himself that he was making a cold camp because he was afraid of the dragon. Still, he could not bring himself to light a fire, even though the night chilled his recently washed jerkin. A fire was visible for miles in these empty spaces—farther if your enemy could fly—and Aleon simply did not know what he would do when he encountered the dragon again. For a long time he sat staring at the stars, trying to recall all he had heard about dragons in those bedtime stories. At the time he had learned to fight, the chance of his encountering a dragon had not seemed great. The instructions given by the scarred and half-blind prior for fighting large beasts had dealt mostly with elephants, not dragons. Now he hoped to remember some forgotten comment by that prior that would tell him how to slay a huge monster that could fly.

Judging by its size, Aleon guessed the dragon was quite

old. Being red, it was also likely to be capable of breathing fire. If his life was not at stake Aleon could have laughed. It was so absurd to be sitting, calmly trying to remember how to fight a beast that surely didn't exist. And yet it did, so perhaps the legends and fairy stories were true. A giant dragon was ancient, and a red one breathed fire. Knowing that, Aleon wondered why it had not simply engulfed him in flame as he rode toward it, or at least after he had struck it with his sword. Perhaps the very size and advanced age of the creature meant its reflexes were proportionally slow. He'd never heard that in any of the tales, but there might be a chance.

Then there was the matter of language. In the legends most dragons spoke at least some of the languages men could pronounce. Should he have stopped to parlay with the beast? How do you parlay with a dragon? He'd have felt foolish threatening such a massive opponent, yet what else was there to say? Leave and I'll not slay you? He'd never heard of a dragon laughing, but suspected that bold approach would give him the opportunity to hear one.

Aleon searched his memory and his imagination for some way other to fight the monster. His nursemaid always stressed that dragons were incredibly greedy. Perhaps he could offer it some treasure to depart and leave his lands alone? The problem with that plan was simple. He was a Templar, sworn to poverty. His entire personal wealth consisted of his tack, two gold coins and fifteen silver pennies. Aleon concluded dismally he didn't have any treasure a dragon might want.

No, the Templar resolved with a long sigh, they would battle to the death. Which of them was likely to win was apparent. Aleon cringed at the thought of dying. Still, there really was no other choice. He was a Knight Guardian of the Temple of Jerusalem and they did not negotiate with evil. They destroyed it.

But how did you destroy something so large and powerful? He hadn't found an answer when exhaustion allowed him a few hours of fitful sleep.

For three days Aleon stalked the dragon. Cautiously he watched from hilltops as the great reptile returned each evening, circled over the nearby valleys, and then disappeared into the mountains beyond. Several times the knight was sure the dragon saw him, but it seemed to pay no attention. He saw no choice and each morning moved in the direction he had last seen the dragon fly. Fortunately it flew straight toward the same point each evening.

After three more cold, hungry days Aleon had spotted its lair. It was late one afternoon with a cloudless sky that almost glowed blue as the knight climbed higher, and saw the great beast fly into a gap in the side of a shattered mountain. The next morning the young knight crouched low under a spur of rock and watched the dragon leave its cave and fly away. He scrambled among the boulders toward the opening.

The entrance to the dragon's cave was halfway up a sheer stone wall. The stone around it was black and sharp edged. Long ago this part of the mountain had been the inside of a volcano. The cave itself, though Aleon neither knew nor cared, had been formed when a massive bubble of sulphurous gases had burst from within the hardening rock.

Feeling exposed and vulnerable, Aleon glanced constantly over his shoulder as he crept along the valley floor toward the gaping entrance. Even ten body lengths below the dark opening he could smell the dragon's scent. A scorched spot on the already black rock showed where someone or some*thing* had paid the ultimate price for disturbing the huge monster.

Finding the lair gave Aleon a sense of accomplishment . . . for about ten heartbeats. Then he realized that though he knew where to find the dragon, he still had to find a way to kill it.

*   *   *

Aleon was thirsty. He had been working under the hot sun for most of the day and his waterskin had been emptied early. Still, he didn't dare stop even to rest. Exposed and unarmored on the gentle plateau a spear's flight above the monster's cave, every moment increased his danger. The dragon had flown off at first light. The red wings glinted brightly in the morning sunlight. He'd been observing the lair from above now for three days. Despite the fear it evoked in his belly, the knight always watched as the beast soared into the air. It was a magnificent sight few men saw and lived to tell about. He hoped to do more than that. All depended on his present efforts. He returned to the shoulder-high boulder he had levered from its bed in the sparkling dust.

The beast was most likely off to pilfer cattle from another farmer's field, a farmer who depended on Aleon to fulfill his oath and protect him. The thought encouraged Aleon to push harder as he used his staff to lever the huge stone a few inches closer to the edge of the cliff. The boulder was almost round and formed of a grey stone speckled with minute red and blue spots. Aleon had grown closely familiar with the rock that had been the focus of his last two days' efforts.

After studying the glistening stone face that held the lair, Aleon had reluctantly concluded there was no way to climb it without special tools he hadn't brought. But he *had* noticed that high above the entrance the mountain's side seemed to recede. It had taken him nearly an entire day to find a route up the other face of the mountain. There he had found a broad plateau strewn with rocks. The last two days had been a nerve stretching combination of hiding in shadows or crevices whenever he saw any movement in the sky and straining to roll the massive rock toward the edge.

Finally the boulder was in place. For the last three evenings he had gathered his courage and watched the dragon's return. It had always flown back to the lair just before sunset. On the first night Aleon had speculated that the creature might not see well in the dark and maybe he should use a rope to enter and slay it at night. But the fact remained that once in the cave, he had no route of escape and such a combat would pit his sword against the dragon's claws and teeth. He wasn't there to fight the dragon and die. He was there to destroy the monster and live. He needed to devise some other stratagem: hence, the boulder to fall from above.

If it stayed true to habit there would be some time before the dragon returned. Aleon leaned wearily against the massive rock. A gentle wind descending the mountain cooled his skin. He tried to relax. His legs and arms shook from the effort he had demanded of them. His hands were blistered and torn. Even with the use of a stout pole, he had barely been able to move the large boulder. Several times he'd considered using one that was smaller and easier to get into position, but anything smaller was unlikely to seriously hurt a creature as large as this dragon.

Settling in the shade on one side of the boulder, Aleon rested. There was little left to do. He could get back into his armor, but the thought of even that much effort brought an involuntary groan. He was tired, hungry, and still not sure his plan would work. But just before sunset he would find out.

Crouching on the edge of the cliff over the entrance to the dragon's cave, Aleon was able to see the great beast returning against the darkening sky. Cautiously but quickly, he hurried behind the boulder and braced himself against the pole. The knight had wedged a smaller, knee-high rock behind the pole and now forced the thick branch under the boulder itself. With this improvised lever he would be able to send the boulder plummeting off the cliff's edge.

Looking around the large rock, Aleon saw the dragon was following the same pattern that he had observed before. Its silhouette increased in size until Aleon realized how overwhelmingly massive his opponent was. For a brief instant he worried that the monster might notice the large rock that had not sat above its cave that morning, but decided that there was nothing he could do but accept that risk. The knight resisted the urge to crouch down and hide. He had to launch the boulder at just the right moment, or his attack would fail. As the monster approached the black wall that held its cave, it threw its lower legs forward. This forced the wings flat and they acted like sails to rapidly slow its flight. Aleon had seen this maneuver before and expected it. He knew what would follow. In a roar of air driven ahead of its great red wings, it would virtually stop in midair. Then barely moving, the dragon would regain its normal flying position and enter the cave. It was a spectacular show that he'd watched fascinated the two preceding evenings.

All the Templar had to do was time the fall of the rock so that it struck the monster's head while it hovered below him. The fall wasn't far, but the heavy stone should strike with enough force to kill or, at the least, stun the dragon. If stunned, Aleon had a rope he would use to scale down the cliff and finish the kill with his sword. It was not sporting, but in a sporting fight he would lose.

When the now familiar rush of wind began, the knight strained against his lever. For a brief instant the boulder didn't move at all. Then with a rumbling scrape, it rolled that last few feet to the edge of the slope and toppled from sight.

Aleon knew he had hit his target when the air shook with an enraged roar. He hurried to the edge of the cliff just in time to find himself staring into a very large, angry eye. In that instant he thought he saw in it a spark of recognition among the anger, but everything was happening too fast to be sure. Before the Templar could even react, a gout of flame leaped across the small plateau.

There was no time to stand and run. Aleon rolled away from the searing heat. An intensely hot stream of fire splashed near the young knight, crisping the thin wool of his jerkin against the skin of his back. To the young knight's surprise the smell left by the flames was pungent, but more like fine spices than brimstone. By the time he could scramble to his feet the monster was soaring high overhead.

There was a hole toward the back of one wing. His boulder had fallen to one side, missing its head. Rather than striking solid flesh, it had torn through the leathery fabric in the back of the dragon's left wing. As Aleon watched, he could see it was favoring that side during its powerful downstrokes. As a result the monster was circling gently as it climbed higher.

Reaching the relative safety of an overhanging ledge under which he'd hidden his armor, Aleon paused to regain control of his breathing. One side of the overhang was near a gradually deepening cut in the side of the mountain. He had scouted this area thoroughly before beginning to move the boulder. It was well he had, because just as the Templar finished fastening his greaves, he felt the rush of air that warned of the dragon's approach.

Glancing from beneath the ledge, Aleon saw the monster would fly directly over where he stood. When it saw the young knight the dragon let out an understandably annoyed screech and dived. Knowing that the beast would be over him in a heartbeat, Aleon abandoned his gloves and helmet to dive into the shelter of the cut.

Once more the intense heat of dragon's fire made breathing almost impossible. This time, when the narrow pillar of flame ceased the pungent odor was punctuated by the musty scent of cracking rock where the dragon's fire had splashed against a stone wall.

For a long time Aleon did nothing. He could only hope that the dragon thought he was dead. Anything caught in that fiery column would have been incinerated. There was no way the dragon would find anything remaining from such a victim. Dragons had to be used to breathing fire and worrying no more. He hoped that this meant it wouldn't look to confirm its kill. More importantly, he was completely hidden from sight in the cleft. Even if it waited, when he didn't reappear, it might assume he had been killed.

It was far into the night when Aleon risked even a quick glance above the edge of the narrow ravine. It took most of his courage to just raise his head above the edge and look. He half expected to find himself once more eye to eye with the giant monster. It took two attempts before his arms obeyed the command to pull him upward.

Nothing moved among the shadows of the plateau. Knowing how well sound carried in the mountains, the young knight then removed his wooden-soled riding boots before climbing out. Once he was standing on the plateau he considered going to the edge and looking over at the monster's lair, but decided that was tempting the threads of fate to snap once too often. Instead he made his way carefully down the cut and to a much smaller cave he had found earlier. Less than an arm's length across at the opening, it was barely large enough for him to sit upright once inside. But the opening faced another stone wall only a few feet away. He was hidden from anything that was anywhere but directly outside the entrance, a space too small for even the dragon's head.

Once inside the cave Aleon took stock. To his disadvantage he was hungry, sore, exhausted, bruised, burnt, and shivering from the cold, the night chill having arrived with the sunset. His horse and pack were half way down the mountain and unobtainable without risking being seen. And the dragon still lived. What he had gained was having actually damaged the dragon. He had hoped to kill the monster; instead he had just managed to arouse its wrath. If he could get away, Aleon decided that he might as well go back to the village. The same trick wouldn't work again so there was no use staying in the mountains. A few days of rest and real meals should make things clearer. At least Aleon hoped so, because at that moment, the young knight didn't have the slightest idea of what he should do next.

The Patriarch's village was the largest in the valley. That meant it was home to over four hundred people. Most of these were farmers or those engaged in the trades, such as the smiths and merchants, needed to support farmers. It wasn't important enough to have an inn, but one shopkeeper sold home-brewed beer from a large barrel. The tallest building was the temple itself, with a tower that was intended to hold a bell, but only served as a watchtower until the townsfolk could afford to commission one. The tower wasn't very impressive by most people's standards, but it looked wonderful to the battered knight as he led his tired horse into the stable.

It wasn't until he was actually entering the village that Aleon realized how he must look. His clothes were singed brown across the back, half his equipment was damaged or missing, and his formerly profuse brown hair was burnt to within a finger length of his skull in the back. He also looked as tired as he felt.

"I thought you were lost," the Patriarch greeted him, trying very hard to sound cheerful.

"I nearly was," the Templar admitted.

"What happened?"

"I fought the dragon twice," Aleon started to recount the story and then paused at the disbelief evident in the Patriarch's expression.

"Twice it nearly killed me," he hurried on, "and I wounded it, slightly, but failed to kill it."

"We know that," a smith Aleon knew was a close

friend of the Patriarch agreed loudly. "It's been seen almost every day between here and the mountains."

The Templar went on to explain how he twice wounded the beast, exaggerating only by leaving out his horse's panic as the cause of his first charge. Telling it all took several minutes during which someone brought him bread, cheese, and beer. While he'd been fed what they would spare by a few farmers on his journey back, the full meal tasted fabulous. When he'd finished the tale, most of those who had gathered drifted off. The Patriarch, who had been surprisingly silent, then furtively gestured for him to enter the chapel.

Once alone the older man placed a friendly hand on his shoulder and gestured to Aleon to sit. The motionless, wooden bench felt good after three days of hard riding in a raspy saddle. Within a few seconds Aleon could feel himself getting drowsy. A few words from the Patriarch later, he was once more wide awake.

"I didn't want to say anything in front of that crowd, but you are probably the cause of the dragon's activity. It was most likely searching for you. I've had reports of it circling over all parts of the valley. The farmers are frightened and I've had to talk swiftly in order to convince a few to stay. The reports of missing cattle and burnt farms have ended though, so perhaps you accomplished something," the cleric observed without gratitude. "Dragons are rarely bested, or even harmed. When you have wounded one, it is best to kill it quickly. Otherwise, you might say that it takes the insult very personally, boy. The only way something as intelligent as a man, that's the size of small castle, and breathes fire, takes being wounded is very personally. It is most likely seeking revenge for your audacity."

Aleon felt his stomach twist and knot. His heart raced with the thought that the colossal monster was intent on evening the score. Somehow he felt assured it wasn't merely going to punch a small hole in his arm, exchanging the proverbial eye for an eye. He swallowed hard to drive the taste of sour beer from the back of his throat.

"Then I'll have to go out and face it again," the young knight said, trying to keep any quaver from his voice. He almost succeeded.

"There's another problem," the Patriarch added almost apologetically. He seemed genuinely sorry to be the bearer of more bad tidings.

"Worse than a dragon intent on exacting revenge?" Aleon wondered.

"Possibly," the cleric warned. "Do you remember the young nomad you killed near Orzcrev's steading?"

The Templar realized he hadn't thought much about the dead youth for several days. The dragon had taken up most of his attention. Whenever the thought had arisen, he'd tried to concentrate on something else. He still wasn't sure whether to be appalled or satisfied at his victory. The Patriarch continued.

"You certainly seem to have gotten yourself into a lot of trouble. It seems that was the oldest son of one of the vilest of the Tartar chieftains." The older man shrugged as he spoke. "Word has come that he has sworn vengeance. That's a blood oath among the horse nomads. He can do nothing else until the death is avenged. They could arrive here anytime, but it will likely be another ten days before they search this far."

"Long enough for the dragon to get me first," Aleon observed, feeling weak. He probably sounded as frightened and depressed as he was, but was too weary to care. Somehow his concerns of a few hands of days earlier about proving himself to the Patriarch now seemed unimportant. It appeared that all he could accomplish now was to determine how he would be remembered after he was dead.

That evening, the exhausted knight tried to think of some way to deal with either one of his problems, but his mind was too fogged to allow clear thought. After an appropriate prayer of thanks, and a short request for aid for his survival, Aleon stumbled into his small dormitory and collapsed. He awoke the next morning with an idea that, the more he considered it, was a good one

Several boys, probably in expectation of getting to fire at his dragon, had been practicing their archery against the wooden wall of his room. Eventually the Patriarch appeared and put them to rout, but the sound of the arrows had inspired a vivid dream. Aleon was on the walls of a great fortress located where the village now sat. A line of nomads mounted on dragons was surging toward the fortress. When they were close Aleon had blown a bugle and hundreds of other Templars had suddenly stood and fired ballistas that had been concealed on the wall. The ballista, he was to later explain several times, resembled a massive crossbow that fired an arrow two feet long with immense force. A bolt had struck each of the attacking dragons with a sound just like the arrows were making on his wall that morning. When each bolt hit, a dragon disappeared.

Remembering the dream, Aleon considered if he had been sent an answer to his prayers for assistance. The longer he considered using a ballista on his dragon, the better he liked the plan. He could recall a text in the Patriarch's library that contained a diagram of a Roman ballista. The smith could make any metal parts needed and there was plenty of good wood nearby. He had even fired one of the ballistas that sat at the corners of the grand priory as part of his training, once.

It turned out to be both harder and easier to construct the weapon than Aleon had expected. The smith was quite happy to attempt the ironwork, once the Patriarch had guaranteed payment. It had taken more persuasion to convince a forester to find and cut the exact woods needed. Finally he had been able to get the village carpenter to assist by agreeing to serve as his assistant until they finished. The knight quickly found that an assistant's tasks included all of the heavy lifting and most of the hard work. That, at least, kept him too busy to brood about vengeful nomads.

It also took time for them to construct the weapon. Each day another message would arrive, often brought by a family of distraught farmers, reporting another sighting of the dragon. It never seemed to do anything, but now was seen everywhere, and the terror was spreading. The Patriarch began hinting that Aleon was using the ballista as an excuse to avoid another encounter, and the knight wasn't really sure if that wasn't true. Occasionally, to add to his nightmares, a merchant would complain about a savage band of nomads he'd seen on the road.

By the fourth day they were ready to assemble the ballista. This aroused a great deal of interest in the village. The weapon was something few had seen. There were very few castles, and less sieges, in their isolated corner of the Worzclaw. It was, without question, the most unusual construction project anyone there had ever engaged in. Under their gaze the carpenter had become energetic, and he pushed Aleon aide to assemble the giant crossbow himself. Not to be outdone, the smith had joined in the assembly. Each time a joint failed to fit well, each would loudly blame the other, but then they worked together to solve the problem. Both were sweaty, but proud, when it was finished. As the last piece was put in place there was an immediate cry for them to try out the weapon. Seeing how proud the craftsmen were of their work, Aleon agreed. Almost forty people braved an unusually hot afternoon sun for the first test.

The weapon stood as high as a man's chest and was as wide as most could reach. The inch-thick, metal bowstring was cranked back using a system of levers that had been copied from the Patriarch's manuscript. While roughly cut, to both Aleon and the carpenter's great relief, everything stayed together when they released the empty bowstring for the first test. Aleon had helped produce five bolts. The Templar tried not to show how concerned he was that the weapon would work. Yesterday there had been reports of a band of heavily armed Tartars riding around villages instead of raiding them. He would have at most a few more days to deal with the one problem before the other arose.

The metal-tipped wooden bolt, when fired, flew steady and straight. It burst through the two-inch-thick board they used for a target, then buried itself almost entirely into the ground some fifty paces further. The villagers cheered. All were sure a single bolt from such a weapon would slay anything. Aleon thought rather sourly that only those who had not personally seen the dragon were impressed. He wasn't sure, but he hoped.

He was happy they had been able to construct the weapon, but now he had to go out and face the dragon again. There was no question that he had been lucky to survive his past two encounters. Chances were he wouldn't live through another. Somehow the thought that it didn't matter, since the nomads would get him later if he did survive, didn't give any solace.

The villagers' enthusiasm extended to helping Aleon load the ballista onto a cart. After an appeal by the Patriarch, four foresters and two former soldiers agreed to accompany the knight to where he expected to confront the dragon. They would help him unload the weapon and prepare it to fire. None would be armored and their arrows and soft iron swords could do little damage to the monster. All agreed that should the dragon attack, they were to flee singly and return to the village. Aleon bravely promised to distract the dragon while they fled. The next morning, as they prepared to leave, word came that a large band of horse nomads had been seen close to the village.

The Templar discovered it was easy to act as if one had courage when you have so little to lose. It was, Aleon decided, as if he had already accepted death. Even the gift by the Patriarch of a new helmet and gloves failed to arouse any emotion. Was this a form of courage? Most likely he was being cowardly, the Templar decided, but couldn't generate any emotional reaction to the conclusion.

The problem was that he got no satisfaction from it. He couldn't even muster any enthusiasm for slaying the dragon. Where everyone else seemed motivated for revenge, he acted out a sense of duty. The creature, though evil, was so magnificent—more beautiful than angels, and maybe more powerful.

Aleon staked his own armor out on a pole as bait. The arms and legs were stuffed with straw, and old boots hung from the pants. Waiting at the edge of the forest fifty paces away, Aleon and the six villagers sat nervously under piles of freshly cut branches. Insects landed and bit, but no one risked so much as a slap. None of them was sure just how keen a dragon's hearing was, and were less than anxious to find out. They had been sitting unmoving for hours and the normal sounds of the woodland had returned. Aleon found himself enjoying the songs of the birds and insects, and regretting how short a time he was likely to have left to hear them. His enthusiasm waned as the day dragged on. By the afternoon he doubted that the single ballista would kill the dragon. His remaining hope was to wound it seriously enough that it would abandon his valley, the valley he had sworn to protect.

The Templar tried not to think about his own fate. Any time he considered the future, he had to resist the urge to simply flee the area. But his oath held him, and the knowledge that, if frustrated, the Tartar chieftain would exact a bloody revenge on the farmers and villages. Still, while waiting to fight a dragon, any concern about being killed by nomads seemed unimportant. Aleon knew that this time the dragon wouldn't settle for flying off injured. One of them would have to die here, or somewhere similar to here, very soon. The only thing Aleon really feared was that the nomads would arrive to take retribution before he could try the ballista on the dragon. That would be so unfair.

Everyone watched the sky for any sign of the monster. They had seen the giant beast on the horizon flying south early that morning. Twice before it had flown over this road junction on its return. There was a good chance it would do so again.

When the sun was only a hand above the horizon and all seven men had grown stiff, it did. One of the foresters was first to see the dragon approach, soaring high over the edge of the forest some miles away. He whispered for everyone's attention, not trusting that the monster was too far away even to hear a shout. After a few heartbeats the dragon must have noticed the bait. It banked sharply and sailed toward them.

Once he was confident his dragon's attention was centered on his decoy armor, Aleon stood up slowly and made sure the ballista was aimed to a spot just above the armor. The monster still wasn't committed to passing where he could fire the clumsy weapon, and the ballista would be of no use if the dragon spotted it, so Aleon kept one branch hanging awkwardly over his shoulders and left several more leaning against the weapon itself.

The dragon gave a deafening cry as it drew closer. Two of the villagers stirred as they crossed themselves, but to Aleon's relief, none fled. The dragon was close enough now that he could feel the wind pushed ahead of the monster's wings. It made the straw-filled arms of the empty armor move realistically, waving the wooden sword fastened to one glove. To the knight's surprise birdsong rang out from a nearby tree. The small flyer was evidently unaware or cared nothing for the larger one. The Templar tried to concentrate on its melodious sound and not the loud, rapid thumping of his heart.

He had expected his dragon to fly over the armor and destroy it with one of its fiery breaths. There would have been no risk for the dragon and anyone standing there would be incinerated. His plan was to fire when the monster passed above the armor. Aleon bent over the ballista and tried to gauge how far he would need to lead the shot. To his surprise the dragon raised the top joints of its wings and slowed to land gently before reaching the suit.

Had its keen eyes determined the ruse?

This was hard for the Templar to judge. The monster was fifty paces from the bait. It must have noticed there was no face inside the mask. Why was it just standing there? What was it watching? The dragon hadn't turned toward the forest where they hid, but its eyes were on the sides of its massive head. It could see them clearly without facing their way. No one moved, or even risked a breath. Even the songbird went abruptly silent.

The dragon took a step halfway to the armor. By the way its head angled and back arched, there was no question that it had now discovered the suit was empty. Before thinking about it, Aleon threw his shoulder into the side of the ballista and shifted it to point at the dragon. Branches cracked as the heavy weapon pushed them aside. The monster reacted to the sound by turning just as quickly to face the forest.

To Aleon the dragon seemed once again uncomfortably close. He hesitated. Staring into the dragon's giant, inhuman eyes frightened Aleon. But again, rather than anger, its eyes seemed to contain some glimmer of recognition. He expected that would be followed by anger, but saw instead surprise. The tableau remained frozen for what seemed a very long time, so long that the bird returned to trilling its song. Then the dragon must have noticed the ballista. The expression in its eyes hardened, and suddenly the wings snapped open and began to flap.

Aleon cranked madly and fired. There was little need to aim carefully. The massive dragon filled the sky. The bolt sped forward with an angry buzz that ended with a solid thump. The young knight risked a glance upwards even as he scrambled to simultaneously both crank the weapon and fit another bolt in the firing groove.

The first bolt had flown true and buried its iron head deep in the front of the dragon's shoulder. The great beast made no sound as it turned to examine the wound as it hovered over the empty armor. Aleon got the impression that it was more annoyed than hurt.

As soon as it was ready the knight fired the giant crossbow again. This time the bolt sped toward the monster's chest, but it skittered along the thick scales there until it drove into the softer muscles at the wing joint.

This brought a bellow of pain and the monster moved slowly towards the knight. As it approached, the Templar could once more smell the spicy odor of its breath. He yelled for the others to flee for their lives, but all had anticipated him and were already crashing through the forest.

Aleon hurried to prepare to fire a third time. Before he had finished cranking back the bowstring, a line of fire marched across the edge of the forest. There wasn't much he could do. Throwing himself to one side and rolling away, the knight escaped with only another singeing.

The ballista was less fortunate. It exploded in the intense heat of the dragon's flame. A quick glance assured the knight that nothing remained of the weapon except charred stubs of wood. Aleon rolled to his feet and dashed into the woods. The dragon bellowed a second time as the knight scrambled toward the thickest section of trees. Once in thicker cover, he risked a look back.

The monster had bent its head around and was using its teeth to draw the second bolt from its wing joint. This time the missile had buried itself much more deeply. The action must have been painful for a third, even more intimidating roar followed.

Turning to continue his retreat, Aleon felt the buffet of wind that told the dragon had taken to wing. For the next few minutes Aleon lived the nightmare of fighting his way through the thick forest undergrowth while overhead a dragon circled and occasionally breathed fire. Twice trees within a few paces of the Templar burst into flame and showered him with hot ash. Other trees suffered as well until Aleon understood that the monster was simply attacking every time it saw some movement. Still there was no way he could stop and hide. The fire drove him forward, and soon the growing conflagration was as great a threat as the circling monster.

The Templar pushed forward with no regard for the branches that slashed into his exposed face and arms. Before Aleon expected it, he emerged not far from where he had staked his horse under the shelter of a giant willow. The mount was pulling at the rope that held it and whinnying in terror as the forest fire drew closer. This was no time for niceties. Aleon used his sword, which he didn't remember drawing, to cut free the tie rope as soon as he had mounted. As he expected, the horse bolted. He clung to the saddle, not caring where the beast fled so long as it was away from the dragon.

It took several painful jounces before he was able to sheath his sword and start to bring the horse under control. Scanning the sky he caught sight of the dragon. He had ridden for only a few dozen heartbeats after calming his horse when a new problem became apparent. At first the knight was upset because the six villagers had not scattered as planned. Instead they were cowering in the shelter of a small clump of oaks. The cart they had arrived in was nowhere to be seen. Aleon waved and yelled for them to split up before the dragon took them as a group. Instead of fleeing, they all began to gesture toward the sunset.

Aleon's anger quickly gave way to fear. There, riding quickly toward them was a band of almost a dozen Tartars. Reddish sunlight glinted off their armor. The horse nomads' distant war cries could be heard even over the sound of the burning forest.

Aleon had to quickly make a hard decision. He had to assume the dragon was still searching for him. If it had been upset before at its cave, then it would be enraged now. He couldn't outride a flying dragon. His only hope would have been to find someplace to hide. But to stop anywhere meant death at the hands of the Tartars. Searching the evening sky again, Aleon spotted his dragon. Almost overhead, it was rising higher by flying in circles inside an updraft. The knight felt somehow it was watching him.

When the great beast didn't swoop to attack, the Templar turned his attentions to this other threat. The Tartars had gotten closer than expected when the young knight turned to face them again. They were riding hard and it was apparent they knew who Aleon was. He could now see they were all heavily armed with lances and their peculiar horsebows. There was a chance he could at least outpace them. He hoped that they had been riding hard already and their horses would be tired. His own had rested all day, except for its recent panic.

One of the Tartars shouted and pointed at the gathered villagers. Aleon turned his horse and literally rode for the hills. If he could not outdistance the nomads, then he would at least draw them away from the poorly armed villagers.

Spurring his mount, Aleon galloped away from the nomads. As the pursuit lengthened he wondered why they ignored the dragon circling overhead and worried that perhaps his two enemies had formed a pact against him. Though how this made things worse he couldn't guess since he could not think of any way his situation might be worse. The horse nomads' cries increased as they recognized a chase and saw it as great sport. A few fired arrows at him, but he saw them fall short. For the first time Aleon regretted leaving his armor on the far side of a burning forest. Without it he was less a burden to his horse, but its lack meant that they wouldn't need to actually catch him to kill him. If they managed to close the gap between them, the Tartars could shoot him from the saddle.

Aleon's back hurt. So did his hips and the inside of his legs. The muscles in the back of his neck hurt worse from straining every few moments to look over his shoulder. He had been riding or hurriedly leading his steed all through the night, unable to stop for any real rest. Twice he had stopped to water his horse and nearly been overtaken by the Tartars. With the approach of night the dragon had screeched and flown away. Aleon was too exhausted for coherent thought. He rode on because that was what he was supposed to do. Fear had long ago given way to fatigue.

The Tartars had lost sight of him in the darkness. Still, even now Aleon could hear their war cries echoing off the low hills. He knew from experience their strategy was to drive their prey onward until it dropped from exhaustion, and it was working.

The sun had just risen. Its growing light caused the jumble of rocks and scrub to throw red and blue shadows. Shaking himself out of a walking drowse, Aleon knew he couldn't run much farther. With the coming of the light the nomads would find his trail. Their wiry ponies seemed never to tire. The next time they saw him he would not escape.

He considered an ambush. But with no bow and a dozen skilled warriors pursuing him that would be suicide. The lone horse and rider were picking their way across a stone-covered slope when the shadow passed over them. Without looking up Aleon knew the dragon had returned. He braced himself to dodge another fiery breath, but none came. Evidently it was still content simply to watch him flee from other enemies. Resentment fought its way through his exhaustion. The dragon was playing with him, watching him scurry away from the Tartars while knowing it could pluck him from his saddle at any time. In an impulsive act of defiance the knight halted for a brief moment and watched it circle. It was impossible not to watch the magnificent beast in flight. He drew his sword and challenged it to fight, but the great beast ignored the gesture.

Silently the dragon glided up the side of a nearby hill. The flyer then rose, circling overhead in a tight upward spiral. It roared once and Aleon spurred his tired destrier from a slow walk to an exhausted trot, then pulled it to a stop when nothing happened. The monster's attention seemed to be on something other than the knight and his challenge. After a moment of confusion Aleon knew that it must have spotted his pursuers. As he plodded on he realized that the Tartars would not need to find his back trail. His location was being marked to everyone for miles around.

The Tartars weren't long in appearing. They had ridden past him in the dark. That was hardly a surprise considering the slow time man and horse had been making. They appeared at the crown of the hill above Aleon and his destrier. Several of the nomads fired from the saddle even as they spurred down the slope towards him. Their horsemanship was impressive, but fortunately their marksmanship was less sure. Most arrows went long, but one glanced off the neck of the Templar's horse.

That was too much for the abused animal. It was too exhausted to buck, much less run. Whinnying with pain, the horse rolled on its side. Aleon pushed himself from the saddle, managing to avoid having his leg crushed beneath the horse. The ground came up hard under him, and a pointed rock bruised several of his ribs. The knight could feel that in a short while the bruise would begin to stiffen. But then the pain in his side faded as he discovered that he didn't have any time left. The triumphant cries of the horsemen greeted the young knight as he stumbled to his feet. Drawing his sword, he turned to face them.

The Tartars were all dressed in leather and unmatched pieces of Frankish armor. Most were short and had small, dark eyes. Each carried a long spear that could be used as a lance. There was a string of hair fastened to the tips of their lances. Earlier, from a distance, the knight had thought this to be horsehair, but as they closed he saw that the hair was too light and fine. It had once graced the heads of their human foes.

Most of the riders had put their bows away and leveled their spears at Aleon. They were riding forward at a leisurely pace, calling out to him in the singsong language he didn't understand. That was probably just as well, though the intent of their comments was plain. His would not be a pleasant death.

When the horsemen were fifty paces away Aleon could see them tense for the final charge. He raised his sword in defiance and looked about for some miraculous chance for escape. There was none. On the rocky, gentle slope their steppe ponies could ride a man on foot down within heartbeats. Nor was there any place to hide. The Templar knew that all he could do now was fight back well enough to force them to give him a quick death.

Before the nomads charged, their chief barked an order. He was older and better armored, wearing an intricately decorated and gold-plated cuirass with what might have been a battered Roman eagle on it. He was demanding the right to kill Aleon alone. Aleon realized this was the exact reverse of the battle he had killed the man's son in. Then he had been mounted and more heavily armored; now the other man had the same advantages. The other nomads eased back in their saddles and smiled. They were not pleasant smiles. Then the old Tartar shrieked and drove toward the dismounted knight.

Ducking and only defending with his sword, Aleon managed to deflect the first attack. The sheer force of the spear as he blocked it threw him over backwards. The rocks hurt and the Templar nearly lost his grip on his sword. The nomads cheered their leader while Aleon scrambled clumsily to his feet. The chief was obviously enjoying himself, raising his spear in salute to his bodyguards before dipping his lance and charging again.

This time Aleon was more prepared. He managed to step aside from the lance at the last instant and brought his sword down on the end of the wooden shaft as it passed. The very end of his blade cut through the wood, separating the iron tip and an arm's-length of shaft from the rest.

The nomads didn't cheer this time, and several looked restless. Again the old chief barked an order and those who had again raised their bows lowered them. When he turned to face Aleon, the chief's grin was gone. It was replaced by a determined and deadly look. Visibly angry at his failure, the old Tartar threw the rest of his spear to the ground and drew his own sword.

Unlike a spear, even at the gallop a rider can shift a sword instantly. Aleon knew that there was no dodging aside from the next blow. The heavily armored chief actually rode back past his men to allow his horse room to reach a full gallop. Pulling his shield over his back the Tartar chieftan turned the animal without using his hands and Aleon had to admire the horsemanship. There was little else he could do.

The Tartar came at him in a blur. Aleon was just able to raise his own weapon to deflect the old nomad's swinging blow. They hit with a musical note that hung in the air after the two warriors had parted. The speeding horse had added so much force to his opponent's weapon that the knight's sword was torn from his grasp. The nomads cheered as the weapon clattered to the ground several steps from the Templar.

Alerted by their cheer, the Tartar chief turned his pony in another impossibly tight circle and rode back toward the disarmed knight. Aleon lunged toward where the sword had fallen, but the nomad spurred between him and it. Then he rode directly at the unarmed knight and Aleon was barely able to avoid the blow by diving between the Tartar pony's legs. The chieftain turned and swung again. Aleon danced back, stumbling on loose gravel as the other nomads' cheers grew more enthusiastic.

The old chief was grinning again. It was the same humorless, deadly smile with which he had started the battle. He was clearly enjoying himself. His shouted comment made the other nomads laugh. Aleon tried to yell back defiantly, but could barely speak. His mouth was too dry.

The old nomad's smile grew broader and more menacing at Aleon's feeble croak. He raised himself in his stirrups and chanted something in his own language. The others echoed the same phrase a few seconds later. If he had to guess, Aleon would have said the old man was calling on the spirit of his son to watch his death be avenged. That meant he was hoping for a kill soon. The young knight could feel panic threatening to block his vision. He had been driven even further from his sword. The urge to run was powerful and only the knowledge that he would be easily ridden down let the Templar stand unmoving.

The old Tartar repeated his cry six more times. Finally the nomad charged. Aleon was prepared to dive to one side, even knowing that the skilled horseman would still be able to follow. There was little other choice that might buy him a few heartbeats more of life. The Templar kept his eyes on the approaching chieftain as he shuffled back a few steps and heard a clink at his feet. Risking a quick glance down the knight saw the spear tip he had cut free earlier.

As the grinning nomad spurred past him Aleon surprised the man by not fleeing, but instead falling flat. The Tartar's sword whistled a finger length above the knight's head. As he dropped the Templar grabbed what remained of the spear shaft and drove the point into the pony's rear leg. The weapon stuck and was torn from his grasp, but the horse's leg collapsed sending the chief into a tumbling roll. The animal screamed, kicked, and screamed again. Aleon dodged backward.

Without turning to see where his opponent fell, the knight dashed up the hill to recover his sword. As he began to run several of the bodyguards raised a cry. An arrow bounced off a rock at his feet and another cut a channel in Aleon's shoulder blade. He continued to run toward his weapon, waiting for the sound of hooves.

Instead the beleaguered knight heard a familiar, but even more frightening sound. The dragon was back. With a sinking feeling Aleon realized that it must have decided not to leave the final kill to the Tartars. The massive beast had arrived to claim its prey. With a growing sense of hopelessness Aleon grabbed his sword and turned to face the new threat.

To his surprise, the dragon wasn't facing him, but had landed between him and the bodyguards. A few of the startled horsemen fired arrows, which bounced off the thick, red scales. The dragon responded by breathing fire in front of the nomads' horses' hooves. The ground it played upon couldn't burn, but the intense heat and mansized column of fire was enough to cause every pony to bolt. Before Aleon could react to the sudden change in his situation, only three Tartars remained on hillside.

The dragon turned, its eyes bright, and settled visibly back onto its haunches.

It took the Templar several long moments to assess what was happening. It appeared that the great beast was helping him. He might live! Aleon stood unable to decide what he should do next. Then depression returned. Hope was foolish, he told himself. The monster was just playing with him. It wanted the kill for himself. When it tired of the game, he'd die. It hardly mattered whether he was killed in this lonely place by a dragon or a Tartar chief.

The knight stood, unsure which enemy represented the most immediate danger. Whichever he faced meant turning his back to the other. Even sitting passively, the hulking mass of the dragon intimidated Aleon. The chief answered his query by shrieking his anger and charging at him. Reluctantly he turned his back on the monster and faced the nomad.

After the initial crossing of swords, Aleon was relieved to see that fighting on foot he held an advantage.

"No smile now?" he taunted the old Tartar as they exchanged blows and thrusts.

The man responded by uttering a wild shriek and attacking without concern for protecting himself. Twice the old nomad's wild swings nearly tore past Aleon's guard. The young knight wasn't wearing any armor and any blow that got through would have killed or maimed him. The few times he managed to land a blow of his own they had been stopped by the nomad's chain mail or cuirass. Then, at the end of another series of frenzied attacks, the chieftan's blade pulled the small man off balance and the Templar saw an opening. Almost before he realized what he had done, Aleon drove his own blade into the Tartar's throat.

The chieftain fell without a sound.

With a wailing cry the three remaining Tartars abandoned the top of the hill and disappeared. Quickly gathering up the nomad's weapon, Aleon turned to face the dragon with a sword in either hand.

"Haven't you fought enough for one day?" it asked. The voice was deep and rumbling with a softness to it Aleon had not expected. But then he had not expected it to talk at all.

"Have you?" the knight asked as he approached the dragon. He found it hard to sound menacing being dwarfed by the dragon's massive bulk.

"I think I'd had enough a long time ago," Aleon was surprised to hear from the red monster.

"Why?" the knight finally asked, gesturing at the fallen nomad and his fleeing followers.

"You were a valiant opponent," the dragon rumbled back. "And you fought to defend your land, not to rob my hoard."

Aleon could only stare, not really ready to understand what was happening. The dragon continued.

"After you dropped that boulder on me, I was quite upset." The dragon spoke calmly, though loudly, as if dealing with some theoretical situation. Aleon found himself almost unable to accept that he was having a conversation with a beast whose very existence he had doubted less than a week before. The dragon, however seemed to find nothing unusual in having a chat with a human while squatting on a hillside next to a dead body.

"Then I found your rope and the scrape marks on the plateau above. I realized you must have been there for days."

"Three," Aleon managed to confirm.

"Yes, three," the dragon agreed, "and you never tried to pillage my lair."

Aleon nodded. The Templar had simply never thought of it. Though perhaps he should have. The legend, but then he was talking to that legend, was that dragons slept on gigantic piles of gold. The booty he might have taken could have outfitted mercenaries to assist him. It also would have returned him to Normandy in style. Choosing discretion, he said nothing.

"I searched you out then, wishing to see what kind of knight can resist the call of a dragon's treasure trove." It paused and waved a clawed 'hand toward the sky. Aleon suspected he had seen the dragon equivalent of a shrug.

"When I thought I'd found you it was your trap," it continued glancing at the wound in its shoulder. "I wondered if I'd judged you wrong. Then I saw you lead those horsemen off to save the others."

Again Aleon decided this was not the time to explain why they were after him alone.

"I watched the chase." It shrugged again. "You have courage. And I have no further desire to do battle with you. We need a truce, you and I. I have a need for a human that I can deal with honorably."

The Templar hesitated as he began to realize the incredulity of his situation. He was standing on a hillside two months hard riding from his relatives in Normandy, having a blood feud with the Tartars and in a conversation with a dragon. When he returned they would never believe any of this happened. Aleon discovered that he was thinking again about living and just how much he wanted to continue to do so. His earlier acceptance of death gone, the knight's heart began to race as he looked up at the gigantic creature standing a few paces away. Why was he talking to a dragon? Was cowardice inspiring his words or prudence? Aleon thought for a long moment and then spit out his challenge before he was unable to say it.

"I cannot make a bargain with a minion of the devil."

"The devil?" the dragon wondered aloud. The knight would have sworn that it was amused at the thought. "Maybe you and your spreading hordes are my devils, but I assure you I have no pact with your evil gods."

"Will you agree to leave this land?" Aleon demanded. He wasn't sure where he was finding the courage.

"Certainly not," the great beast protested mildly. "My kind lived here before yours learned farming. When I heard the land had been abandoned after the plague emptied it, I decided to return."

"Then we must fight," Aleon concluded reluctantly. He looked up at the mountain of muscle sitting a few paces in front of him and realized that he had unconsciously moved to place himself in the shade of the monster's great shadow. The Templar's legs began to weaken as he regarded the beast he had just challenged. The dragon was so large he probably couldn't even reach high enough to strike a vital organ. Certainly not before it simply squashed him like a bug. Then again it had only to breathe its fire and nothing would remain of him at all. There were no caves or cuts in the rock he could hide in this time.

"You can't win," the dragon's words echoed his thoughts. "And you're likely to be busy for some time in any case. The old fellow you just killed is likely to have more sons and dozens of cousins."

Sudden Aleon felt very tired. Nothing was over. It had just begun.

"I didn't move to those isolated mountains to fight," the dragon explained.

The knight raised his eyes again. He was getting tired of facing imminent death and then finding things had changed. Though that *was*, he immediately reminded himself, better than the alternative outcome. The dragon continued.

"I am old and have fought my battles. Now I wish to study the mystic arts and philosophies. When you live so long as I have, you begin to wonder about things that shorter-lived creatures rarely consider."

"What does a dragon need to wonder about?" Aleon asked, confused. This wasn't like any confrontation with a dragon he had ever heard about.

"To learn enough to ask the right questions," the

dragon replied in an even more distant voice. "I've lost interest in wealth and glory. That was a fantasy of my youth. Though many of my kin still value gold and gems above all else. Maybe I just have enough."

Again Aleon regretted that he had not raided the lair and fled with sacks of treasure.

"Perhaps there is a way we can leave each other in peace," the dragon offered in the silence. "Considering that at the moment I am in less danger than you, the offer seems reasonable."

"I can make no contract with a minion of the devil," Aleon objected.

"The devil, again? Hardly! Then a truce perhaps? I have no desire to kill you. I'd prefer to have men of honor, or at least limited greed, around my lair. Once you're gone the nomads will ride freely and eventually find my home. Then I'll have to fight or move again and that's very disruptive."

"You're letting me live because I'm convenient?" the Templar wondered aloud. He was too tired to feel outrage, but was sure he'd just been insulted.

"And because you are rather heroic for one of the little ones. That interests me."

Aleon could only stand and stare. He didn't feel heroic. He felt sore, tired, and the cut on his back stung horribly. He didn't feel he had any real leverage, but if he was to even consider the dragon's offer it had to be something that was tolerable by those he was sworn to protect.

"The farmers cannot afford your raiding their herds. Even if I were to agree they could compel me, or another like me, to seek you out," the knight explained. He wasn't sure why he spoke. If the dragon wanted to let him live he was a fool to argue against that.

"I'll not apologize for needing to eat," the dragon insisted. "Along with the game, I'll need perhaps one or two of your farm beasts in cycle of the moon. How many cattle has your valley lost to those Tartars?"

"Dozens," Aleon admitted sullenly. It was an admission of failure.

"So if those raids stopped, your valley could easily have enough extra cattle and sheep to satisfy my needs," the dragon argued.

"True, but we can reach no agreement," the Templar maintained and wondered why. He wanted to make peace with this dragon. It had just saved his life and he wanted to live.

"Let us say that since I fly every day, should I see any intruders, I might make them unwelcome. How long before they choose to raid somewhere else rather than fight against the two of us?" the dragon offered.

"One farmer's stead burnt or herd scattered and I'll have to come after you," Aleon threatened, raising both swords. But there was no menace in his voice and Aleon found himself smiling. He was looking forward to the look on the Patriarch's face when he told the old cleric that he finally had the much more experienced and powerful protector his station deserved. It just wasn't human.

"Never," the dragon agreed pulling back in mock fright. The motion made the great beast's shoulder hurt where the bolt had torn into the flying muscles and it added "of course" more thoughtfully. Then the dragon rocked back against its closed wings as if frightened off its feet by the man standing before it. The ground shook as tons of dragon shifted. Dust rose and then the dragon feebly kicked its legs, mimicing panic.

Finally, Aleon had an ally; he had to laugh. So did the dragon.

THE POWER WITHIN

by Mickey Zucker Reichert

Joshua leaned against an olive tree, its intermittent branches supplying scant shade from the broiling sun and its reflection from the desert sand. Sweat rolled down his face, plastering black hair to his forehead, stinging his dark eyes, and drenching his loose-fitting shirt. He ignored the discomfort for a greater one that bore no relation to the weather. As general of the Chosen Ones' army, the burdens of a nation lay, aching, on his shoulders; and braving the midday heat seemed the only way to steal a moment alone. Though months old, the Lord's words still echoed in his head: "The lands of the Children of Israel will stretch to the banks of the sea. And you shall lead them." The advance and its myriad wars had already begun. *So many dead, enemy and friend alike. So many dead at my command.*

Remorse twisted through Joshua, twining uncertainty through the stalwart faith he needed to appease the God he loved and served, usually without question. Now belief seemed as much a burden as the formidable task

133

that lay mostly before and partially behind him. He imagined his obligations as a weight, a seamless casting of the scarce steel that only their Hittite enemy managed to gather in bulk, an impenetrable shielding that even his problems could not breach. But the responsibilities remained, trapped inside the armor with him. Frustration and doubt fostered rage. *Who is Joshua to doubt the word or intention of the Lord God?* No answer came, no guidance from the One above.

Still clinging to the image of his armor, Joshua sought escape elsewhere. He was a soldier first and foremost. He would find his solace in killing and destruction, in defeating a goliath enemy whose strength and power seemed indomitable. Though only a daydream, the satisfaction of that one perfect soldier's act would displace the negative ideas and thoughts he wished to escape. Having decided his course, he sought a form and figure for the bitterness and uncertainty that plagued him with this restless need to slay. An ancient memory surfaced. As a toddler, he had feared the yellow streaks of lightning that ruptured trees and set cottages to flame. The thunder's boom had sent him skittering and quivering beneath his blanket. Then, his imagination had created a sentience to the storms that terrified him. The jagged flashes became a monster that streaked across the sky, the thunder its roar, so mighty it threatened to tear the world asunder. Over the years, he had tamed the beast he called Ohr, meaning *light*, then befriended it, riding through the gale-chopped night sky, a warrior on missions of God.

Now, Joshua decided, he would borrow the look of the imaginary friend that had once seemed so real in his infantile ignorance. He could conjure nothing more terrible in adulthood than the figure crafted from a child's terror. He could think of no monster that could better personify the inseparable mixture of frustration, anger, and misery that tore at him now. Closing his eyes, he lost himself in the illusion. He imagined that the evil creature had kidnapped a fair, young maiden named Faith from the Children of Israel; and the great warrior Joshua must slay it and all it represented, restoring Faith to her proper place in his heart and among the people.

A presence awakened the dragon in his cave, even before the faint clink of mail diffused through birdsong to his ears. He sighed, breath hot against his foreleg, not bothering to rise. Massive, red eyes glided open to the familiar darkness of his cave and the distant glow of treasure long owned and no longer appreciated. Once, those trinkets had reminded him of the days of glory, when he and his human friend had rescued them from the clutches of enemies, swooping down on the unworthy like a golden revenant. Now, the storm world of Eshem lay emptily placid, glazed to a quiet, grey calm that matched the tedium of an eternal life grown dull. Despair hounded him. Hope had died years ago. Only a mindless, routine charade goaded him to clamber to his feet. He stretched each leg until the claws splayed, slithering his tail across the stones to work the kinks from every joint, then lumbered toward the mouth of the cave.

As the intruder drew nearer, the dragon analyzed it from habit rather than interest. Though it had not yet come near enough for his keen vision to carve its figure from relentless gloom, he read its nature from its thoughts. Human, it seemed, at least nearer that than anything else with which he had ever had contact. The creature worried the concept of time the way only a mortal could. It also bore the tragedy of understanding death, clutching to concerns about its own and others. It seemed burdened to the point of breaking with responsibilities the dragon could not sift into context. Over all, uncertainty pervaded every thought, and it seemed most focused on the need to destroy a beast of fantasy to place its life back on the even keel it sought. The dragon suspected he was the newcomer's target. And he did not care.

Human. The oddity spurred a long-buried spark of interest. The dragon glided forward, awaiting the approaching figure at the mouth. Within moments, it came around a bend in the pathway. It stood erect, obviously human, though nearly twice the height and three times the weight of his one-time companion. It far more resembled the many foes they had defeated together, dressed from head to toe in metal. A helmet covered all but the eyes that peeped through slits. Iron encased him, jointed to allow for movement that seemed ponderous compared to the natural armored grace of a dragon. He wore a cloth tabard with a blue, six-pointed star on its front, and a sword lay slung at his hip. Any other clothing was buried beneath the protections. From helmet point to boots, he stood barely as long as the dragon's neck.

The dragon remained still, a breeze stirring beneath his scales and the triangular plates drooping along his back. As the man approached, the dragon could taste the bitterness that fueled a murderous rage and the man's intention to quell feelings of helplessness and uncertainty with killing. The dragon wondered who or what had taught him to respond to circumstance in such a violent manner. The enemies of his human friend had seemed little more than parchment cutouts, caricatures of greed who tumbled like flotsam beneath the dragon's roar. The dragon's friend had been an innocent, incapable of the thoughts that plagued the man who faced him now. He had waved his wooden sword without malice, believing in triumph through faith and friendship, without understanding war's link to blood or destruction.

The man marched directly to the cave and drew his sword, shield strapped to the other arm. "Beast! Come out and fight."

The dragon sucked in a deep breath, then blew it out in a sad sigh, steam twining from his nostrils. From experience, he knew men's vision could not compete with his own. To the stranger, he looked like a shapeless blur in surrounding shadow. "No," he said at length.

The response seemed to baffle the man. The command left his tone, replaced by confusion. "No?"

"No."

The man partially lowered his sword, clearly unprepared for such an answer. More of the anger funneled into perplexity. "Why not?"

"Why?"

"Does it matter?"

"Of course it matters."

The man considered, obviously irritated by the need to think about instead of simply enacting the mindless violence he had sought to uplift his spirits. The dragon understood that the man simply assumed a creation of his own imagination would behave precisely as he decided it would and with no more provocation than himself, so opposite the expectations of the child who had befriended the dragon years ago. "Because . . ." the man cried. "Because you've captured a beautiful woman, and I've come to rescue her."

The dragon smiled for the first time in longer than two decades, managing to find a hint of lost enjoyment in the man's discomfort and the game. "No, I haven't."

"You haven't?"

The dragon shook his head. His jagged, iridescent horns rattled against stone. "What would I do with a human woman?"

The man's brows beetled, barely visible through the eye slits. Clearly, he had never considered the details of such a thing before. "You'd defile her, of course."

The dragon snorted a smoky, derisive laugh. "Imagine that." Through the mental bond, the dragon watched the man struggle and fail to do so.

Instead, he changed the reason. "To eat her."

"Bleah." The dragon crunched his face at the thought

of devouring humans. "If I've eaten her, then you're too late, aren't you?"

Frustration raised new anger in the man. "Fine! No woman, then. Good needs little reason to slay what's evil."

The dragon's head drifted through the opening, sunlight gleaming from clean, yellow scales. He fixed one sorrowful, scarlet eye on the man, cocking his head for a better look. "What makes you so damned good?"

The man raised his sword and lunged for the eye.

The dragon jerked back. The blade skimmed his cheek, scraping a line of scales and skin. A drop of blood fell to the ground as the dragon retreated back into his lair with a startled cry. "Ow!" Instantly, he struck back, foot shooting from the cave with a suddenness intended to startle. The man blocked the claws with his shield, but one slipped beneath his defense. The dragon stabbed the toenail through a breach in the warrior's armor, poking without raking. He zipped his foot back into the cave. "There. I do as you do. See, we're both good." He drifted back into the cave, annoyed by the man and tired of wasting his time on one so unworthy.

Shocked, the man said nothing.

Giant tears welled in the dragon's eyes, splashing to the stone despite attempts to control them. He felt foolish. Twenty years had passed since he had last seen his human friend, twenty years that had passed like twenty thousand. He dared to hope he had discovered another who might share the world that friendship had made glorious: colorful with flowers and rainbows, misty from ever-present rain, the sky a blue-gray playground of clouds through which they flashed, flew, capered, and exchanged thunderous war cries. Yet, he had discovered nothing but a resentful, ugly man who bore no relationship to the child with whom he had played. His back seemed empty where the boy's warm body used to fit, every breeze a cold reminder of his absence. The dragon slumped to the cave floor, all will to play or fight disappearing. If the man chose to kill him for his own invented reasons, perhaps death would prove less painful than a tiresome, lonely eternity.

Lost in his own sorrow, the dragon did not notice the change that gradually washed over the man outside until he recognized deep-seated memories painfully dragged from the man's distant past. Hostility faded, replaced by cautious excitement.

The dragon froze in place, knowing joy and sadness at once. He leapt up and whirled suddenly, tail slapping against stone, then roared a greeting that sent every stone in the world to shaking. "Josi?"

"Ohr," the man whispered, the sound audible in the intense silence that followed the dragon's call. "That can't be you." His defenses slipped only slightly, just enough to barely reveal the familiar child trapped beneath the weight of responsibilities, warped and changed by circumstance.

Ohr poked his head through the opening again, this time cautious.

The man hurled his sword to the ground, and his helmet followed swiftly. The face was unfamiliar, broader and coarser than Ohr remembered. The eyes did seem the same, but only in color and depth. He did not recognize their harshness. The unruly mop of black hair had been clipped short, as his imagination. "It can't be. How can it be?" Realization crowded in, an understanding that he had conjured more than just an ancient picture into which he could force any personality or intention he wished. This was not just an empty mental image to fill and distort on a whim. This was Ohr.

The dragon surrendered to some bitterness of his own. "How could you leave me? I thought we were friends."

"Friends," the man repeated distantly. "Friends, yes." The repetition seemed to jar him from his thoughtful silence. "They call me Joshua, now. Josi was a childhood nickname."

"I am called nothing," Ohr returned. "A lonely dragon needs no name when there is no one to speak it."

The man hung his head, truly remorseful if only momentarily. Rationalization quickly welled up to block the guilt. "I'm sorry, Ohr. I loved you, you know."

"Loved?" The dragon fished for more.

He did not get it. "Loved." Joshua met one huge, red eye with his own. "I will not lie to you. I have not thought of you for longer than a decade. I don't know if I still love you."

"Oh." The dragon hung his head, vision lost to a blur of moisture. A lump filled his throat, sending steam out his nostrils, and he found himself unable to say more. His creator, his god, and his friend had forgotten him.

Joshua took over where the dragon failed. "I'm not sure I can explain it in a way you can understand." Nevertheless, he tried. "Mortals die, so we change in short spans of time. I just grew up."

Ohr shook his head, trying to read the thoughts as well as the words; in the days when they had wound through the stormy skies together, they had had little use for spoken communication. Now, the bond between them, mentally and emotionally, had weakened, perhaps beyond repair. "You got bigger. So you abandoned me. And Eshem."

Joshua heaved a sigh, obviously frustrated by a point that seemed so obvious to a human yet nearly inexplicable to Ohr. "It has nothing to do with size or appearance. It's here." He tapped his temple with a finger. "And there." He made a broad gesture apparently meant to encompass the world. His world, not Eshem. "We begin innocent and ignorant. Time and life bring us experiences, and commitments we can't escape. I was a child when I romped with you. I became a man, and the obligations that age brings left me no room for an imagined playmate."

Ohr scratched at his scales with a hind leg, and his claws clicked against them. "Imagined?"

Joshua shrugged.

"And you like this adult life better than what we had?" Ohr tried to anticipate.

"No," Joshua admitted. "Most any man would rather spend his years frolicking in endless childhood. Your world allows that but mine doesn't. Day to day, lives hinge on my decisions. Men die by my hand and my decree, and I often can do nothing but hope more enemies die than friends. I look to God for guidance, and he gives it. But, at times, I wonder if he is any more real than you, if the lands he sends me to conquer, at the price of myriad strangers lives, is really ours to take. Am I Josi, or am I one of the enemies you and I defeated together? Are you the evil dragon who burns innocents and captures maidens, are you the lightning and thunder that frightened me as a child, or are you the beloved companion I created to allay that fear?"

"That last is easy," the dragon replied, still sorting the complexities of Joshua's explanation and hurting from timeworn need. One thing seemed strong and certain: his old friend was suffering. The pain was tangible, the twists of his logic less simple to follow. "I am Ohr."

"Yes," Joshua said, and the load seemed to lighten slightly. "You are Ohr."

"Stay here with me." The edges of the horizon had reddened, the first color the dragon had seen since Josi's disappearance years ago. Rain pattered to the stones, its sound lost for so long that its return seemed loud as an avalanche. His great heart ached for the past, and the only one who could bring joy and succor stood before him dismissing the bond they had once shared so completely. "There are no troubles here but those we create and defeat together."

Rain dragged strands of hair along Joshua's forehead and rattled against his armor. He studied his old friend, thoughts delving into distant memory and fantasy at once. Ohr knew he gave the invitation long and appropriate consideration, and the dragon followed his line of thought through decades of knowledge and battle. At last, the man found an answer, one filled with pain and hope. "Someday, old friend. When the autumn of my life turns to winter and my people no longer need me. If the Lord allows it, I will return to the one true love I ever had. We will dance again through the turbulent night sky, and my memories of life will seem as faded as our time together has now become."

Ohr smiled through misery, buoyed by distant dreams. He would spend more time alone, but it would pass quickly, assuaged by the certainty of happiness in the future. He had glimpsed the changes that mangled his friend's conscience. Once, Josi/Joshua would have sought out a dragon for assistance and companionship; now, he sought comfort from violence instead. Ohr would not let the burdens of manhood destroy what little remained of his friend's youth. Without some reminder, the man might forget his vow as easily as he had suppressed their triumphs in Eshem. "Promise me one thing. When things seem their darkest, remember me. Believe in the magic that once was so easily yours, and I will be there for you. Just once. Until your return here."

Joshua smiled, and the first genuine ray of trust flickered through his darker thoughts. "I will." He hefted sword and helmet, heading back the way he had come.

Occasional rays of sunlight slithered through a dark layer of clouds, and the desert smelled of damp. A dreariness settled over the city of Jericho and its wall, so massive many of the shops and dwellings perched atop it, fused to its mighty construction. Joshua sat, cross-legged, amidst his army and silently marveled at the structure.

They would breach it; he did not doubt God's decree for a moment. The lands of the Children of Israel would expand to the banks of the sea. Yet, one question burdened him until its weight seemed like more than any packhorse, let alone human, could bear: *How many will die as the price for this land?*

It was not a question God would answer. The Almighty explained his conquests and desires in terms of generations, rewarding or punishing his followers and enemies en masse. The details fell to those he chose as his leaders, men like Moses and, now, Joshua. God would ascertain victory or defeat, but the details and strategies fell to Joshua. He only hoped he could live up to the task: the Chosen Peoples' bronze weaponry and scarce protections against Hittite steel. He wished his followers had access to the seemingly limitless iron stores of the enemy and wondered if the world together would ever discover enough to create the solid core of armor he had worn in his fantasied attack against a dragon who had turned out to be a childhood friend.

Soldiers and rabbis shifted, preparing themselves for the nightly circumnavigation of Jericho's fortifications. This time, the ritual called for them to circle seven times where they had done so only once each day for the previous six. No man dared to break the silence that had endured since camping outside the walled city, and Joshua appreciated having no need to chat or speculate. Tonight, they would expect a miracle, granted to Joshua from God.

But the spark was not there. All contact seemed to have left Joshua, as if the One Deity, He who had guaranteed success, had left him. A quiet loneliness gripped Joshua in a hold that seemed suffocating. He felt incomplete, as if he had cast aside a part of him too primal and dear to ignore. It went deep, eternal, and seemed to have haunted him for decades instead of days. It was not the Lord whom he missed. His faith remained too strong to doubt that God would take care of his Chosen Ones when the need arose. Joshua missed Ohr.

Sandwiched by warriors, the rabbis headed for the city. Wind gusted, hammering sand against the ramparts and into the faces of the soldiers. Joshua rose, shielding his eyes with a hand, driven to pace, though he did not. To reveal his inner turmoil would only distress his soldiers needlessly. He would stand stalwart, keeping his discomfort and uncertainty internal as he always did. Though surrounded by followers who adored and trusted him like a father, he felt very much alone; the only one who truly understood him was a figment of his own imagination.

The rabbis and soldiers made their circuits as rain dribbled from the sky. A few silent, curious eyes occasionally peered at them from over Jericho's fortifications. As commanded by Joshua, the Chosen Ones kept their circle wide, beyond bow shot of the city, safe from all but those who might charge them from Jericho or spies hidden outside who escaped the searches of the Children of Israel. But no one challenged the somber ritual. As the rabbis completed the seventh cycle, their robes soaked and their eyes averted from the sand, they headed back toward camp. Joshua still felt no fresh bond with the Lord, received no command, and worried.

The contingent returned too soon for Joshua. The seven rabbis clutched their ram's horn *shofars*, awaiting their general's command. He gestured for them to blow as the guarding soldiers returned to their places among the army. They played as one, each tone different enough to distinguish from the others and made musical by the steady rhythm of the rain. Every note dawned crisp and clear, though the blend made a strange cacophony over the wind. And, when each had finished and the music faded into obscurity, Joshua commanded the Children of Israel to let out a mutual shout.

The Chosen Ones gathered breath and called out at once, the sound mellow and unfocused in the wake of the rabbis' chorus. All eyes locked on Jericho as the community battle cry built to a rumble and died, the silence deeper and more terrible for its breaking. Yet, the city had not changed.

Sudden horror gripped Joshua then, the same he always knew in the presence of God. The lonely hollow in his gut seemed to wrench and tear within him, and God spoke in a voice so thunderous he thought every soldier around him would hear: *The power to defeat Jericho is not a miracle I will grant. It is already within you.* Then, the presence disappeared, and Joshua's loneliness and uncertainty trebled. He knew what he needed to do. He needed to call upon that part of his mind that had been a gift from God, the childhood innocence that created an enduring and eternal friend.

"Ohr," Joshua whispered so softly even he could not hear the call. But another did. As it had throughout his boyhood, his mind touched the loving beast with whom he had played, the only one who cared for him unreservedly, the only one who never judged.

Ohr! The dragon's head whipped up. Rain pounded the rock, drumming a symphony on the roof of his cave. Elation pierced him like a red-hot arrow. It was Josi, not Joshua who called, at least in spirit. The unshakeable faith and unconditional love of a child caressed Ohr in glorious waves that drove him nearly mad with pleasure. He flashed from his cave in an instant, cutting between worlds as he had not done since Josi's absence had plunged him into despair. His golden body lashed the night sky. "Josi!" he rumbled in reply, so loud his voice distorted the name. As lightning, he cleaved the clouds in a jagged trail. *JOSI!* Thunder blasted, a roar of fierce joy whose echoes, equally loud, refused to die.

The ground trembled beneath the sound, roiling and tumbling the Children of Israel like a child's reed fort in a gale. The river Jordan bucked into a tidal wave that blotted out the northern and eastern horizons. To the south, the sky went black, filled with the waters of the Dead Sea. The colossal wall of Jericho shuddered, as if it alone might thwart the dragon's might in defiance. Then, it seemed to hop from its foundation. Stone crashed and toppled. Buildings on the ramparts folded, and chips of granite, sand, and thatch filled the air.

Assailed by a wave of human terror and agony, Ohr hurled himself between the quaking rubble and the Children of Israel. Debris pounded him, and a flying stone snapped a horn at its base. Gritting his teeth against pain, he remained in place, shards stamping bruises the length of his body and delicate wings. Unconsciousness hovered, but still he remained in place, idly wondering what came after death for an immortal.

Then, suddenly, the barrage stopped and Joshua's soldiers no longer needed his shielding. Ohr took a dizzy step. Fire seemed to flow through his legs, yet he managed an awkward step. He flapped his bent and bleeding wings, surprised to find they could still support him. They ached with every beat; but he flew, gliding back toward his cave to wait in eager solitude until his childhood playmate became as permanent a fixture in the land of Eshem as the dragon who bore the name Light.

The slam of stone seemed soundless after the dragon roar that had deafened Joshua. Dust filled his eyes and choked him. He coughed, rolling on the ground in agony, blindly rubbing grit from his eyes.

It seemed like an eternity before voices replaced the ceaseless aftermath of ringing in Joshua's ears and tears washed the last of the stabbing fragments from his vision. Shakily, he rose. The Children of Israel sprawled, stood, or crouched at their camp, gazes universally locked on Jericho. Having ascertained their safety, Joshua turned his attention to the city as well. Shattered stone and wood littered the plain on which the mighty city had once stood in defiance. Glimmers of iron, bronze, and clay glittered amid the wreckage. The battle was over, even before it began and, apparently, the Chosen Ones had not taken a casualty.

Joshua gestured to the rabbis, and they led the Children of Israel in a fervent prayer during which his voice rose unhesitatingly above the others. Only after they had finished and he sent the soldiers to dispatch survivors and pick through the rubble did he tack on a single other phrase. Grinning like an infant, he whispered to the whistling wind. "I love you. I know now I always have."

A haggard jolt of lightning returned the sentiment.

BIRDIE

by Mike Resnick and
Nicholas A. DiChario

I sleep.

Eventually the heavy oak doors of the wine cellar screech open, its iron hinges sprinkling detritus upon my earthen floor.

The slow *creak-creak-creak* of wary footsteps descend the rotted wooden staircase that has not borne the weight of Man since—hmmm, let me think about this—Robert Darwin? God only knows how many years ago that was, and *BOOM!* The wine cellar doors collapse again, leaving in their wake a young human boy, standing at the bottom of the cellar steps, trembling in the soft glow of a single flickering candle.

"Is there a dragon down here?" says the lad.

"Anything's possible," I answer.

The child gasps, and I see his white face turn a shade or two paler, and when he finally lets out his breath, out goes the candle. I seem to recall Robert, when he was

149

a lad, making the same blunder—but when Robert blew out his candle he scrambled up the steps and pounded on the wine cellar doors, begging to be freed, screaming like a banshee that the dragon was about to devour him alive.

But this one just stands up straight, straining his weak human eyes, eyes that were not made for seeing clearly through the darkness.

"What year is it, lad?"

"The year is 1817," he says. "I thought Father was fibbing. I mean about you. Of course, I can't see you— so you could be fibbing, too. This could all be part of my punishment. Are you a man pretending to be a dragon?"

"Why in the world would I want to do that?"

"Maybe Father is paying you."

"I am not so easily bribed." I flare a nostril, and reveal just enough of my flame to illuminate the corner of the wine cellar where I lie resting.

The youngster edges closer.

"Well, my boy," I say smugly, "do I pass the test? Man or beast?"

"You do look different. Is that green fur?"

"Land scales, actually."

"And that big head with the long nose—"

"Snout."

"And those long floppy—"

"Wings."

"I think your ears are bigger than my whole head," he says, his voice filled with more curiosity than awe. "Do you have four legs or two?"

"Two hind legs. Two front forearms. Fourteen digits in all." I wiggle my fingers and toes.

"Those are awfully small arms," he says. "And awfully big legs. And just look at the size of your toenails!"

"Talons."

"And there's that fire in your nose, too. I don't know of any man who can light a room with his nose."

"Snout." I haul myself up to get a better look at the boy. He doesn't back off, even though I'm as tall as two men and as round as ten. He's a skinny cub, but handsome for his race, nothing at all like the other Darwins I've seen. Erasmus was ugly as sin, and Robert was a fat pig of a child, an awkward, weary specimen with nerves like glass trinkets. The Darwins, historically, have been an absolutely hideous-looking clan. "If it makes you feel any better to believe I'm a man, then I'm a man."

The boy frowns. "You smell different, too. Like ... like ..."

"Wine?" I suggest.

"How many years have you been down here?"

"That's a good question." I pause. "Let me think. I was sleeping under a tree, and when I woke up this wine cellar was all around me. I don't remember much before that."

"You mean we built Mount Darwin right on top of you?"

This seems to upset the lad, although for the life of me I can't understand why. I lie down and get comfortable again, resting my chin on the floor.

The boy strides right up to me, sticks his candle in my snout, and lights the wick. He reaches out and touches my land scales. "They don't feel anything at all like fur or fish scales. They feel like ... I don't know ..."

"Peat moss."

"You can put your fire out now if you like. It must be painful for you to have it burning inside your nose like that." He stares at me. "Do you get headaches? Father gets them badly sometimes. Where do you come from? Do you have any family?"

"My fire is not painful; I don't get headaches; and I don't come from anywhere, nor do I have any family."

"Everybody comes from somewhere."

"Is that so?" I retort. "Says who?"

The lad sits down cross-legged on the hard-packed dirt

and holds the candle out in front of him, inspecting me. I shut down my nostril, and a small cloud of smoke wafts in the air between us. A pensive look crosses the cub's face, too serious a look for a young human boy—at least from what I can remember of them. I've come across a few in my lifetime. They always look a little stupid and very frightened in my presence, never pensive. In any event, I am intrigued, as much by the boy as by the fact that I seem to be carrying on a conversation with him.

"What are you doing down here in my wine cellar?" I ask him.

"Father is punishing me for making too much noise in the house. He's always punishing me for something. I think he doesn't like me much. He says I'll never amount to anything. He says I lack *ex-pe-di-en-cy*, whatever that means. Just now he told me I've pushed him to the limits of his endurance so he's locking me in the dungeon until after dinner."

"The dungeon?" I repeated. "Is that what he calls it?" The boy nods. "What's your name, lad?"

"Charles. Charles Darwin."

"You father wouldn't happen to be Robert Darwin, would he?"

"Do you know Father?" he asks.

"I've met a few members of your lineage. Apparently it is a Darwin tradition to punish their cubs by banishing them to the wine cellar—excuse me, the *dungeon*—where the sight of me is supposed to terrify them."

"I don't find you scary at all."

"Come to think of it, I don't find you scary either," I say.

The boy nods, apparently satisfied with the arrangement.

"Expediency," I say. "A concentrated effort in pursuing a particular goal or self-interest with efficiency and haste."

"I think you might be a very big bird. Do you come

from a family of birds? Do you know how to fly? Are you lonely down here all by yourself?"

"I prefer solitude."

"Or maybe you are a fish, because of your scales."

"*Land* scales. I'd rather be a bird, anyway. I don't know how to swim, but I *do* know how to fly." I try to flex my wings, but it has been such a long time since I've used them that they flap just once, awkwardly and stiffly, so I give it up.

"I promise you, when I get out of here, I'll figure out where you come from," he says with exaggerated pride, tucking his thumbs under his suspenders.

"What if I don't want to know where I come from?"

"Everybody wants to know where he's from."

"I wouldn't bet my last shilling on that."

The boy puffs out his candle, and curls up on the wine cellar floor. "Do you mind if I take a nap, Birdie?"

Birdie?

In a matter of minutes he is sleeping peacefully. I smile. I do not ever remember smiling with any of the other Darwin stock. This one is different.

Charles Darwin.

"This is an incredible opportunity, Birdie! I must go, I simply must!"

Charles is talking about the expedition, of course, as outlined in this letter from the botanist, John Stevens Henslow. Charles, only twenty-two years of age, has been recommended by Henslow to a Captain FitzRoy, R.N., commander of Her Majesty's Ship the *Beagle*, preparing for a journey to survey the coasts of Patagonia, Tierra del Fuego, Brazil, Chile, Peru, and several islands in the Pacific, to record chronometrical measurements around the globe. The short of it is, FitzRoy needs a nature lover who can keep meticulous records.

"A trip around the world! And listen to this. Henslow

recommended me as 'The best qualified person he knows likely to undertake such a situation.' "

"Not exactly a rave review," I say dryly. "You could well substitute 'madman' for 'person.' "

He ignores my sarcasm. "There's more, Birdie. Henslow says Captain FitzRoy is 'A public-spirited and zealous officer of delightful manners, and greatly beloved by all his other officers!' "

"And were you the first chosen to undertake this *situation*, Charles?"

"Well, no," he admits.

"Others turned it down?"

"Well, yes. Henslow himself turned it down, but he didn't want to leave his wife, and Leonard Jenyns is a top-notch naturalist, but he is a clergyman first and foremost and he doesn't want to leave his parish in the lurch."

"Might I remind you that you are a clergyman, also?"

"I am not," he replies heatedly. "Well, not yet, anyway. And you're not going to talk me out of this expedition, Birdie. I've already discussed it with Father, and I've sent my letter of acceptance to the captain. This is the perfect opportunity for me to document new species." He paused and stares at me. "Don't you see what this means, Birdie? At last I might be able to pinpoint your origins!"

"Ah-ha! You're doing this for me, aren't you Charles?"

Silence. Of course I am correct. Ever since the first moment he saw me he has been driven to discover who and what and why I am.

He became interested in natural history, in minerals and sea shells and fossils, in pigeons, in marine life, always searching for clues to my origins. The Greek and Latin that Dr. Butler tried to teach him at Shrewsbury Grammar School made no impression upon him whatsoever.

When Charles turned sixteen, his father gave up on

the boy ever gaining a classical education, and decided to send him to Edinburgh to study medicine. Alas, the sight of blood disgusted him, and he hated inflicting pain as much as most men hate bearing it, so he began to cultivate new and more interesting hobbies—zoology, geology, botany—and without the support or encouragement of his family or his masters at school, Charles continued to pursue my past, even though I constantly tried to dissuade him.

"Give it up, Charles. Get on with your life," I would lecture him. "I was here a long time before you were born, and I'll be here a long time after you are gone. I don't need to know where I came from. I will survive."

"I'll find you somewhere, Birdie. You'll see. I'll find you."

After Charles' failure at Edinburgh, old Robert Darwin began to think that the clergy might be the only respectable career left to his son—a fate, as far as I was concerned, that did not frighten Charles nearly enough. So, in 1828, off to Christ's College, Cambridge he went, just in time for the Lenten term. Mathematics, theology, languages—how frustrated poor Charles became at this sacred institution of higher learning! The administration had absolutely no use for his true love, the natural sciences, and excluded them from the curriculum.

He wrote me from Cambridge about how his father, on one of his visits to the college, had berated him: "Father said I care for nothing but rat-catching, and that I will forever be a disgrace to myself and my family."

But Charles kept on.

It was at Christ's College that Charles met Henslow, and the opportunity for this boat ride came about.

As I look at the lad now, young and strong and healthy, full of red-faced determination, I see that his curiosity is stronger than any of the opposing forces in his life, and in a way I am almost jealous of his sense of urgency and wonder and purpose. What would it be like to feel such feelings?

"As I mentioned," Charles says, sitting cross-legged on the wine cellar floor, reminding me of the little Darwin who could so easily make me smile, "I have already sent my letter of acceptance to Captain FitzRoy, on one condition."

"One condition?"

"Yes. That I might be allowed to bring my faithful dog along with me, for comfort and companionship. It is a two-year expedition, after all."

"You don't own a dog."

"You noticed," he grins.

So in the end, I agree to the expedition for Charles as much as Charles agrees to it for me.

It is a bright, December morning, in the year 1831. Charles and I stand on a hill in Devenport, overlooking the dockyard where the beleaguered *Beagle* sits half-sunk, looking more like a shipwreck than a ship. I appear in the guise of a dog: there is no limit to what dragons can do when they set their minds to it.

"She may appear to be in dire straights," says Charles, "but Henslow has assured me she's seaworthy."

"Ah, yes," I say. "Your dear friend Henslow, who so graciously turned down this commission so he could offer it to you."

"The *Beagle* has been five years at sea, so she's a bit battered, but she's been rebuilt from the inside out."

"How reassuring," I mutter.

"She used to be a three-masted, twenty-five-ton brig, carrying up to ten guns," he says as we walk through the shipyard and up to the *Beagle*, where some of the crew are busy loading supplies by winch and crane. Their sharp voices cut through the crisp morning air.

As we walk up the gangway he whispers to me,

"Remember, don't talk to me in front of FitzRoy or the crew. You're supposed to be a dog."

"Aarf!" I say, and he shoots me a behave-yourself glare.

I entertain hopes that this FitzRoy might just be bright enough to deny me passage—the sea is no place for dead weight, after all—but when we board the regal *Beagle*, FitzRoy, dressed in a spectacularly clean English Naval uniform, rushes up to us, salutes us both, and shakes Charles' hand.

"FitzRoy, Captain FitzRoy!" he exclaims, scooping a monocle out of his breast pocket and slapping it over his left eye. "And you must be the young Darwin chap I've been expecting. And this must be your dog. What's her name?"

"Birdie," says Charles.

"Birdie, yes, of course, Birdie!" FitzRoy reaches down and scratches my snout. I snarl.

"What strange green coloration you have, and what a unique short-hair fur, the likes of which I have never before felt on any animal!" He adjusts his monocle, which makes his eye appear larger, while simultaneously making him squint. He smiles at me, then turns to Charles. "You'll have to keep her in the aft holds, below sea level."

"I understand," says Charles, without asking my opinion.

"One last thing before you board, Darwin. I run a clean ship. That means no rum or whiskey or spirits of any kind, including wine. Do I make myself clear?"

Charles is taken aback for a moment, then he nods. "Ah, yes, that smell. That's just Birdie. I gave her a wine bath before we arrived in Devenport. When I was at Edinburgh studying medicine, our professors discussed this new theory that alcohol might actually be used to sterilize—"

"Ah, say no more!" FitzRoy raises his hand. "We don't

want the beast in heat. Progressive thinking, Darwin. We're going to get along just fine, you and I."

So I'm led by two members of FitzRoy's crew into the bowels of the ship, where I'm shoved into this dark room, and the hatch is slammed shut and padlocked over my head, at which point I gratefully assume my true shape. I can hear the tired old wood of the hull creaking against the waves. The hold smells of seaweed and mold.

I can only hope that this trip makes Charles happy, that he finds the treasure for which he has so earnestly been searching all these years. My origins. He's a good lad, after all, but he suffers from the same incurable ailment as all the others of his race: restlessness.

I curl up in the corner, and sleep.

"It's about time you woke up," says Charles.

I yawn, stretch my arms and legs and wings. It's so hot and stuffy in the aft hold I can barely breathe, but the heat has made my wings more flexible, and for the first time in centuries I am aware of their strength.

"Is it morning already?" I ask.

"It's *July* already," he replies with a touch of disapproval in his voice. "We're in Maldanado, in case you're in the least bit interested." He stares at me and frowns. "I never knew you to be such a sound sleeper."

"I was hoping I would sleep through the entire expedition. If it weren't for this infernal tropical weather, I might have been able to do it."

"Honestly, Birdie, I don't even know why I bothered bringing you along."

"Nor do I. All I've done is trade one dungeon for another."

I notice Charles is almost as pale as the first time we met, and he's sitting on the floor in a rather hunched position, as if ill. He rubs at the dark circles under his eyes.

"What's wrong, Charles?"

"Would you like something to eat?" he says without lifting his head. "The seamen have been netting shark for two weeks."

"No, thank you."

"Don't you ever get hungry? I don't believe I've ever seen you eat. To tell the truth, that bothers me. Are you a carnivore? Are you going to suddenly burst into a feeding frenzy and consume the crew?"

I search my memory. "I seem to remember eating once, a long time ago. Something makes me say a spinach salad, somewhere in France. Now why don't you tell me what's really bothering you?"

"Would you really like to know?" he says, raising his voice, glaring at me through glossy, red-streaked eyes. He pushes himself up off the floor. "I've been seasick since the first day we set sail. FitzRoy is an ass—that's right, an ass! He's a *Creationist* for God's sake, Birdie! He thinks God snapped His fingers and created all living things in their past, present, and future forms, just like that!"

Charles tries to snap his fingers but he's shaking so badly he can't quite pull it off. In this day and age, ardent Creationists aren't scarce enough, as far as Charles is concerned, and those who believe in Progressionism are just as bad. Progressionists would explain fossil discoveries and archaeological finds as proof of nothing more than successive intermittent catastrophes, with God destroying and replenishing the globe with new species after each cataclysm, Noah's flood being the last of them. ("The existence of all species can be explained using the sound principles of science," Charles once told me. This from a graduate of Christ's College, Cambridge. Amen.)

"And that crew!" Charles raves on. "You'd think a bunch of seamen who have sailed to almost every known port in the world would have something a little more stimulating to discuss than food, ale, and naked women!"

Charles begins to sob. I reach out and take him under

my wing. "There, there, Charles, everything will be fine. The longer they're at sea, the less interested they'll be in talking about food and ale."

"Try to stay awake, will you, Birdie?" he snuffles. "Just so I have someone intelligent to talk to."

I get him to relax a bit, and then I get him talking, which is something he seems to need desperately.

He tells me about the lofty mountains of Porta Praya, and their groves of cocoa-nut trees and tracts of lava plains and herds of goats. He tells me of the octopus that sprayed him with a jet stream of water on the rocky shore of St. Jago. He tells me of the stark-white rocks of St. Paul, the vast Brazilian forests, the reddish-brown sea of the Abrolhos Islets. He tells me of the vampire bats in Engenhodo and how they bite the horses there, and how the large black-and-ruby spiders of St. Fe Bajada feed upon prey ten times their own size.

All of this between bouts of tears, while I rock him gently in the crook of my wing.

And then, exhausted, in the middle of a sentence about a sparkling apricot-and-flamingo-colored sunset in Rio de Janeiro, he falls fast asleep. I feel his fragile body shivering beside me like that of a tiny butterfly. The heat is stifling. The *H.M.S. Beagle* rolls helplessly in the waves, like a wine barrel, and I think: *Oh, how I miss the sweet smell of wine!* I smell nothing here but salty sea water and fish, fish, fish, like a Venetian summer (although how I remember a Venetian summer I do not know). Charles is feverish. Why did I ever allow him to go through with this?

In the days that follow, Charles' spirits brighten under my care and attention. He is excited about leaving the ship and traveling by land from Bahia Blanca to Buenos Aires. He is reluctant to leave me behind, but I assure him that I will be fine.

When he finally meets up with the *Beagle* again, he

seems more energetic. He has collected hoards of specimens, some to dissect, some to stuff, and others merely to observe. He seems his old self again—enthusiastic, inquisitive, determined, even expedient. He has returned with a gift for me, a bright, jade-crimson-turquoise-colored blanket, woven by a half-naked woman of some South American Indian tribe. It's big enough to fit around me like a shawl. Much to my surprise, I adore it.

I notice he has returned with something else as well. His skin is covered with red bumps, some of them swollen, some of them scabbed, and he cannot stop himself from scratching. "We were attacked by large, black bugs as we crossed the Pampas."

"What kind of bugs?"

"Benchuca, I believe."

"What can we do for the itch?" I ask.

"Nothing. Nothing can be done. The bumps will disappear soon. You can stop mothering me now." And then he smiles and winks.

"Welcome back," I say.

So the days turn into weeks, months, and so on and so forth . . . the Falkland Islands, the Strait of Magellan, Chile, Peru, and the Galapagos Archipelago fall behind us. Once in a while, late at night, Charles will sneak me on deck where I will watch the waves roll beneath the ship, look up at the bright moon and the vast canvas of stars, and feel the salty spray of the sea upon my face.

Charles' gloominess returns only when he finds it necessary, ever so often, to inform me that he has still found no clues to my origins. On such occasions he hangs his head low and speaks into his chin and cannot look me in the eye.

This infuriates me. Why can he not let go of this childhood obsession with the origin of my species? But I keep my anger to myself. Charles needs my support. He has dealt with more defeatism and opposition in a quarter-century of his life than I've seen in eight or nine centuries of mine.

I am a dragon, I remind myself, and Charles is only a man.

When we set sail for Van Diemen's Land, Australia, the crew begins to talk about something more than food and ale, more even than naked women, and I don't like what I'm hearing. Apparently the aborigines there were run off by the white settlers only a few months ago, and since that time raids and burnings and robberies and murders have become commonplace, the aborigines striking back with small ambushes whenever and wherever possible.

When we drop anchor, I tell Charles, "I don't want you going ashore. The natives are restless."

"Nonsense, Birdie. The town is secure and most of the natives have been deported to another island. We'll be docked for ten days and I'll need to make some excursions inland to examine the unique geological structures of the area."

"You've got more than enough—"

"Birdie, this expedition is nearly at its end and I've still found no clues to your origins! There are some highly fossiliferous strata in Van Diemen's Land, and I must take every opportunity to—"

"My origins! *My origins!*" I feel the heat rise into my snout. I rear back on my haunches, and my nostrils begin to flare. "Why can't you just give it up?" I can't remember the last time I've been angry enough to smolder like this.

Charles takes a step back. For the first time in all the years we have known each other, he is afraid of me. Why do I worry so about Charles? I am a dragon. What do I care for the ephemeral pursuits of Man? And yet I *do* care about Charles.

The heat of the moment passes. I plop down on the

floor, let my nostrils fizzle out, and pull my Indian blanket up around my neck and shoulders. "I'm sorry," I say.

Charles exhales slowly, trying to pretend he was not frightened, though we both know he was. "It's been a long voyage for us all," he says. "I think everyone is tired, including you. Just remember to keep your voice down. We don't want FitzRoy catching on to us this late in the game."

"FitzRoy couldn't catch a mountain if Mahomet dropped it on him."

"Have you ever met Mahomet?" he asks.

"Possibly," I answer.

Charles climbs out of the aft hold, leaving me to stew for ten days.

Only it's not ten days when the trouble begins. I hear the explosions of black-powder rifles. My ears perk up. Men are shouting. I smell smoke.

"Charles?"

I climb the steps of the aft hold. The hatch is padlocked shut. I feel the anger rise within me. My belly churns like a furnace and I feel my throat burn with red heat. It has been so long since I've erupted, it almost frightens me. My body trembles. My throat tastes like coal. My saliva drips like hot tar. I am appalled at the digestive system I must house in order to manage such an internal inferno.

I rear back and belch, blowing a fire hole through the hatch.

There is nothing left to do but burst onto the upper deck.

It is a pitch-black night. The *Beagle* has been abandoned. All hands are on shore. It seems that the aborigines have attacked the town.

Charles!

I leap overboard, splash into the sea. The water drowns my fire, and I sink like a stone. I suddenly remember that I can't swim. But I know how to fly, so I start flapping my wings. Higher, higher, higher I rise—and finally I break the surface.

Into the great mysterious night I fly! It has been so long. Centuries! Up over the *Beagle,* over the sea that ripples the gold-orange of the burning town below me, up over the town itself, I fly.

The aborigines are withdrawing. They've killed. They've taken prisoners. The townsfolk fire their balls aimlessly into the dark. But I am a dragon and my eyes can see everything. I can see the dancing spears of the natives, their hurried retreat, their wounded victims and struggling prisoners . . . *and Charles!* Charles has been taken at spear point, his hands bound behind him, driven like an animal by a dozen aborigines into the black forest. If they reach the thick of the woodlands, I'll never find him, I'll never see him again.

The fire screams within me!

I dive!

"Chaaaaaaaaaaaaaaaaaarles—!"

My fire rakes through the aborigines, setting the field of their retreat aflame. They scream. Charles screams. I make my pass and my wings caress the air and I circle back, a trail of fiery phlegm cutting through the black night, and I dive again. One native, two natives catch fire and roll in the grass. The others run for their lives. Charles has fallen. Smoke billows. I circle and dive and circle, giving the natives a damn good look at me. I shall live in their nightmares for the next ten generations! But I must save Charles before the fire or the smoke take him. So I dive once more, and like a hawk snaring its prey I pluck Charles out of the grass with my talons and take to the air again

He looks up at me with stark terror in his eyes, and his lips form the question: *Birdie?*

I glide low to the ground, as silent as the wind. I drop Charles in a safe field near town, and head back to the ship, without so much as a word to the poor boy. There is nothing to say. Charles has finally seen me for what I truly am, a dragon. It will take him time to adjust.

When I land on deck, I scorch a few more areas of the bulwarks to mask my escape and make it look like the aborigines tried but failed to burn the vessel, and then I climb down through the ruined hatch, back into the aft hold, and curl up on the floor with my blanket.

In the morning, after order has been restored, rumors pass among the crew of a flying creature all ablaze, a beast the size of a country cottage, storming through the nighttime sky and wreaking havoc among the aborigines. But it was dark, and there was so much confusion and so many fires that most of the seamen do not believe the tales, or if they do, they aren't willing to admit the truth.

Charles is uninjured, but it is three days before he comes to the aft hold to tell me so.

"I never should have gone ashore, Birdie."

"Wisdom is hard learned," I tell him.

But at least Charles has come to me. I believe this is a gesture of acceptance. Man, I have come to learn, is a creature of metaphor.

The two-year expedition runs five years in all.

When we return, I retire to the Darwin dungeon. It is my home, after all. I curl up with my Indian blanket and sleep.

Charles visits me often in that first year, and together we compile his *Journal of Research Into the Geology and Natural History of the Various Countries Visited by H.M.S. Beagle under the Command of Captain FitzRoy, R.N.* It's Charles' bright idea to include FitzRoy's name in the title, a point on which he refuses to compromise in spite of my objections. Otherwise, I edit the manuscript for him, suggesting some stylistic enhancements, all of which he agrees to, including striking all references to his faithful Birdie, a point on which *I* refuse to compromise because I insist upon protecting his scientific integrity.

After the publication of the *Journal*, he is lionized by London's intellectual society, his career as a scientist catapults, and I know I'll never have to worry about Charles settling in as a country clergyman in some obscure backwoods parish.

Still he visits me often, to tell me of an exciting speaking engagement, or of a treasured new colleague, or of an admiring letter from some American naturalist, and one day when he comes, he tells me of his cousin, Emma Wedgwood, to whom he has proposed marriage.

Even after he is married and moves to Upper Gower Street in London, he thinks to visit me occasionally. He comes to tell me about his children, and how he will be among the first generation of Darwins not to punish his cubs by banishing them to the dungeon on Mount Darwin.

One day when he comes, he is so ill he can barely lift the wine cellar doors and make his way down the steps. He is weak and nauseous and suffering from heart palpitations. He does not stay long.

It is many months before I see him again, and when I finally do, he tells me his symptoms have worsened, and I can see he has lost weight and appears deathly pale.

"I am not likely to improve, Birdie. I am suffering from the attack of the Benchuca, the great black bug of South America. Do you remember the day I returned to the ship riddled with bites, after my hike through the Pampas?"

I remember, but I say nothing.

"The disease carried by the Benchuca is fatal," he says. "It can also be long and painful. I had hoped that after having gone so long with no symptoms, I might not have been infected, but it was not to be."

Charles carries with him a stack of notebooks and papers he can barely hold in his arms. He spreads them out on the floor and stares at me. "I have been working on a theory," he says. "Will you help me?"

Among the volcanic outcrops known as the Galapagos Islands, off the coast of South America, each island claims its own distinct population of birds and animals. Although there were obviously common ancestors, the fauna of each island developed separately, despite only a modest oceanic separation.

When Charles traveled across the islands, he noticed that the finches have become so distinct from one island to the next that they can no longer interbreed.

Charles has read Lamarck's hypothesis, dating back to the eighteenth century, that all living matter has an inherent drive toward increased complexity. This intrigues him, as does Buffon's theory, which suggests that environmental conditions as well as the struggle for survival might lead to the extinction of some species, and the succession of others.

"We also must consider Lyell's belief in uniform geological change," says Charles. "As geological alterations occur, this must bring about changes in the natural habitat of all living things."

We assemble the evidence, piece by piece, until it all finally makes sense.

Global changes. Genetic mutations. The struggle of all species for survival. Natural selection.

Evolution.

It is not *my* origin that Charles has discovered during the voyage of the *Beagle*, it is his own.

And yet just when the theory of Man's evolution becomes so absurdly obvious that neither of us can ignore it, ignore it is exactly what we do. We push aside our papers and relax to the smell of wine and cedar and moist earth, and spend most of our time together talking about death.

"I am looking forward to my death, Birdie," Charles says. "Death is the last great challenge of Man."

"You have always been too curious for your own good," I tell him.

Charles slides a Chilean cigar out of his pocket. I flare my nostril for him. He sticks the cigar in my snout and puffs hard on the butt, then succumbs to a coughing fit.

"Charles, I want you to know that I am very sorry."

"Sorry about what?"

"In many ways I am responsible for your malady. If not for me, you never would have gone on the expedition, and you never would have been attacked by the Benchuca."

"No, no, don't you see, Birdie? You have given me my life, not my death. If I had not met you, I never would have been driven to explore, I never would have lived through such exciting adventures. Death is merely a consequence. That is the way of Man, Birdie. We pay for our lives with our deaths."

I nod, but I do not understand. How can I?

"Because of you," I say, "I was able to share in that adventure." I am surprised to discover that this matters to me.

"You know, I could have died at the hands of those aborigines. I have never properly thanked you for saving my life, Birdie."

"Think nothing of it."

"I'm sure it is a point of less concern to someone who has lived centuries, probably eons." Charles coughs. He does not possess the lung strength to keep the cigar lit, so he stubs it out in the dirt. "Man needs to believe in his life after death. Man must have his gods."

Ah, yes. Charles is afraid of the changes his insights might bring about among his species. He is afraid of how his race might suffer without the comfort of the Book of

Genesis. He does not see what I see. He does not have the perspective of centuries.

"Charles," I say. "What does your theory tell you about Man?"

He looks at me blankly.

"*Adaptation,* Charles," I explain gently. "If Man needs new gods and new beliefs, I promise you that he will devise them. It is not only the body that evolves, but also the spirit."

"But does Man *want* new gods?" he asks dubiously.

"I cannot say," I answer. "If he does not, rest assured that he will create new reasons to believe in the old ones."

"I am very tired, Birdie," he says. And this is the last thing he will ever say to me.

Charles is supposed to visit me today, but when or if he arrives, I will not be here. I have decided that I cannot watch him die.

So I am alone in the wine cellar when I scribble Charles Darwin's name across the cover page, and affix a title to our manuscript: *Upon the Origin of Species By Means of Natural Selection, or Preservation of Favoured Races and the Struggle for Life.*

I don my Indian blanket and tuck the manuscript under my wing and climb the stairs of the wine cellar. I push open the doors and step out into the bright morning sun.

I think I shall take the train to London—or perhaps I shall fly—to Albemarle Street, and in my human guise, much as I hate corsets and bustles, I will personally deliver the manuscript to the publishing company of John Murray. I was impressed by the job they did with the 1845 edition of the *Journal,* quite a money-maker from what I understand, and I am certain they will be eager to print Darwin's newest work. In any event, I must do what Charles cannot. I must offer Man the truth. It is essential, I think, for the continued development of his species.

Then I shall find another place on the Earth to live. Mount Darwin will never be the same without Charles. The future Darwins, like those before him, seem a dull lot. I am a dragon: I can fly, I can set a field aflame with my breath, I can see things clearly in a way that men, even so gifted a man as Charles, cannot, and I have needs of my own.

The boy has overcome his initial surprise at seeing me, and now sits down on the floor, cross-legged, a few feet away.

"Why have your parents locked you down here?" I ask.

He stares at me uncomprehendingly, and I switch to German.

"No one locked me here," he answered. "I often come here to think."

"And what do you think about?" I ask.

He shrugs. "It is difficult to express," he says. "They are very big thoughts," he adds seriously.

A warm glow suffuses me. "Sometimes I think very big thoughts myself." I pause. "I think we are going to become friends."

"I would like that."

"What is your name, boy?" I ask.

"Albert," he says.

"Albert," I repeat. "That is a very nice name. And I am Birdie."

I wrap my Indian blanket around me. I am content.

FOG OF WAR

by William R. Forstchen

November 22, 1805

On the distant horizon he could see the campfires of the Russian pickets, their glow reflecting off the low hanging clouds. He pulled the collar of his great coat in tight around his throat to ward off the evening chill.

Damnable country, he thought. In Corsica it'd still be warm this time of year.

"My Emperor, it is not safe here, we're beyond our own lines."

He looked back at the circle of staff officers following him, not sure who had spoken, interrupting his thoughts. He stared at them coldly, ready to snap out an angry reply. In the gathering shadows he could see their faces, young, so damn young most of them. My children, fearing for their Emperor. No, he couldn't get angry, not with them.

"Go back to the camp, leave me alone for awhile."

"But, my Emperor—"

He forced a smile.

"Our pickets are out ahead of us," and he pointed off towards the distant fires, "I want to be alone, to think."

Though he smiled, he set the proper tone to his voice, the tone that expected instant obedience, the tone that could send thousands to their deaths without hesitation.

The staff turned away reluctantly and started down the hill, gazing back over their shoulders with anxious looks before disappearing into the twilight.

Good. If there was a problem with being an emperor it was finding even a moment to be alone, truly alone. He walked on, hands clasped behind his back, looking out towards the shadows, pondering his next move.

So far, it had all gone to plan. With the beginning of this war, the Austrians had moved forward, out of Vienna and into Bavaria to meet him, not bothering to wait for their Russian allies. Ulm had been the result, yet another triumph, and from there to Vienna but a quick victorious march. But now, now was the real challenge. The Russians had pulled back out of Vienna, and even now were gathering in their strength, not thirty kilometers up the road to the east, the rest of the Austrian army not trapped at Ulm moving to join them. He would be outnumbered now, his own army still strung out behind him on the road back to Vienna.

What to do?

He walked on across the Pratzen Heights visualizing it all as it was drawn on his maps. The road back to Vienna behind him, to his left, the high dark Moravian-Switzerland mountains, foothills that continued on up into the Black mountains of Bohemia. Wild country, primitive, almost medieval, a strange land this.

"Emperor Napoleon I presume."

Damn, now what. He turned to see who was intruding. *"Mon Dieu!"*

He felt the hair at the nape of his neck prickle straight up, his knees going in an instant to jelly, shaking uncontrollably.

The shadowy figure drew closer, standing up on its hind legs, head rising up on its long neck, turning slightly to gaze at him from its bulging red-hued eye.

Napoleon Bonaparte started to back up, ready to run. "Would you let it be said that the great Emperor Napoleon was afraid of something and ran away?" the shadow asked, drawing yet closer.

Napoleon stopped. The trembling in his knees was still uncontrollable, yet now there was a flicker of anger. A coward? Never, death was always preferable to that.

Surprised by his own instinctive response he nevertheless made the sign of the cross. That action alone caused him to seize control of his fear. He could imagine the Pope, the pompous fool, chuckling over the great Emperor trembling, making the holy sign and then blubbering out a quick Pater Noster.

The trembling stopped.

"Ah, that's better, do you mind if I sit?" the shadow asked.

Though the trembling had stopped, command of his voice was still questionable and Napoleon merely nodded a reply.

The dragon sat down on his rear haunches, resting on his stubby forelegs, head looking straight at him, still cocked to one side. Its scales rustled like the creaking of old armor, its breath washed over him, smelling of ancient damp smoke.

It sighed, stretching, like an old weary dog.

"What are you?" Napoleon whispered.

It laughed softly, a deep rumbling chuckle that sounded like distant thunder.

"Ah, what am I? A devil perhaps? Do you believe in devils?"

"At the moment, I'm not sure."

"A good answer. Perhaps I am Mephistopheles, you are my Faust and together we shall bargain for victory. How does that sound?"

"I don't need a devil's bargain for what I can take on my own."

The rumbling laughter was even louder now.

"Well spoken, my Emperor; what I would expect from you. But no, I am not a devil."

He felt a sense of relief for that indeed had been his first thought and he knew the temptation would have perhaps been too much, to exceed even Alexander and like him march to Persepolis and the seas of India beyond.

"A dragon then?" he finally ventured.

"Very good, my Emperor. You do remember your children's tales. Yes, a dragon. Gar of the lineage of Bakga," and it bowed its head low.

"I dare say that you might even consider me to be of royalty. I hope that does not arouse your Republican instincts. But then again, I think I can let you in on that secret, seeing that you are now an Emperor yourself."

Napoleon smiled. This was far too fantastic. If I were an eater of opium, he thought, then I would believe this. No, it must be a dream. Yet he could feel the warm breath. On impulse he stepped forward, reaching out with his hand, touching its face.

"No, I am not a dream."

"This is fantastic."

"That's what some people would say. But there are others," and it growled softly, turning to look back towards the east.

"Damn Russians, nothing but ignorant peasants, and the locals around here, those damn Bohemians, do you think I'd stand much of a chance with them?"

"I take it you don't like Russians then?" Napoleon asked softly, in a friendly, understanding voice.

The dragon growled, a low rumble of rage, and turned its head.

Though he was used to wounds, it still startled him. The dragon's right eye was swollen shut. He looked at it intently. A saber wound slashing across his face, narrowly missing its eye. He reached up to touch it and the dragon winced, pulling back, rumbling with pain.

"You're hurt."

"A brilliant observation," Gar snapped.

"A Russian?"

"Damn cossack. There I was, minding my own business. If there's one thing a dragon knows, especially if he wishes to survive, it is to lay low when you humans are marching about fighting one of your wars. Especially with those new weapons of yours which don't even give us a fair chance. This cossack, however, comes poking into my hole, catching me asleep and gives me this," and Gar raised his forepaw to point at the wound.

"What happened to him?"

"I ate him."

"Oh."

"I hate eating Russians though. Too greasy. Frankly I prefer Turks myself, but it's been a long time since they showed up around here. Now as for Mongols, it's been five hundred years since I've seen one of them; they were too stringy."

Gar paused, looked at Napoleon and chuckled.

"No, I won't eat Frenchmen. It goes against the code."

"The code?" Napoleon asked quietly.

"You have a code, I heard it's developing out rather nicely by the way, and so do we. We only eat those who bother us. Sort of an issue of honor. Also, if we made humans a steady diet, they'd get upset and hunt us in earnest. But if you leave us alone, we'll leave you alone, though I don't know how my cousins living in the French Alps feel about you. I just wish you humans felt the same about us as far as codes go."

"I didn't even believe you existed," Napoleon said softly.

"That's the whole intent," Gar replied. "However, it's getting rather difficult of late. Too many of you people.

And then you have these damned peasants, like the Russians and the locals around here. Do you think I'd come up to them for a talk like this.?"

Napoleon started to reply but Gar cut him off.

"Hardly likely. If they had one of your guns they'd shoot first, run, and then get the villagers out for a hunt. Now with their armies tramping around on top of it, it's getting downright dangerous. My sister's youngest was killed by several Russian lancers just last week. She's beside herself with grief."

"I can imagine," Napoleon said softly. "She has my sympathy."

Gar looked at him intently for a moment.

"I think we can talk a little business you and I."

Napoleon smiled. If this is a dream, then so what. But if it is not, he reasoned, making alliances was a pastime he enjoyed. Beyond that, he knew it was best to humor whatever it was sitting next to him, especially when one considered the size of his fangs and claws.

"How might I be of service?" Napoleon responded smoothly.

"I like you French. I rather like your revolution as well. Get rid of the old superstitions, bring in an age of reason, of science, of progress. I like that," Gar rumbled, now settling down to stretch out on the ground, motioning for Napoleon to sit down beside him.

"One of the reasons I learned French, I thought you people might come by here some day. You see there's still a lot of us old ones left around, hiding in the mountains, the swamps. But you people are taking the rest, making it more difficult every day. Now there's some that I think would be decent types, say some of those English. More than one of my cousins have had fair dealings with them."

Napoleon shook his head angrily.

"Perfidious lot."

Gar laughed.

"Still, from our viewpoint they're not all that bad. But these Russians, the locals here, that's another story."

Gar's voice rumbled into a language Napoleon could not understand, but as an old soldier he knew cursing when he heard it and Gar was letting go with a long pent-up stream of it while looking back towards the glowing campfires to the east.

"Can I be of some assistance to you in your vendetta with the Russians?" Napoleon asked smoothly and, as he did so, he even reached up and took hold of Gar by his ear, tweaking him gently.

Gar turned and looked back.

"You do have a way about you, my Emperor," Gar said, settling back down, "but I am not one of your old grumblers, your guardsmen whom you can tweak like that."

"My apologies."

"Accepted. But as I was saying about your revolution. My cousins and I like the idea. Bring your humans out of the Middle Ages, get rid of these foolish superstitions, settle things down a bit with some progress. If we dragons helps that to happen, perhaps a ruler, a truly enlightened ruler, might finish up his, how should I call it," Gar paused for a moment, "his Napoleonic Code with a little subclause regarding the rights of dragons."

"The rights of dragons?"

"Well, why not. You French are talking about the rights of man. That's what you claim your revolution is all about. Don't you think my kin and I are entitled to some rights around here as well?"

Gar rustled slightly, his scales flexing out, rattling.

"Oh, but of course."

"You promised those damn Poles to the north a free country and, let me tell you, I don't like them any more than I like the Russians. Well, if you're going to give them rights, what about us?"

Napoleon smiled.

"The Poles. A good people and firm allies willing to fight by my side."

Gar chuckled.

"So now we come to the bargaining."

"Yes, the bargaining."

"I offer an alliance, Napoleon."

Napoleon looked appraisingly at Gar. As a shock weapon he'd be ideal. He was easily the size of a heavy mount for a cuirassier. He looked closely at Gar who was now barely visible in the darkness.

There were even wings. Wonderful, better than a Montgafer balloon for looking behind enemy lines. A dragon regiment for heavy attack in the Imperial Guard with a light scouting regiment to range behind enemy lines. Why, it'd throw the Russians into a rout the first time they saw them.

Wonderful!

"I offer you the rank of general in command of your own dragon regiment," Napoleon said excitedly. "As for your uniforms, we can fit you out in something like a hussar's outfit. You'll look grand."

Gar shook his head and growled.

"My dear Emperor, I know what you are thinking here. I have no desire to charge a grand battery firing grape-and twelve-pound-solid shot."

"How about for scouting then?"

"You don't seem to understand. Our whole purpose here is to avoid contact. You humans might relish a grand charge but, then again, you can kill a million or two and be none the worse for wear. One good charge like you did at Marengo will wipe us out. No, we are not volunteering for that."

"Then how can you expect to earn your rights?" Napoleon snapped peevishly. "Even the Italians are fighting beside us!"

"There are ways of serving, and there are ways of serving. Personally I think I and those of my kin living nearby can be of help. We know that you had hoped to smash the Austrians and the Russian armies independently. They're linking up together, right now," the dragon nodded back towards the east.

"You are telling me nothing that I don't already know," Napoleon said quietly.

"You are outnumbered. Winter is approaching and with each passing day your enemy will grow stronger while you weaker. If your campaign continues another month, your supplies will start to become scarce. What you are looking for is one overwhelming victory, a battle of annihilation to knock the Austrians and Russians out of the war before the Prussians decide to join in. If they can hold out long enough, your situation will grow increasingly desperate."

Napoleon nodded, not replying. The dragon was right, though he would never admit it to him.

"Are you offering me something?" Napoleon finally asked.

"First let me make an understanding from my side," Gar replied.

"Go on then."

"If we help you to end this current campaign with a total victory, then in return you will do a service for us."

"Which is?"

"Recognition in your code of laws protecting the rights of dragons. Second, that certain preserves be created, we won't ask for much, a mountain here, a swamp there. Finally, that diplomatic recognition be extended to us as an autonomous group independent of humans."

Napoleon leaned back saying nothing.

"You know, it might create problems. You say you have cousins scattered in different areas?"

"Yes."

"Where?"

Gar laughed.

"I'd rather not say. My cousins might get upset if I revealed just how many places they were located."

"I can see a problem here. I'm fighting a war. Even I will admit that we are not popular in all places that we take. Local populations might not agree if I start to set aside land here and there for your sanctuaries."

Gar nodded sadly.

"I can see that."

"What about after the war is done, when all of Europe is united under my, excuse me, I mean living together under one rule."

Gar remained silent for ar moment.

"Let me phrase it this way then," Gar finally replied. "If my clan here can provide you the means of obtaining victory in your current campaign, when the war is done will you in return meet my requests?"

"You think you can influence this campaign even though you refuse to fight by my side."

"There are more ways of fighting then simply charging their line," Gar replied.

Napoleon hesitated for a moment and then smiled.

"Done. My code of law, at such time, will be amended to treat the rights of dragons as equal to the rights of man."

"Fine." Gar stirred, reaching up with his forepaw into a small satchel dangling under its arm. He pulled out a sheaf of paper and handed it to Napoleon along with a stick of charcoal.

"Shall we place this treaty in writing?"

Napoleon laughed and nodded.

"I think my handwriting might be better than yours," Napoleon said quickly. He took the stick of charcoal and, resting the papers on his knee, began to write, while Gar emitted a small flame from his nostrils to provide some light.

With a dramatic flourish Napoleon finished off the two copies of the treaty and signed them both. Gar looked down at the paper, squinting at it with his one good eye and then finally nodded an agreement.

"My reading of French is not the best but all looks in order here."

Gar took up the charcoal stick and drew, in letters Napoleon did not recognize, what appeared to be the dragon's signature.

He took one copy of the treaty for himself and handed one back to the Emperor.

"I think, my Emperor, that for the present this should be a secret concordat."

"Why?"

"Suppose you lose, even after our help. Then where will we be? I dare say that the crowned heads of Europe would hunt us down to the death in vengeance."

"I will not lose."

"But just suppose you do. No, it will be our secret for now. And for heaven's sake don't let that damn Tallyrand find out. First off, he'll be upset that he wasn't in on the negotiating and, secondly, all of Europe will know if he ever finds out."

Napoleon could see the point. The propaganda value of this agreement was difficult to judge. Chances were the pope would claim that dragons were the minions of Satan; it might arouse Italy and Spain. No, it was best to keep it quiet.

"So how do you plan to honor your part of the bargain?" Napoleon asked.

The dragon stood up and stretched.

"This place you humans call the Pratzen Heights used to be nice ground. Several hundred years back it was all woods, until the damn peasants came and cleared it. There was a time when some of my clan lived under this very ridge in some rather comfortable caves.

"There's a good stream nearby; they call it the Goldbach," he pointed towards the west where the stream came down out of the Moravian-Switzerland mountain, "and a couple of ponds that the stream runs into. The fish in there were wonderful to eat until the peasants moved in," he then pointed towards the south and southeast.

"Now, if only you could move your army forward, then turn around, fake a retreat, and lure the Russians and Austrians back to this ground. Do that and my clan and I could prepare the means for victory."

As he continued to talk Napoleon listened and smiled. Within minutes they were both down on their hands and knees, scratching out a map on a piece of paper.

December 2, 1805

The thunder of artillery rattled with a crescendolike roar. Pacing, with hands behind his back, Napoleon cocked his head and listened, then turned to look back at his staff as a mud-splattered courier came up the hill.

"Word from Davout?"

Gasping for breath, the courier rode up by Napoleon's side and saluted, handing over a dispatch. Napoleon read it and then looked back at his staff.

"The pressure is still building on the right; they're falling for it."

The staff looked at him anxiously, barely visible in the swirling mist. The battle was almost invisible. To the south, he could see occasional flashes of light where the fog was thinning out. Straight ahead, the Pratzen Heights were all but invisible as well. To the left the fog was thinning out slightly but still holding.

Excellent! Just as the plan had been worked out two weeks before. He had moved forward the morning after his talk with Gar, advancing thirty kilometers eastward to the area where the Russians and Austrians were massing. Then he had turned, as if already beaten and retreated. They had taken the bait, sensing victory with their superior numbers, and pursued him. Next he had committed an act which he knew the enemy would view as a supreme folly, he had conceded the Pratzen Heights to them, pulling back to the Goldbach River. With that move they would believe he had committed the ultimate folly by giving away the high ground, thus allowing them to have a secure and apparently impregnable ridge to form their center on.

He then extended a weak screen to the right, making it look vulnerable. The right flank was an open invitation for an enemy attack. He knew they would see the weakness to the south and fall upon it, hoping to break through and then cut his line of retreat. As the battle continued, they would strip more and yet more out of their center to push the issue home. What they did not know was that during the night he had secretly reinforced the right with reserves forced marched up from Vienna.

There was a nervous cough behind him and he turned.

"Sire. You can tell by the sound that the right is hard pressed. Don't you think it is time to send the attack in?"

Napoleon angrily shook his head.

"What did I tell all of you two weeks ago?"

They looked at him nervously.

"Go on, what did I tell you when I came back from my walk on those heights?" and he pointed to the east where the shadow of the Pratzen could be dimly seen.

"You announced, my Emperor," one of them said, "that the war would be decided on those heights."

"Then have faith," Napoleon replied, and he reached over to the aide and pulled his ear playfully.

"Look at this fog," he announced, "that was in the plan as well, don't you remember. I told you that the ground below the heights was marshy, that a mist would rise up before dawn from there and out of the river and it would conceal our main advance until the time was right. Give it just a little more time to play to our advantage. Let them strip their center."

He went over to his field chair and sat down. Behind him the staff paced nervously, but he ignored them. He kept an ear cocked towards the battle, listening intently as a roaring volley rippled across the fields. Yes, they were committing more. The trick now was to make sure he didn't wait too long and lose his right flank even as he gained the center. To the north the battle had started as well, the sound increasing with every passing minute.

He looked straight up. He could see clouds now, patches of blue sky. The air was getting warmer. The sun climbing. Flashes of light flickered on the heights, reflections of swords, bayonet points, the fog down below starting to burn off.

Another minute.

He could almost sense, rather than see that the Russians and Austrians smelled victory, moving yet more into their attack.

Well I smell victory, too. The dragon and his clan were doing their part. He had to give them that. Their breath was bubbling out from their lairs into the river and ponds, turning them to vapor, cloaking the front of the heights as they had promised. Yet they could not do so forever.

"You will know when the time is right," Gar had said. "After all, you've won every other battle on your own till now."

Napoleon stood up, shading his eyes. Yes, the sun was about to break through.

"Now, you may send them in now," he finally announced, looking back at his staff.

With a wild shout couriers set off at the gallop, racing into the swirls of mist, and then minutes later he finally heard it, the sound sending a corkscrew shiver down his spine, the drums playing out the *pas d'charge*.

He could feel the vibration in the air as the divisions started forward, the mist giving the sound of a ghostlike quality. The rumble of fighting started to flare up ahead and to the left as the advance slammed into the north flank of the Austrian-Russian line, crashing into it, rolling it back.

The mist was breaking, the Pratzen Heights now standing out clear.

He extended his telescope and focused on the hill. The standards of the Russian guard studded the hill, their numbers not as many as before but still a strong force. It would be shock that would have to break them; if they held out long enough the enemy could still recall its commitment to the right.

"Send in the Imperial Guard," Napoleon announced, and yet more couriers galloped off.

"Just a couple of more minutes, Gar," he whispered softly.

The drum rolls of his Imperial Guard signalled the advance. To the southeast all was now clearly in view, his own line buckled, barely holding on, the bulk of the enemy moving in for what they thought would be the kill.

And then, from out of the mist, he saw his own divisions sweeping up the forward slope of the Pratzen, the Russian Guard deploying into line to meet them.

"Now, hit them now," he whispered, hands clenched behind his back, flexing nervously.

As if a curtain was drawn back, the fog in the valley started to melt away, the sun, a golden orb now shining clearly behind the heights. And up out of the mist, advancing at the double, emerged the Imperial Guard of the Empire, tricolors snapping in the early morning air as their bearers ran to the fore, the chanting of the troops rising up . . . .

"Vive l'Empereur, Vive l'Empereur!"

The Fog of Austerlitz disappeared to be replaced by the Sun of Austerlitz. The Russian guard wavered, breaking, a few heroic souls struggling to rally them and then they melted away beneath the morning sun, the lines buckling, breaking apart in panic as the feared troops which had carried a score of fields came upon them, rising up out of the mist.

He heard cheers around him as the tricolors gained the heights and then pivoted, turning south, splitting the allied army apart. His cuirassiers, the heavy cavalry of the guard, storming through the center to widen the breach, sowing panic into the rear while the infantry continued its turn, now racing south down the length of the heights, driving the panic-stricken enemy before them.

Within minutes all semblance of an enemy army south of the breakthrough disappeared. The panic grew, rippling down the line, for how could this be? But moments before the valley below was empty, filled with fog, and now even as it burned away the bulk of the French army had risen up out of the concealment to render into shreds the dream of victory.

He could see them running, throwing away their muskets, tearing off packs and cartridge boxes, fleeing in terror. But there was no place to go except the frozen ponds, where peasants and, before them, dragons had fished.

The mob broke out into the ice, running, and though the thought of it made him feel cold at heart still he gave the order, looking back at his staff.

"Have the artillery bombard the lake," he said, and then turned back to watch.

Within minutes his guns were turned sending their shot bounding and screaming across the frozen lakes. Sprays of ice showered up and then the lake started to fracture. He tried to tell himself that it was the weight of the panicked mob, but he knew that his enemies would call it callous brutality against an already beaten foe.

The ice cracked, shattering under the weight of the men and the hammer blows of shot. It seemed that within seconds what had once been solid was now liquid, thousands upon thousands falling into the freezing water. He watched in silence, it did not take long. The heavy wool coats soaked with water pulled their numbed bodies down into the depths .... Gar and his cousins would have good fishing on Russians and Austrians for weeks to come. It was at least a form of payment for services rendered.

The battle roared about him, cheers, screams of triumph and pain echoing, mingled with the rattle of musketry, the thunder of the guns, all of it a glorious ovation to what he already could see would be his greatest victory.

"There is still work to be done on the northern flank," he said, and he motioned for his staff to join him and ride.

December 3, 1805

Even in the cold winter air, the stench of corruption hung heavily about him, yet he would not let it steal from him this moment. Less than a day ago, all Europe would have believed him defeated and now, now there was already the glory, the legend of Austerlitz. Already his old grumblers, the Imperial Guard, had built it to a myth, how he, the Emperor, had so clearly seen that here would be the place of victory weeks before the battle was joined. Already it was said in the camps that he had even foreseen the fog, and knew its beginnings and its endings. Upon such legends more victories would be built, for in war men were nothing, a man everything. If a man becomes legend, victory will follow victory. His old grumblers, and his foes, would believe the legend of Austerlitz, how out of the fog of war the Emperor had foreseen and seen all things clearly. Such beliefs would come to shape battles yet to be fought.

He walked along the base of the hill, around him now,

nothing but the dead. At least for this moment his staff, at his orders, had withdrawn.

"My Emperor."

Napoleon turned and the shadow drew closer.

"You served me well today, Gar. If you were a man I would make you a marshal. The fog you and your clan made worked to perfection, a marvelous perfection!"

Gar bowed his head low in reply.

"Thank you for the dinner. I suspected you bombarded the lake to provide a little extra treat. Though Russians are greasy, a dipping in chilled water seems to help the taste. We try and fish out the Austrians first, however, their meat is softer."

Napoleon shuddered inwardly at the thought and Gar rumbled a laugh.

Gar drew closer.

"Though I did not serve you merely for meal," Gar said, "I expect the treaty to be honored."

"Oh, but of course, my friend. I came here to thank you for your service to me, and to assure you that it shall indeed be honored."

Gar looked at him, a thin smile creasing his jagged jaw.

"You know, it is said by some that we can read the souls of men."

Napoleon looked at him unblinking.

"I would like to think that your Republican sentiments of your youth still burn within, that you will link the rights of dragons to the rights of man."

"Once the wars are over, so it shall be as I agreed to in our treaty."

"Wars?"

Gar looked at him curiously.

"Yes, wars. That is exactly how it is written on both my copy and yours," and Napoleon reached into his breast pocket, pulled out the document and unfolded it.

Gar looked down at the paper, a brief flicker of flame

fanning from his nostrils to provide light. He squinted at the paper intently, gazing at it with his one good eye.

"Wars. I don't recall it being phrased that way. You humans have fought wars from the beginning, one endless series of wars."

"It says right here, and I quote, 'upon the conclusion of the wars.'"

Gar looked down at the contract and nodded.

"Ah I see, the plural form of *guerre* is in writing. My reading of French was never the best, though I do suspect that you knew that."

Napoleon said nothing.

"So it shall be awhile," Gar said softly.

Napoleon looked at him the way he found he could now look at so many. If only the victory had not been so spectacular, so legendary in its proportion. To reveal now the truth about the Fog of Austerlitz and the already famous prediction of how it would be fought two weeks before it happened would steal from the legend, his legend.

"Upon this victory so many others will come," Napoleon said, "upon this moment we have been made all but invincible in the eyes of my own people and our enemies."

"And the story of a dragon might detract from the legend."

"My friend," Napoleon said with a smile, again coming up to pull on his ear, "I fight this war to create a new Europe. It will take years yet, perhaps a generation before the monarchies are laid into the dirt. Now take the English, if only you could get your cousins in England to do something useful. Say burn some of their ships, or blow up a storm, now there would be a real service to ensure the rights of dragons."

"I cannot speak for my kin over there. Perhaps they might feel partial to their Englishmen. No, I can't bind them to that in order to bring about a treaty already agreed upon between you and me which made no prior mention of a need for their services."

"Ah, you see," Napoleon said quickly. "So it will be some time yet. I must, if need be, march to Whitehall itself to force them to the table. And then there is Moscow as well and Madrid before much longer and even Constantinople."

Gar shook his head.

Napoleon looked at him, his features softening for a moment.

"Come, my friend, you have done well by me today and I shall do well by you in return. My army is already leaving here. The only Russians you will see here now are ones for your dining table. And when it is all done, I promise you the rights of dragons will be assured upon my final victory."

Napoleon looked up at him and as he spoke he actually believed in his heart what he said. He liked this creature; it's just that the foolish thing should have read the treaty a little more carefully. And besides there was the legend to maintain.

Gar drew away, forcing Napoleon to let go of his ear.

"When your troops are trapped upon the roads of Spain, cut apart by their peasants, do not look for us there. And if you should ever march to Moscow, and find the road of your return frozen, do not look for us to warm you with our breath. And do not cry for me to carry you on my wings if you find yourself, at last, chained like Prometheus to a rock. I am sorry, my Emperor. I will not eat you out of vengeance for, after all, we dragons at least do live by our code.

"Adieu."

Gar disappeared into the night, as if he was made of nothing more than mist.

Napoleon looked around, as if he had, indeed, been talking to nothing more than the fog. He looked down at the treaty still in his hand and for a moment he thought to call Gar back and to strike off the plural at the end of the word *guerre*.

But there was the legend now. The legend of Austerlitz. That was the thing of the moment. Moscow, Spain? They would fall with the legend alone riding before him. And then he would honor his word as he had promised to when he wrote it out. He folded the paper up, tucked it into his breast pocket and walked away. He would file it with all the other papers once he returned in triumph to Paris.

The moon rose, pale and crescent, its ghostly glow reflecting off the upturned faces of the dead that lay heaped around him.

IN THE HEAVENS
AND ON THE EARTH

by Christopher Stasheff

The Dragon of China heard the bray of a trumpet
from afar. It was harsher than those played by the people
who were his bone and muscle—it was piercing, and
seemed off-pitch. In irritation, he lifted his head from
his claws—he had been uncommonly weary lately; his
blood had seemed to grow thin. Those barbarians from
the steppe had been spicy indeed, and had invigorated
him long after he had digested them and spat them out—
but after a century and a half, that surge of energy had
dwindled, and he had become sleepy, very sleepy,
scarcely able to waken to greet the sun each morning
before he lapsed back into torpor. He had roused himself
briefly so that his people could fight those wild men from
the north, those Manchus, but he had fallen into lethargy
again quite quickly, and began the work of digesting
them, absorbing them into his bone and blood. "Conquerors" they called themselves; fodder, he found them.

But they lay like lead within him, scarcely invigorating him at all; there was too little of the new in their ideas, too much of the old. They made the Chinese who were his body wear pigtails as a sign of servitude, but other than that, they seemed to have very little to offer, and he absorbed them almost at once.

So, everything considered, he welcomed the notion of something new.

Looking up, he saw a man riding toward him with a long lance, one that flared out to guard his hand. Strange indeed he looked, clad all in metal that gleamed like silver in the sunlight, riding across the clouds with a banner emblazoned with a cross. That shell would be a bother; the Dragon would have to peel it off him before he could dine.

The little man saw the Dragon and gave a shout, levelling his lance and kicking his horse into a gallop.

The Dragon stared in indignation. Could this insignificant insect dare to challenge the mighty cloudrider? Negligently, he lifted a claw to flick the challenger away . . . .

The spear stabbed into his foot, and the dragon roared in pain and surprize. He flicked indeed, and the lance went spinning. Then he drew his talons back for a blow that would knock the temeritous barbarian tumbling—but the shiny little fellow raised his hand and cried, "Hold!"

Out of sheer surprize, the Dragon withheld his blow. Then the novelty of it caught his interest; anything that would alleviate the boredom of millenia was worth investigation. He lowered his vast head to the rider's level and demanded, in a voice that rattled his silver clothing, "Wherefore should I hold?"

"Because I am England!" the rider cried. "Know, decadent serpent, that I am Saint George, and the power of God resides in me!"

The arrogance of the creature, the sheer, overweening

pride of him! But he was amusing, so much so that the Dragon ignored his bad manners and asked instead, "The power of god? What god is that?"

"The Lord Most High!" the little rider cried. "Jehovah of the Thunders! The One, the only God!"

"There are hundreds of gods." The Dragon was disgusted by the barbarian's ignorance. "And the One is the Tao, the summation and whole of which all things are part. The Ch'an call it 'Buddha.' "

"Blasphemy!" Saint George cried, and drew a silver sword.

With a flick of his claw, the Dragon knocked it whirling from his hand. "You are rude indeed, barbarian. Know that it is you who blaspheme, by daring to challenge the Dragon of China!"

"You shall submit to God's will! I shall wrest that submission from you, for I am a saint!"

"What is a 'saint'?" the Dragon asked, interested.

"Why, it is . . . ." The rider floundered a moment, then demanded, "Are you so ignorant that you do not even know of God and sainthood?"

"You try my patience,' the Dragon said in irritation. "Beware, for you cease to be amusing. Tell me plainly what a saint is."

"A saint is a soul that has won to Heaven, and the presence of God!"

The Dragon recognized the concepts, if not the words themselves. "Ah. One who has achieved nirvana, one who has become one with the Tao. A bodhisattva, a sage."

"You speak gibberish!"

"You bore me." The Dragon flicked the little rider away; he spun rolling across the clouds. His horse whinnied with alarm and sped after him. The rider struggled to his feet and cried, "I shall subdue you! My lance shall pierce your heart!"

"Then you had better find it first," the Dragon said, and lowered his head to his paws again, as the rider went searching frantically through the clouds for his spear. He ceased to matter to the Dragon, who sank back into tranquility . . . .

But not into sleep. There was a strange thrumming in his blood, and when he did lapse again into unconsciousness, the germs of concepts sprung from the thrust of the lance percolated through his blood. Unseen, invisible, they began to spawn new ideas, in the heart of China.

There had been others who had come, similar to this barbarian, but they had not disrupted the Dragon's sleep. Minor pinpricks they were, traders at the edges of China, borne by the sea or having toiled across the desert. Long had the Dragon imbibed the traces of nourishment borne by such men, with their strange hairy, nobby faces and round eyes. Their holy men had labored in both court and village, but had disguised themselves and their ideas so much in the cast of China that they had not waked the Dragon. Only this brash Englishman had had the effrontery to challenge him outright.

But perhaps he would have his uses. The Dragon would absorb him, as it had absorbed all who had sought to conquer; they who came to slay, made excellent dinners. Perhaps, in his blood, this "saint" would cleanse him of those presumptuous Manchus, who dared claim they had the Mandate of Heaven.

How ridiculous! As though Heaven could choose any barbarian to rule the Middle Kingdom! They were a cancer in the blood. This Englishman would be so, too, and perhaps the two cancers would cancel one another.

But the Englishman was only the vanguard; when the Dragon woke again, he saw Saint George riding at the head of a band of half a dozen—and their names were Saint Andrew, Saint Mark, Saint Ignatius, and Saint Louis. There was also Emperor Frederick with a long red beard, who was no saint. The Dragon knew all this, because the men shouted their names and titles as they came. He all but laughed at the notion of this crude barbarian daring to call himself an emperor. He restrained himself only by remembering that these poor ignoramuses had no idea of the grandeur of the Son of Heaven.

They had grown larger, too.

"Avaunt, demon!" they cried. "We shall slay you, we shall free your people from your depravity!"

This was too much, too rude. The Dragon reared back, bellowing in anger. The riders—still small to him—shouted incomprehensible prayers to their God and spurred their horses. The Dragon flailed at them, sending a horse rolling away, a rider head over heels—

But lances pricked him.

The stabs only angered him further; he thrashed about him until he had knocked them all away, all the little shell-men—but they were big enough now that they might make a meal. He plucked one from the ground—Saint George, by his cross—and husked him. The barbarian howled in anger, still trying to strike with nothing but fists, as the Dragon popped him into his mouth.

He stuck in the Dragon's craw. Something sharp sent the lightning of pain shooting through the Dragon.

The Dragon bellowed in pain and spat him out. The little beast had drawn a hidden dagger, two hidden daggers, and had ripped the Dragon's throat. Now, at last, the Dragon's anger turned white-hot, and he raised a paw, hovering over the horseman . . . .

But before he could strike, a strange lethargy crept over him—not the weariness that had beset him for decades, but a heaviness of limb and mind that dulled his senses and sent him sinking back into torpor. As he sank into the paralysis of trance, he realized that the daggers had been poisoned.

In the trance, he saw ships laden with poppies sailing from India to Canton, but as they sailed, the poppies grew smaller and smaller until they had condensed into bricks—and the ships were the outlandish half-circle craft of the west, with their square sails and single flags. Most of those flags bore the cross of Saint George, but for some odd reason, it was laid over the X-shaped cross of one of the other new saints, that Saint Andrew, as he called himself . . . .

The ships dropped anchor in Canton harbor, and round-eyed sailors rowed their cargo ashore. At first they had to persuade Chinese peasants to buy it, so cheaply that they all but gave it away. Soon, though, the Cantonese were buying the opium of their own accord, then buying it frantically, and paying whatever the Englishmen demanded. The more they bought, the deeper into torpor the Dragon sank . . . .

But the Manchus stirred within his blood, the Manchus and, through the civil service, their Chinese servants. The governor of the province was outraged (on behalf of the emperor) that he was not receiving a share of this lucrative traffic, so he imposed a tax, a tariff, in the emperor's name.

The English squalled protest, a protest that their consul filed with the governor—or with his agents; the governor was too busy to confer with a lowly barbarian. But while the consul protested, the Scottish and English captains smuggled the opium into Canton.

Finally, the emperor (or his servants) told the governor to enforce the tax.

The Dragon waked, to find the knights grown amazingly, grown by half and more, and Saint George largest of all. He roared in surprize and anger, rearing back to rend them with teeth and claws.

Saint George couched his lance, called upon his God, and rode full-tilt against the Dragon.

This time the huge claws only rocked him in his saddle, only made his steed swerve from its course. The beast was immense, far heavier than any horse the Dragon had ever seen! It would make a good meal, and the Dragon was hungry, he thought, even as he opened his vast jaws and lowered them, to gobble the temeritous knight . . . .

The lance pierced his tongue, ran over it into the back of his throat. The Dragon roared in pain and anger and reared back, yanking the lance out of the knight's hands. His mouth filled with blood, but the knight shouted and attacked him with his sword. The stabs were only pinpricks, but they irritated the Dragon sorely. He threw himself down, curling about the knight and his horse, cutting them off from his fellow knights by the impenetrable scales of the Dragon's back. His belly was not quite so well-armored, but well enough to withhold all but the strongest pricks of Saint George's sword. The knight whirled about, stabbing frantically, isolated and contained, while the Dragon watched balefully.

The governor's men sealed the warehouses where the British stored the opium they had smuggled in—if unloading ships in broad daylight can be considered smuggling. Chinese officials announced to the English that the opium had been confiscated.

In return, British gunboats sailed into Canton harbor and began bombarding. The Chinese cannon were poor things in comparison to the British, far out of date, and the forts fell quickly. The British pressed a treaty on the Chinese that was just as the British wanted, and the governor's staff signed it. Thus ended the Opium War, with the British firmly ensconced on the island of Hong Kong and with trading rights clearly spelled out for the European nations, in Canton, Shanghai, and a few other treaty ports.

But the Chinese mandarins drew rings around those ports, and ignored them. A few missionaries penetrated the interior, a few merchants, but the mandarins ignored those, too. Surely they were too few to matter, and too unsophisticated; after all, they were only barbarians . . . .

The Dragon watched the little horseman's sallies and

charges with amusement as Saint George struggled to break out of the huge living ring that contained him. The Dragon grinned, reflecting that when his mouth healed and the blood within dried up, he would have a very full meal.

But the wound festered, and the pinpricks released new germs that percolated through his body—more new ideas, more new concepts. The one that would do the greatest damage of all was the strange religion that insisted there was only one God, though he had a Son . . . .

In the south, a hill man named Hung Hsiu-Ch'uan came to Canton to take his examination for the civil service. There, a strange man dressed in the robes of the Ming Dynasty, the last with emperors of Chinese blood, gave Hung a small book containing excerpts from the Christian Bible. When he failed the examination and was carried home in delirium, Hung dreamed that the One God gave him the task of expelling the demons from China and bringing the whole world to His worship.

But the one God was named "Shang-Ti," the first father-god of China, though his son was named Jesu.

For Hung Hsiu-Ch'uan, a few years later, went to a missionary, learned of Christianity, and read more of the books of the Bible, then went home and began the cleansing of China.

Saint Andrew took up Saint George's lance and sword and drove both beneath the Dragon's scales, into his flesh. The monster roared and whipped about, his body fighting against itself in agony, due to the foreign life in his blood.

Of course, he was no longer a living ring, and Saint George rode free again, his sword and lance once more in his own hands.

Hung Hsiu-Ch'uan gathered a band of men to worship Shang-Ti and Jesu; he marched them into temples and broke idols. But when the emperor sent soldiers against him, he found that the only way to continue the cleansing of China was to declare himself to be emperor—and the emperor was the Son of Heaven. After all, Hung knew that the Mandate of Heaven had passed to him. He declared a new Empire, the Tai-Ping Tien Kwoh, the Heavenly Kingdom of Great Peace, and went out to wreak war upon the land. He defeated the Manchu armies; he conquered city after city, province after province, until he held most of southern China.

The watching saints applauded. "Christianity conquers China!" they cried. "Our God is invincible indeed!" Then they sat back, to watch the Dragon's convulsions.

Hung Hsiu-Ch'uan made Nanking his capitol, then sent armies north, to attack the emperor himself. They came within forty miles of Peking before they were driven back. Then the Taipings sat, ruling the south, for ten more years, with constant skirmishing along their border with the Manchu emperor. Gradually, though, they began to weaken.

Finally, a Chinese general of great ability arose. Little by little, he began to push back the Taipings.

The saints watched as the Dragon shuddered and snapped in delerium. "He is weakened," said Saint Andrew. "Perhaps we should attack now."

"No, we should not." This one was no saint, but a somber figure in dark clothing and a stark white collar, with knee pants and white stockings, steel buckles on his shoes, and a flat-topped conical hat with a wide brim and another steel buckle. "Surely thou dost see that, ill or not, the monster is still formidable. See how his eyes do blink, how his jaw doth snap! He doth dream, but were we to descend on him, he might take us for figures from his nightmare, and spring upon us."

"Surely we can defeat him, all of us together, my son!"

The black-clad man glared at Saint George. "If I am thy son, I am estranged indeed, thou Papist! Nay, I have declared my independence of thee; I have conquered half of the New World, and am a nation to be reckoned with!"

"An upstart nation," the saint scoffed, "and one whose empire is small indeed, compared to ours."

The Puritan favored him with a black regard. "Wert thou in my Salem, thou wouldst find thyself quite quickly in the stocks! Nay, I have experience of the paynim; I say, withhold our hand."

"I like not your manner," Saint George grumbled, "but your advice is sound."

The Dragon whipped in waves, his whole body clashing against itself.

"See! The Chinese general smites the blasphemers!" Saint George cried. "And blasphemers they are, for Hung Hsiu-Ch'uan has declared himself to be the Younger Son of God! There can be no doubt now that we should strike against them!"

"And no doubt that we shall be on the wining side," the Puritan said darkly. "Well, one of my own nation has begun it; let one of yours pursue, to take the credit for the defeat."

And so General Gordon did—in the eyes of the Western world. But the Chinese knew better.

"He defies us!" said Saint Louis. "Do you wait for his blood to boil if you will—we shall attack his head!"

"Nay, I shall lead you," Saint George averred, and even as the Dragon's body writhed in fever, the knights rode with lances levelled at his huge brain.

There was fire in the Dragon's blood, as Hung Hsiu-Ch'uan committed suicide by swallowing powdered gold and his capitol of Nanking burned—but there was fire in the Dragon's head, as the English burned the Summer Palace. He awoke roaring in anguish for, though the Manchus might have bathed in its luxuries, the fabulous park had been of Chinese making, and had been a Chinese treasure. He awoke, and turned on his tormentors. One huge paw drove them back; talons raked open their armor. Huge teeth closed on Saint George, the Puritan, and the others, and held them fast.

The emperor's favorite concubine had borne him a son who had become emperor in his own right—a very weak emperor, cut off from the world, immersed in pleasures. When he died, the dowager had her nephew declared emperor, and ruled while he grew. But when he came of age, the young emperor took power into his own hands and strove to modernize China, to eliminate the corruption of the officials and restore the prestige of the Manchu Dynasty. But the dowager empress organized a coup, deposed him, and ruled as regent. Now she dealt smiling with the Western ambassadors—but in secret, she nurtured a secret society that had learned the fighting techniques of the Shao-lin Temple, but not its spirit. They erupted in rebellion, killing Europeans and driving them back into the foreign enclave within Peking. The Westerners, not knowing the terms for Chinese martial arts, saw only that when they fought without weapons, the "rebels'" techniques resembled boxing, and called them "the Boxers." They manned the parapets and held their enclave for fifty-five days, while their ambassadors sent urgent messages to the empress dowager, which she ignored, and Western gunboats massed to press inward. They came to Peking; they met the Boxers, and wiped them out. Finally, the empress agreed to prosecute the "rebels," and thanked the Westerners for saving China from them.

Blood welled from the Dragon's head, but still on his feet, he faced the saints, roaring, claws slashing.

"We can never defeat him," Mark warned the others, "but we may tame him ..."

"Do not counsel gentleness, I pray you." The Puritan had discarded his conical hat and shoe buckles; he now wore a frock coat, trousers, and a beard with no moustache. "We have only to keep our distance and harry him from all sides; he shall wear himself out."

But within the Dragon's bloodstream, new ideas were percolating. Even as he advanced and retreated, roaring and slashing with huge claws at targets that sprang away from his blows, the fever mounted within him as new armies sprang up, and troops of bandits grew in size to become armies in their own right. Finally, fever overwhelmed the Dragon, and he sank back into torpor as Sun Yat-sen, a descendant of a Tai-Ping rebel, armed with ideas from the West and gathering armies by the glittering splendor of notions of human rights and government by the people themselves, overwhelmed the Manchus and drove the last emperor from Peking.

"The empire has fallen apart!" Frederick cried. "Now may we loot it at will!" He raised his sword to strike.

"Hold!" Saint Louis caught his arm. "It is my missionaries who have borne the risk; it is I who shall have first fruits!"

Frederick threw him off with a snarl, but Saint George caught Saint Louis and together, they charged the emperor. The saints fell to fighting among themselves, while the Puritan watched until finally he, too, was drawn into the melee.

The Kuomintang was not enough in itself to hold all of China; as World War I racked the globe, its afterechoes disrupted Sun's government. Mandarins gathered armies and hacked their way to power; whole provinces fell under the sway of warlords who ruled as petty kings.

And an idea more virulent even than Hung Hsiu-Ch'uan's Christianity took hold in the heartland of China and began to grow apace—the idea of Communism, and the warlord who raised its red banner was Mao Tse-Tung.

Still, he was only one warlord of many, and as Sun Yat-sen died and his lieutenant Chiang Kai-Shek rose to power, the Kuomintang steadily lost its hold, Chiang too becoming only one warlord out of many. For decades China writhed in the anarchy of internal strife, while villages burned and peasants starved. Western missionaries scurried among them, trying to save lives, to stave off starvation, but they were few, so very few . . . .

"We should put him out of his misery," Saint Louis said. "He has grown so little now!"

The Dragon still dwarfed any one of them, but no longer dwarfed them all together. He slept, but his sleep was racked with nightmares; he growled and moaned, and his whole body shivered with the fighting within.

"Shrunken or not, he is still too big even to think of cutting him into pieces," Saint George objected.

"It is not he who has diminished," Saint Mark pointed out, "but we who have grown."

"We can at least bleed him," the Puritan said. "It might lessen his fever . . ."

"Dragon's blood is a prized commodity, eh?" asked Saint Andrew.

But before any of them could approach with lance or leech, a new figure stepped near the sleeping behemoth. He wore square-skirted armor and a flaring helmet with upsweeping points on the front, like horns. With a harsh short cry, he slashed his sword into the sleeping monster. The Dragon waked roaring, slashed feebly at the armored figure—then sank back into torpor.

"What is this?" the Puritan cried. "A Chinese attacking China?"

"Not Chinese!" the attacker shouted. "I am a samurai of Nippon!"

"Nippon? Oh, are you mean Japan!"

"Nippon!" And the samurai slashed the dragon's side again, for emphasis. Scales that could turn the best steel the West had to offer, gave under the second blow of the samurai's sword. The Dragon muttered in his sleep, gave a short howl, but did not wake, for the fighting within him was so furious that it kept him in a coma. The samurai shouted and slashed, again and again.

*   *   *

The Japanese had conquered Manchuria. Now they invaded China, dismembering the armies, attacking civilians. Chiang Kai-Shek hung agonized in a dilemma, unsure whether to continue his fight against the Communists, or to turn all his forces against the Japanese. Finally, his generals virtually forced him to make peace with Mao so that he could turn and fight the army from the eastern islands.

"How base a deed, to attack one who sleeps!" Saint George cried.

"We cannot let him kill a sleeping beast," the Puritan stated.

"Surely not," said Saint Mark, with a cynical smile, "for if he did, there would be nothing left for us to dismember."

With a shout, the samurai turned and slashed at the Puritan. The monochrome man cried out, leaping back as he raised a forearm to shield his face. But he did not leap quite far enough, for the arm came away with blood spreading over the cloth.

In the middle of the Pacific, Pearl Harbor burned, and the people of the United States, who had been determined to stay out of Europe's war, found themselves clamoring to fight the Japanese. President Roosevelt asked Congress for a declaration of war.

"There is no doubt who we must attack *now*," the Puritan said grimly, and his clothing metamorphosed into a military uniform.

The knights shouted and attacked with their lances.

The Puritan attacked with a rifle.

But the samurai's armor deflected both lances and bullets, and his marvelous sword actually pushed the Europeans back, then back again, before the Puritan shouted "Nuts!" and bore back in, his rifle turning into a machine gun. The saints followed him, lances turning into machine guns, too, and foot by foot, they drove the samurai away from the Dragon, marvelling at the way his sword whirled, almost invisible, deflecting blow after blow—but some of them pierced his armor, enough so that he retreated and retreated again, to his home islands. There he raised a howl and set himself, both swords high, and the Europeans paused, knowing this would be a battle to the death—the samurai's death, and their own severe wounding. They were not at all sure they wished to kill so valiant a fighter.

The Puritan settled the matter by throwing a grenade.

It arched high, but the samurai tried to watch both the hurtling spheroid and the Europeans, alert for attack—and the grenade landed beside him, then bounced up under his armor to explode. The samurai cried out and fell, wounded; the swords dropped from his hands as he fell unconscious.

The Puritan was at his side in an instant, wrenching off the armor, placing a tourniquet, and binding the wound.

The saints turned back to the dragon, watching the shudders that racked its unconscious body, ready to step in with swords as soon as it raised its head.

Chiang Kai-Shek and the Europeans harried the Japanese; who shifted strength to fight the battle of the Pacific. The Chinese drove the islanders out. Then they turned to fighting among themselves again—and Mao Tse-Tung was all the stronger, for he had held aloof from fighting the Japanese, knowing that Chiang would weaken himself expelling them. Now that they were gone, he renewed his own attack, pressing closer and closer to Peking, conquering one warlord after another, driving Chiang Kai-Shek and his Nationalist Chinese off the mainland and onto the little island of Formosa. Finally, the Red Flag floated over all of China.

The Puritan looked up from his patient, sure he would live, and frowned. "He ain't China," he said. "Not that Commie. That guy on the island, Chiang, *he's* China."

"Neither of them are China." Saint George gripped

his sword and raised his shield over Hong Kong. "The Dragon is China—and now the Dragon has turned Red."

They looked, and sure enough, it had. They stared, watching as the convulsions tapered off into shuddering, which quieted into natural sleep. The Europeans gripped their weapons nervously, for surely, this was a very large and mighty beast. They lifted shields, ready for anything, but deciding that perhaps they should seek trade, not plunder.

Mao consolidated his rule. Transformed into the Party, the ancient Civil Service was invigorated, streamlined— and answered only to him. All of China answered only to him.

And the Dragon awoke.

CALL HIM MEIER

by Roland J. Green

"I have bad news," my mate Evelyn said, as I slipped into the cave.

"Your brother Malcolm has learned to play the bagpipes," I said.

It had been a fine night's flight, taking me well over Ireland. That was the best place in the British Isles for a dragon to stretch his wings in this high summer of the Human Year 1940. Over Wales and Scotland, let alone England, one found too many airplanes and barrage balloons, not to mention eager human gunners both on the ground and in the air.

So I was not as ready as I ought to have been to be a sober audience for bad news. Or as Evelyn thought I should have been, at any rate—if her glare had been flames, I would have sported blackened scales for months.

"Bombs fell where the children were playing," Evelyn said, letting each word drop like a stone from a cliff. "A fragment struck Damar's wing. A foot-span lower, it might have severed his spine."

209

I curled in the entrance to the cave and invoked the Spell of Otherness. This conversation promised to last longer than we could safely leave the cave mouth visible to humans.

Also, Evelyn knew better than to interrupt me while I took us into Otherness. She thought I needed total concentration. That was true once, and I have found it useful to let her think it remained so. It gave me a chance to organize my thoughts and reply like a sensible dragon.

At last we were invisible to any human senses. (I made a mental note to see if the radar both sides were now using could detect an object in Otherness. It was a machine sense, rather than a human one; such have been known to make difficulties for dragons.)

"How is he?"

"Asleep. I cast a binder spell over the wound, then brewed a mild sleeping draught. It should heal. Whether it will heal in time for him to learn to fly before winter comes, I do not know. I am not hopeful."

I went into the chamber where our dragonets slept, to see Damar with my own eyes. He was our youngest, born the year of Edward VIII's abdication; at the time I feared he would be our last. Evelyn was young and healthy enough, but she was reluctant to bring more dragonets into a world growing more hostile every month. From what we knew at the time, I would not say that she was wrong.

Damar was asleep and seemed in no pain, but he would not be taking even his first wing exercises for a while. Our daughter Rhiannon also slept, but as usual Daffyd our firstborn was only pretending.

"Youngster, you need your sleep too," I said firmly.

"But I saw what happened to Damar, and told Mother. Did she tell you?"

I wanted to lie, but Daffyd's magic is Truth-sense. It

is impossible to lie to him—a serious handicap for the parents of such a dragonet as he seemed likely to be.

"No."

He described how a formation of Royal Air Force bombers had flown over the valley. They were slow (Handley-Page Heyfords, he said) and dropped only practice bombs, otherwise he and Damar might not have been able to get away. Fortunately he could carry Damar far enough to be safe, when he did not have to fly high.

"Of course, staying down low helped. I tried to stay over the brown rock. A red dragon shows up against gray or white rock."

I was torn between praising his good sense and wishing I had locked up the *Boy's Book of the Royal Air Force* along with the *Ars Amatoria*. (Not the human version; Ovid's long-suppressed one for dragons, that he wrote during his exile in what is now Romania. It is even stranger than the human one, but what would you expect of a book based on the study of Transylvanian dragons?)

"None of them saw you? None of them came down low?"

He looked pensive. "I suppose their not coming down low doesn't prove much. Those Heyfords are so big, slow, and clumsy that even if they saw all of us sunbathing they probably would not be able to come down and chase us."

"But they might have sighted you and radioed a report, so that the humans will be sending a Limburger—"

"Lysander, Father. That is the one that can fly low and slow, and land even shorter than a dragon."

It was my turn to look pensive. Our lair is far up in the Welsh mountains, surrounded by cliffs and crags that challenge even seasoned rock climbers. (I remember George Leigh Mallory as the human who came closest to stumbling on our cave, and was not wholly unhappy when I heard of his disappearing on Mount Everest. I hope that it was an accident, however, and that the *yetis* have no blood-guilt.)

But humans curious about dragons or suspicious about anything unusual going on, and able to land by plane with machine guns, grenades, and other dragon-slaying weapons—that was a wholly new threat.

Also one I would be able to deal with a trifle better after a decent night's sleep. I had fasted most of the way to Ireland and only taken a single sheep for myself, apart from the two I brought back. (If Kelvin of Aberystwyth had not developed the potions that let us live mostly on vegetation, with only a bit of meat for catalyst, the dragons of the British Isles would long since have eaten themselves out of any hope of survival.)

So I told Daffyd even more firmly than before that he would need to be well-rested tomorrow, and went off to our own sleeping couch. Evelyn was already asleep, and I curled close without waking her. I do not know if she needed the comfort, or even felt it; I know I did.

The Heyfords came back the next day, and the day after that. The third day brought no Heyfords, but another, smaller kind of bomber—Blenheims, Daffyd said.

The fourth day brought no bombers, only Evelyn's brother Malcolm with a bulging sack of gifts for us all. Even in wartime Scotland, Malcolm was a master scrounger.

His new coloration was more of a surprise. He had always been darkish on the bottom; now he was flat black, with barely a trace of scale-sheen left. His upper surfaces were in broad stripes of dark brown and dark green.

"You're in Bomber Command colors!" Daffyd cried, when he got his first good view of his uncle.

"Aye, lad," Malcolm said, and that is about as far as I am going to go in reproducing Malcolm's dialect. He had been nearly two centuries old before he left his birthplace in the Outer Hebrides, to fly with Bonnie Prince Charlie in the Forty-five. It was a minor miracle that he did not speak Dragon Gaelic; an impenetrable brogue was something we had learned to take for granted, and mentally translate.

"It's simple enough," Malcolm went on. "The local humans at least have a good deal on their minds. So if they see something bomber-sized and bomber-colored, they won't be curious about the rest. If they do come close, I pull back my head, kink my tail so that the end stands up like a rudder, and lower my forefeet so they look like fixed landing gear. That fooled a flight of Spitfires, and those lads are about the sharpest in the RAF."

Daffyd insisted on his telling about the meeting with the Spitfires in detail. We went through several mugs of herb tea laced with a bit of Evelyn's mead before he was done. Then Evelyn excused herself to prepare dinner, and Malcolm went straight to business.

"The RAF's converting this territory to a bombing range," he said. "You've been lucky so far. If that hadn't been a practice bomb, or if it had been someone doing low-level work the way they do on the barges over in France—"

"Barges in France?" I asked.

Malcolm shot me one disgusted look, my wall of books a second. "You ought to add a few copies of the *Daily Express* to this museum of old human learning," he grumbled. "The Germans are getting ready to invade England, or hadn't you heard?"

He lectured me about being informed of current events until I was ready to throw a mug at him. Empty or full, it didn't matter. Finally he ran out of ways to parade his knowledge.

"I flew south with that vanload of equipment because I'm leaving the British Isles for the duration of the war. I think you and your family ought to go with me."

The idea of being bombed five times a week and then overrun by the Germans (make that the Nazis: the Germans had usually been friends to dragons except during the Thirty Years' War) did not appeal to me. The thought of leaving everything we had built or collected here over nearly a century since I flew Evelyn across the threshold was even bleaker.

"I'll listen, if you have any ideas about where we should go," I told him. "Believe it or not as you wish, I have been aware of the war. Western Europe would not seem to be a very safe place for us."

"Who said anything about Western Europe?" Malcolm replied. "Ever heard of the Pripet Marshes?"

"Somewhere in Russia—"

"Ah, the Soviet Union. You'll have to be careful about that, when we get to the refuge. One of our hosts is a Pyreneean dragon who thinks he's a Marxist."

My experience was that dragons who took up human religions and ideologies (if there's a difference between the two) could hardly be said to be thinking. But Malcolm would likely take that as an insult to his Jacobite sympathies. Dragon romantics are much like human ones; reasoning with them is a waste of breath.

"Who are the others?"

It seemed that the Pyreneean dragon had mated with a vastly elderly Russian dragon, who had lived for centuries on a patch of dry ground surrounded by the marshes. Perhaps longer—part of her hoard was Kievan gold, hidden from the Mongols. Then there was gold hidden from successive tsars, from the French in 1812, and finally from the Bolsheviks when they took over in 1917.

"She has enough to bribe the local hunters and peasants, as well as any secret policemen who allow themselves to believe in dragons. Good Marxists, you see, regard us as peasant superstitions. They can't seriously go hunting what doesn't exist."

It began to seem that Marxism might be more useful

to dragons than to humans. "Are our hosts offering charity? Or are we expected to bring something?"

"I'll pay for both of us, at the refuge. My father thoroughly examined certain Spanish Armada wrecks. I've collected the gold, and also turned some of the heavier antiques into British currency, which our friends will accept."

"My flame dies from the depth of my gratitude."

I meant the ritual phrase. I had always wondered if I was wise in making my hoard rare books, rather than more traditional and portable forms of wealth. We can't all manage a chest of rubies, like one Cornish dragon I knew (he was on terms with local wreckers who had looted a stranded East Indiaman during the Napoleonic Wars). But first editions of the *Encyclopedia Britannica* and Gutenberg Bibles are hard to both move and sell.

"I never did think too well of your using the Otherness to pile up books," Malcolm said. "Gold doesn't rot."

"You and your sister agree on that," I said shortly. "But that doesn't solve the problem of repayment."

"Oh, I think it's not so great a problem," Malcolm said. His explanation almost took longer than my patience could endure.

The substance was that he had sworn human associate in Edinburgh, who knew several book dealers in London. If I arranged to preserve the books, he would arrange to tell the human of their location, and the human could pass the word on to the dealers. A share of the money for the books would end up in Malcolm's account at the Bank of Scotland, and that would repay him for whatever he spent to settle us in the Pripet Marshes.

I could not say it pleased me, certainly losing the books and probably the cave as well; we would be homeless even after the war was over. But the world was running mad, in ways dangerous to dragons as well as to humans. To lie with one's neck outstretched for the death stroke was a habit most dragons had long ago abandoned.

I could have said, but did not, that Malcolm had certainly been stretching our customs of secrecy in dealings with humans. However, there was never a Scot, dragon or human, kobold or elf, who balked at law and custom when there was a chance of profit.

We left two nights later. Malcolm was true to his word; his pack was a hoard of everything we might need on the journey and to settle in afterward. He had also brought so much gold that it was a wonder he had managed to get into the air.

For the long trip east, we would of course divide everything. All those who were flying on their own wings could carry a share, except for Rhiannon. She was just barely able to make the flight herself. Even though she offered to carry something, we had to refuse.

Damar could not have flown the distance even had he been whole and flight-taught. Instead he rode under his mother's belly, in a carrier that made us all stare, except for Malcolm.

Evelyn tapped it with a claw. "Iron this close to both of us, for so long?" We dragons mostly have enough magic in us that cold iron is like radium to a human—it does not kill immediately, but death comes early and painfully if one is exposed too long.

"Not iron." Malcolm said, "Aluminum from crashed airplanes, and the straps are leather cut from flying jackets and seat backs."

Evelyn still looked dubious. Daffyd launched into a long explanation of airplane construction, which proved he'd read that *Boy's Guide* attentively. I decided that we could take that book along, if he carried it himself.

He couldn't agree fast enough. The rest of the family nerved itself to the hard decisions about what to take and what to leave, and the rest of the time before we left is a blur in my memory to this day.

No, not quite. The last thing I did, as we gathered to

leap into the sky, was a bit of a trick. I cast the Otherness on the cave. Not the full Otherness, where only the dragon who cast the spell can take it off (and there are only a handful of dragons left with the Otherness in their blood). It was a lesser form, that humans could take off with the proper chants and charms.

Chants and charms that only I knew, and would only pass on to Malcolm for the use of his friends in my own good time. Those books were not going to be cast into the whirlpool of a worldwide war, where half of them might end up in the hands of those who did not value them and the rest burned in bombing raids.

Malcolm would be paid at my convenience, not his, and if he grumbled, I would remind him that no Scot ever hatched could truly get the best of a Welshman. Singing is not the only art of the red dragons, as he was about to learn.

Then we strapped Damar into his carrier and the carrier to his mother, and took to the night sky.

We chose a cloudy night for our departure, although we knew that radar could see through clouds. Fortunately few airborne radars were in service at that time, so we had only to worry about antiaircraft guns guided by radar, and even they were none too common. (If we had had to make our flight in 1943, I doubt I would be alive to tell of it.)

The weather turned against us as we were over Denmark, so we found a sparsely inhabited district and settled in for the day. I cast a limited spell of Otherness over the abandoned paddock where we lay, one that would convince a casual passerby that it held nothing but a few sheep. Before I did that, however, I noticed several bombers colored like Malcolm flying overhead, bound west as if fleeing the dawn.

"You said those were British colors," I prodded Malcolm. "What are they doing flying from Germany?"

"Maybe the British have started raiding Germany," Malcolm said. "A little revenge is a natural impulse."

"Oh yes, they could do it easily," Daffyd said, and went off on a long lecture about RAF bombers that could carry bombs as far as Berlin. I listened with half an ear, hoping mostly that we did not meet any of them either going or coming. Their gunners and the German gunners on the ground would both be nervous in the middle of an air raid.

It also occurred to me that perhaps a little camouflage all around would not be a bad idea.

"How do the Germans paint their bombers?" I asked Malcolm.

"Gray bellies and dark green tops," he said, before Daffyd could offer another lecture. "But I do not have the power to change all of us. Coloring myself as an RAF bomber used up all the Coloring power I have until the next full moon."

"Well, we are hardly going to wait here until then," Evelyn said. "What can you do with the power you have? I hope it includes changing yourself, because over Germany those colors of yours will be anything *but* a protection."

Malcolm looked dubious. "I can darken your redness, and maybe take the brown off my back. If I am very lucky, I can make my belly gray. We might look like a German bomber leading a formation of civilian planes."

"As long as we look like something that has business in the sky over Germany, I hardly care if we are blue with yellow stripes," Evelyn snapped. "Begin, and do not stop until you have done all you can."

Malcolm parodied coming to attention and clicking his heels, which is quite noisy in a dragon; we have four heels. I told him that so much noise could make people wonder if we were sheep, and I did not know how strongly the Germans held this part of Denmark. I did not want to learn at the wrong end of a machine gun.

Malcolm did his work well enough so that none of us would have recognized ourselves in a mirror when he was done. How much this helped us with the Germans, I do not know.

We had the promise of clouds if not storms that night, so we took off at sunset, flying as high as Rhiannon could reach and match the others' speed.

This was a mistake.

Dragons are not as affected as humans by lack of oxygen (although above 8,000 feet we cannot flame very well). An adult can cruise at 12,000 feet for days, so we thought that altitude would be safe enough for the few hours it would take us to cross Germany.

We were wrong. Above 10,000 feet we met a brisk west wind, which took us well to the east of our intended course. We were also above two of the four layers of clouds, so that we had only occasional glimpses of the ground for navigation.

We were indeed doing better at finding our way than Bomber Command did at that stage of the war. It could find the continent of Europe easily; it could usually find the right country. Anything smaller, like a specific city, was a challenge, and one not often met—which explains why the Berlin raids before that night had cost the Germans more lost sleep than anything else.

Nonetheless, Malcolm had assured us that we would be flying mostly over undefended territory on our route to the Thuringerwald. (The Black Forest dragons had become too involved with Nazi cult practices to be trustworthy. The Thuringerwald dragons were hearty peasants, who liked to be left alone with their venison and didn't bother their green-crested heads with politics.)

He kept on reassuring us even after we saw searchlights probing up through the clouds. He fell silent when the flak began bursting, although fortunately well below us. (Postwar American experience with the DEW line and Arctic dragons suggests that we make poor radar targets, and the German radar operators at that stage of the war were underequipped and undertrained.)

Malcolm did not lose his composure until we passed over a winding lake with islands strung out along it. Reflected light from the flak bursts and the searchlights showed it clearly, at least to a dragon's night sight.

"That's the Wannsee," Malcolm said. He sounded uneasy.

"Oh?" Evelyn said (or rather called, as we were making a good speed and the wind of our passage blew away anything less than a shout).

"Yes."

"What does it mean?"

"Ah—the Wannsee is in Berlin."

There was a silence, complete save for the wind and the distant flak, but eloquent of wrath to come.

"Berlin," Evelyn said. "The capital of Germany. The most heavily-defended city in Germany. The most dangerous spot in Germany to fly over."

"Except for the Ruhr—" Malcolm began.

Evelyn made an obscene suggestion for disposing of the Ruhr. "What is the best course out of here?" she added.

"The Wannsee is in western Berlin," Malcolm began. Then Daffyd shrieked:

"Plane behind us, Father! Coming up fast! It's a Messerschmidt 110."

I reversed course and hovered to get a look at our pursuer. Also to take the rear position, so that if necessary I could hold this opponent while the rest of the family escaped. Knowing that one would not be the first dragon to meet this honorable fate made it no more appealing.

The plane had twin engines and twin rudders, and apparently two humans aboard. It also had a noseful of guns, and I had an unpleasantly close view of them for what seemed an age. I knew that the humans were as certainly doomed as I was if it came to battle, and readied my breath.

Then the flak gunners, with a solid target at last, suddenly improved. Shells burst all around my family and me, filling the air with sizzling fragments, smoke, and stench. But the fragments had just a trifle too far to travel to strike with damaging force.

Dragon scales, however, are tougher than aluminum. Flames torched from a wing of the enemy plane as a fuel tank blazed up. I saw the human's faces twist into grotesque masks of fury and despair at meeting such a fate at the hands of their comrades.

Then the plane blew up. This time the fragments were not so harmless. I felt my scales gouged in three places and pierced in at least one. A wall of thunder cut me off from the rest of the world, helped by another wall of light and a third of stinking smoke.

Then Evelyn's cry pierced all the walls.

"Damar's falling!"

It seemed that one of the straps of the carrier had been cut by a piece of flak, without Evelyn noticing it. Before she had time to examine the carrier, the German plane exploded. Another fragment gouged Evelyn's scales and ripped through two more straps.

The last one held only briefly, then carrier and dragonet came free and plummeted toward the earth.

At least I hoped it was the earth. Land dragons sink like stones if they strike water, and Damar would not be able to hold his breath long enough to bottom-walk to land. They can endure a good deal of punishment if they strike even hard ground, and treetops are almost a cushion.

The best solution, of course, was for Damar to strike nothing. The whole family folded wings and plunged after him. I doubt that the best flight of Stukas in the Luftwaffe could have dived in a more perfect formation.

We hadn't entirely forgotten about the flak guns, of course. We had merely turned our attention to other matters. It was brusquely turned back when a flak battery almost directly below opened fire.

Fortunately this was a battery of 88's, comparatively slow-firing for work on dragons already below 8,000 feet and diving fast. One shell would have crippled any of us, two would have been the end, but *all* went wide. (I don't know if they saw us and were frightened or were simply not shooting very well.)

We spread out as we dove, to make sure that we would completely surround Damar, in the air or on the ground if we couldn't catch him before he landed. I caught sight of him and lost sight of Daffyd at about the same time. Then I signaled to Malcolm to spread out even farther; he and I were going to dispose of the flak.

That might be sacrificial, but it was certainly necessary. Even if Evelyn caught Damar in the next moment, we were down low enough for the clumsiest Germans to make good shooting. The fewer guns in the area, the better our chances of returning to high flight and getting away from Berlin.

I plunged vertically, then flung out my wings so that even dragonbone and sinew protested. I leveled out just above the treetops, and just outside flaming range of the battery.

But I had lost the breath I'd taken to deal with the plane, so I had to draw another. Malcolm had no such problem. He came down from the far side of the battery, and I saw a mob of frantic gunners, some fleeing, some manning machine guns or snatching up rifles, a few standing by their pieces and trying to crank them down.

All were too late. Malcolm's breath went out in a searing blast of orange flame. Gunners died screaming where they stood, or ran screaming, clothes aflame, to die a little farther away. Ready ammunition exploded, and Malcolm swerved hard to the left to avoid flying straight into the blast.

Half-dazzled as he was, he did not see the power line. His left wing chopped through it as if it had been old rope in a dragonet's claws. Sparks flew, and the two ends of the line lashed about. One of them slashed into a natural-gas tank, rupturing seams and letting gas pour out to meet the sparks.

The sun seemed to rise as the tank exploded. I saw Malcolm above the blast, climbing desperately for altitude, both wings beating strongly. I trusted that he was all right. The touch of iron had been brief, and dragon scales are poor conductors of electricity.

Now I had to find the rest of my family,

In the next moment Evelyn bugled, and the moment after that the scream of a train's whistle drowned her out. I leaped into the sky, fearing to hear Evelyn's scream next.

Instead I saw Damar in his carrier, squalling lustily, and jammed in the iron framing of a railroad signal tower. A train had stopped just short of the tower, and the train crew were pointing at the apparition ahead.

Finding Damar apparently unhurt was a victory that might be snatched away from us at any moment. That it was not, I owe to my mate and daughter.

Evelyn bugled again, and this time flamed. The orange torch seared the casing of the locomotive's boiler, heating steam-laden tubes beyond their limits. Seams dissolved, steam poured out, and most of the locomotive vanished in a white cloud. The engine driver also vanished, leaping from his cab and running off into the shadows.

Burning gas and exploding ammunition had banished darkness. The fireman must have seen what he faced, but was holding a shotgun, aiming it at Evelyn from the right, at a range where a headshot might cost her an eye.

He did not see Rhiannon until it was too late. Her

mother's true daughter, she stayed low to the ground until the last moment. Then she reared, neck at full stretch, and breathed into the fireman's face. Not flame, just the several cubic feet of concentrated methane a dragon's stomach holds.

The fireman did not faint on the spot. But he dropped the shotgun, which went off with a harmless bang, and clapped both hands over his face. He ran off so fast that I am sure he eventually caught up with the driver.

Evelyn had freed Damar and was crooning over him while Rhiannon wandered along the train. I suppose she was looking for something sweet, like a carload of sugar or even a case of candied fruit. I called her back, just as more firing broke out on the other side of the train. I told my family to get down, while I leaped on the top of the train. I could have gone much higher by flying, but I would have risked hanging in the air, an easy target.

Instead I saw Daffyd lying in the middle of a road carried over a small river or canal by an iron bridge. A convoy of military vehicles had started across the bridge when he blocked their way.

As I watched, he flamed the lead vehicle, an open *Kubelwagen*. Daffyd had a weak flame, but he still blew all four tires. The men in the car jumped out before the gas tank caught fire.

The staff car behind backed up sharply, ramming into the front of the third vehicle, a medium half-track. The half-track's driver started backing without looking behind him, and rammed the bridge railing. Rammed it—and pushed clear through it.

With the staff car still locked to its front bumper, the half-track slid inexorably over the side of the bridge, to splash into the water below. This left my son facing the last vehicle in the convoy, a Mark III tank.

Daffyd flamed again. He didn't reach the tank, but he dazzled the gunner and commander. For a moment they couldn't shoot. In that moment I reached flaming range.

They must have had a round loaded, because flame and the commander flew out of the turret. Then the first round set off the ammunition load. The turret flew clean off the tank in a great gout of flame.

After that, the bridge collapsing under the tank was an anticlimax.

The only one of the family not accounted for now was Malcolm, and even he reappeared, favoring his left wing, by the time I rejoined Evelyn. She was hastily rigging new straps for the carrier, torn from uniforms and webbing discarded by fleeing flak gunners.

Briefly, I had visions of dozens of *Luftwaffe* flak gunners running frantically across country, stark naked and babbling of dragons, and hoped they found both clothing and calm before the Gestapo found them. I have no quarrel with killing in a fair fight; the Gestapo and their ilk are slime, to be purged with flame.

But this was no time for dreaming or laughter. We had rescued Damar, but now it was time to avoid losing our victory. Our wings thundered as loudly as the flak, as we took to the sky.

We made the Pripet Marshes safely, although with empty bellies. The Thuringerwald dragons were not inhospitable; they merely had no food to spare. Reichsmarshall Herman Goering, they said, had made it impossible for an honest dragon to come by a mouthful of venison without risking life and wing.

There was food in the Marshes, however, as well as dragons from every land threatened by war. (There were even some dragons from China, and not in even dragons' memory had our Chinese kin come so far west.) Some of them had healing magic, so the hurts we had taken were soon a thing of the past. Nor did any of the healers ask payment, except for a retelling of our story.

Before the snow flies, the Black Forest dragons came in. They met a chilly welcome at first, but they turned their claws to whatever work needed doing and kept quiet.

In time we learned that word of the descent of wrathful dragons on Berlin had frightened the Nazi dragon cultists out of such wits as they had. They began watching the Black Forest dragons closely, then chaining some as hostages.

When they sacrificed a dragonet to Wotan, the dragon's patience snapped. So did the chains, the rooftree of the temple, and the necks and backs of more than a few of the cultists. They lay dying in the flaming ruins of their temple as their totemic beasts took wing to freedom.

Of course, no word of dragons was mentioned in the highest circles of the Third Reich. There our visit was called the first successful RAF raid, on the very capital of the Reich!

On this hangs a tale.

Hermann Goering had publicly declared that if one enemy plane flew over the Reich, the people could call him Meier. That night, enemy planes had not only flown over the Reich, they had struck hard.

At a meeting the next morning, Hitler greeted Goering as "Herr Meier," and went on from there. According to the kobold enslaved to keep the Chancellery's plumbing in order, the Fuhrer went on at great length, exhausting his entire vocabulary of invective on Goering.

The Reichsmarshall, the kobold said, did not look happy.

Two days later he gave the orders to prepare to switch the air raids on England, from RAF targets to London. On September 7, 1940, the first of the great raids on the capital took place. The raids battered London; the RAF was reprieved with only weeks to spare.

No longer did the Sector Stations have to plot raids with one hand, repair damage with a second, and patch wounded with a third. Experienced RAF pilots could get a decent night's sleep; new ones had a chance to learn their craft.

Goering's turning his air armada against London snatched defeat from the jaws of victory. The war was by no means won for civilization, human and dragon alike—as who should known better than dragons who found their refuge in the Pripet Marshes in the very path of Operation Barbarossa, in June of 1941?

But our visit to Berlin had been a first step on the long road to victory.

SAINT PATRICK'S LAST SNAKE

by Judith R. Conly

Forewarned by shadowed antique visions,
I recognized my nemesis, a sheep-shaggy man
clad in ill-cured skins and self-styled holy filth,
armed with weather-warped staff and righteous zeal.
Into my new-wakened need to nest
intruded his blustering illogical accusations
that linked my kin and mythic demons of his faith.
Grimly suppressing the clench-toothed urge
to inaugurate my larder with his flesh,
I withdrew my hope of home to some days' distance,
but before I could amass shelter for a single egg,
a hunting-horn voice heralded the arrival
of the familiar peace-destroying harrier.
At the prospect of endless pursuit and retreat,
self-pity and offended dignity impelled my wings
to bear my body toward distant setting sun

and foresight of an island bought for baubles,
its future filled with countless disbelievers
borne north by silver subterranean steed
branded with the copper monogram of dragonkind.

THE BACK DOOR

by Diane Duane

The Bahnhofstrasse in Zurich is a wide, pleasant street that stretches, as its name suggests, from the railroad station at its top to the lake at its bottom. The street is a bright one, the shifting light on the Zurchersee somehow lingering on the horizon and spreading right down the length of it, into the parks and the cobbled plazas where the tram lines interlace, onto the glittering shopfronts and the cafes. The paving on the sidewalks under the linden trees, and (close to the station) right out into the street, is grey and white granite, highly polished. In wet weather it can be slippery; in bright weather it gleams. It gleamed today, for this was May, and the sun was out, and in front of the Hotel St. Gotthard the "bleachers" had been put up. Tables and chairs were arranged on them, facing the street, one level above the other, so that no one's view of the passersby would be obstructed. It being past noon, the chairs were already beginning to fill up with the usual customers: Japanese tourists hung with cameras, businessmen on their lunch break with beer in front of them and the *Neue Zurcher Zeitung* preserving their anonymity, prim little old ladies having coffee with hot milk and a pastry, and various other city people indulging the Swiss love of having "a little something" every two hours or so.

Two men stood on the corner of Beatengasse where it crosses the Bahnhofstrasse and looked across at the topmost row of bleachers. There, by himself, sat a small man in a dark suit, his hair quite close-cropped. From his face he looked to be in his mid-forties, though his hair argued the point: it was pepper-and-salt, much heavier on the salt. The man had a copy of the *Zeitung* in front of him, but it was folded, and his eyes were on the street; he wore a lazy, bored expression, not at all what you would expect from someone who was awaiting the kind of meeting he was awaiting.

"Doesn't look like much," one of the men said to the other, softly, in English. He was a tall, slender man, fair, ruddy of face, who looked slightly uncomfortable in his suit.

"All the better," said the second: a shorter man, dark-haired but with cool blue eyes, whose suit betrayed by its fit a more expensive tailor, and an owner who considered it clothing and not a costume. "Come on."

They crossed the street and went up into the bleachers. The small man stood as he saw them coming, and hands were shaken, like a meeting of old friends, and there were courteous smiles all around. They sat down, and a white-aproned waiter hurried over. "Gentlemen?"

"What kind of beer have you got?"

The waiter rattled off about twenty names. The small Swiss man reached out and touched the first man lightly on the arm. The first man flinched very slightly: the small man gave no sign of having noticed it. "Try the Gurten—it's local," he said, and sat back.

The two men ordered the Gurten. The waiter went away. "Herr Falera," said the second man, "our time here is somewhat limited, so I'll get straight to it. How much have you been told about what we have in mind?"

The Swiss leaned back in his seat and looked thoughtfully out at the white-and-grey paving as one of the blue and white Zurich trams, the "holy cows", came humming to a stop in front of them and discharged its passengers. It dinged, moved on again. "Mr. Smyth, I think the word used in my preliminary discussion with your contact here was 'withdrawal.' From what facility? One of the big three?"

All there eyes flicked briefly up the length of the Bahnhofstrasse toward Paradeplatz. There the tram lines met, and around that triangle of cobbles were tastefully arranged the main offices of the three great Swiss banks, the SBG, the SBB, and the UBS. "Not any one of those specifically," Mr. Smyth said. "There's a facility that they share—"

Herr Falera glanced at the pavement again. The beer came: they spent a moment while the waiter set it out, and Herr Falera sipped his for a moment, looking at the grey and white stone, watching the pedestrians scurry along it, watching a tourist pause to take a picture of the bright scene, the light flooding down the length of the street from the lake, the new green leaves on the lindens burning translucent in it, like stained glass. The tourist moved on, and a breath of wind came down the lake and stirred all the blown-glass leaves so that their upper surfaces glittered, blinding.

What the tourist most likely did not know, as even some native Zurchers did not know, was that perhaps thirty feet below the grey and white paving, under the service ducts and the sewers and the utility companies' cables, lay a series of buried vaults running the length of Bahnhofstrasse, down the course of the small natural ravine that had been there in ancient times, the one the Romans had called "the frogs' moat" because of the trickle of the old Sihl river tributary that ran down it.

Now that pathway was reinforced with concrete and steel, a chain of huge silent rooms, and in those rooms, partitioned from one another by office dividers—for what need of cages down there?—the gold lay piled. Half the gold in Europe, some people said: half the Swiss gold reserves, anyway—in this massive storage to which the three great banks had access via numerous underground tunnels, and to the upkeep and security to which they all contributed.

Herr Falera turned back to the two men, a slight smile on his face. "Times must be getting hard for you," he said softly, in his odd soft English. It had a southern lilt about it, something hinting at one or another of the Romance languages, though not French as would have been most likely in Switzerland. "Libya backing away the way it has. Well, they have enough embarrassments at the moment: they can hardly afford to be associated with you, after the recent publicity. But I take it the pickings are not as easy in the great houses out in the country as they used to be. Too many of the old Irish families breaking down and installing security systems at last? Not all that hard to crack, really. But with the quality of help you people find yourselves forced to work with—"

Smyth's eyes narrowed. "This is hardly germane," he said, just as softly.

Falera smiled just a touch more at the sound of the other's milk accent briefly showing through the carefully assumed Home Counties English. "It is very much to the point," he said. "The risks your people have been taking in permitting the opportunistic theft of artwork on the mere assumption that you will eventually find a buyer—these have been making the business uncomfortable for others with, shall we say, similar interests. Suddenly there is publicity, suddenly Interpol sits up and takes notice, and the EC starts a Community-wide stolen art database: suddenly the British, who had killed their art theft department at Scotland Yard for lack of funds, now sit up and revive it, because they know it's your organization involved. All very bad. And the effect on the artwork itself—rolled up and wrapped in binbags and shoved into some buried oil drum in Fermanagh, wasn't it, that last Caravaggio? What collector is going to want such a thing after it's been through something that would take a major museum restoration to put right? Very careless, very thoughtless, some of your people."

Falera watched Smyth sit there, quiet. His face was smooth, but his eyes said plainly that he was not a man who normally kept silent while anyone whatever talked to him in such a tone. Yet he was quiet still.

"We have a buyer," he said after a moment, and drank some of his beer. "A collector."

"Mr. Smyth," Falera said, "gold can be had anywhere. If your collector is looking for art down there—" he glanced at the pavement again—"he or she is going to be disappointed. Such things are kept in museums, or private vaults, and not even the vault managers know what they are."

"It more or less depends on what you consider 'art,' " said the second man.

Falera's eyes went to him. "Mr. Harris, your precis as I understand it would hardly make it seem as if art is your chief concern. I had thought you were more in the line of—" He smiled. "Militaria, I suppose, would be the most delicate way to put it."

"It is," Harris said. "The applied side of the arts, if you like." His smile suddenly went purely nasty, but the look sealed itself over after a moment. "And some of what's down here . . . is militaria."

"Ahh," Falera said. "Do you mind if I smoke?"

"I'm gasping for one myself," Harris said. They lit up: Smyth shook his head minutely when Falera offered him a Galoise Bleu.

"So," Falera said. "Your principal will know, of course, that not all of the gold he or she is interested in will necessarily have eagles and swastikas stamped all over it. Much of it will have been recast and stamped with the usual house hallmarks and new assay brands."

"Our principal knows that," Smyth said, "and would prefer some of the material with the original hallmarks. Historical value, after all."

"I suppose it has a certain cachet to people of such a turn of mind," Herr Falera said.

Smyth made a don't-care expression. "But rebranded material will do as well—gas chromatography can confirm the provenance of the gold from the specific percentages of the alloy metals present in the mix." He sat back and sipped reflectively at his beer. "And of course it would be unfortunate for you and your assistants if, after the fact, it should be discovered that we had the wrong material—" He lifted his eyes to Falera's.

Falera let the attempted menace of the look roll off him: his smile went gentle. "Mr. Smyth," he said, "my ancestors were mercenaries, and the terror of Europe, when yours were gabbing missionary monks practicing their penmanship in St. Gall and trying to teach the locals to clone Munster cheese. We fought our way to our freedom despite the interference of every empire on this continent, in the days when there were empires, not the waning power on which you've wasted eighty years of unfocused hostility and bungled revenge. We may look quiet and democratic these days, but it's a thin veneer: threat brings out the worst in us. So don't waste your time trying to frighten me as if my companions and I were the second-rate crooks you're used to dealing with. Our word is our bond, here. Unlike that of some people."

Their eyes rested on one another's for a little while. Smyth would not look away, but the way the tension fell off told plainly enough that Falera's point had been taken.

"Well," Falera said, and signaled for another beer. "It can be discovered where such things are. But I hope you have explained to your principal that your acquisition is going to have to be a limited one." He put up an amused eyebrow. "Less due to the nature of the security involved, than to the nature of the material to be withdrawn. I doubt the two of you could manage more than two bars apiece. You will want sturdy carriers, none of this softside luggage—the stuff will go right through it."

The two men nodded. "Now, about payment—"

"I have an account as the Banca dalla Sutsilva in Chur," Falera said. "There should be a transfer of half a million francs from your bank here within forty-eight hours if you're interested in proceeding any further. If that's the case, I'll need to meet with you down in Chur within the week," he said to Harris. "There'll be some work in your specialty area to be done."

Harris nodded.

"Then, gentlemen," Falera said, "until next week."

They looked at each other, blinked, as if unused to being so dismissed by anyone they dealt with. After a moment, Harris, then Smyth, got up and walked away, back down toward the station.

Falera watched them go, down the bright pavement, briskly, not looking back. It would normally have taken a lipreader at this distance to tell what Smyth was saying, but Falera had other methods. "Funny accent," Smyth said to his partner. "Sounded like Basque, almost."

Harris shrugged. "He doesn't sound like he really knows who he's dealing with."

"Or knows and doesn't care. In any case, I wouldn't care to be used for anybody else's agenda."

"He came up clean in the check . . . ."

"All the same, he might try to grass us after the fact. These bloody Swiss are too mercenary by half . . . he was right about that much. I think it would be wisest if he has some kind of accident afterwards."

"You'll have to check with Upstairs."

"They'll take our advice."

The two passed out of Falera's range, down the escalators that led into the shopping center underneath the railway station. Falera sighed and stretched his legs out under the table, came up with his cellphone.

He dialed. The other end rang and rang, then picked up, and he heard a sound more a growl than a word.

"Did I wake you? Sorry. They're interested. Yes, well, I agree, but they're our best chance at the moment. The market has been slowing down of late . . . . Fine. Well, about another two weeks yet. They have to pay first, and then we have to get into the system and suborn it. It'll take a little while. No, of course no one will notice! When has anyone ever? Right. Yes, Ill give you a shout next week. Fine. *Gruezi* . . . ."

He hung up and looked at the marble pavement, shining in the sun, and drank his beer.

They saw each other next in Chur, on a day of sunshine and showers. Every so often dark clouds would come lumbering over the Calanda mountain and drop five minutes' worth of rain on the cobbled, wet-gleaming streets; then they would roll on south, while everywhere else the sky burned blue and white with cumulus, muttering with desultory thunder. It was through such weather that Harris ran, swearing under his breath, to the rendezvous at the outdoor cafe which Falera had designated. How they were supposed to have a meeting in a place like that, in such weather, Harris wasn't sure, but he found the man there nonetheless, the only person sitting outside, snug and dry under a canvas canopy, working at a small personal computer.

Falera looked up as Harris came: that same dry look, unusually unconcerned for someone dealing with Harris's organization. Harris felt again that brief stab of annoyance at not being given the proper respect, but for the moment he restrained his desire to put a little proper fright onto the man. Soon enough, it wouldn't matter.

"A beer?" Falera said, without stopping his typing, and without looking at the screen or the keyboard.

"Thanks, yes."

"Try the Calanda," Falera said, still typing, as the waiter came by.

Harris ordered, then raised his eyebrows at the computer as the waiter left. Next to it, connected to its modem, was a tiny cellphone, and beside that, a notepad.

"Look if you like," Falera said, typing on. "Did you have a pleasant trip down?"

"Excepting that this place is in the back of nowhere," Harris said, "yes. Two hours on the bleeding train. Why are you based so far down country?"

Falera laughed softly. "Discretion. Or convenience. I've lived here for a long time."

"Dangerous," Harris said. "People get to know you—"

"Not me," Falera said. "I spend a fair amount of time out of the country."

"Syria," Harris said. "We noticed."

Falera smiled. "And were puzzled, no doubt, because you could find no terrorist connections. No: it's a favorite place, that's all. As for why here—" He glanced around him. "This is one of the oldest continuously occupied spots in Europe, didn't you know? From the Bronze Age to the present, people have lived here, without a break. In so hectic a time, doing such unsettled work, it's pleasant to come home to a feeling of continuity, of something stable."

Harris just avoided snorting, having little time for such high-flown notions.

"But there are other reasons," Falera said. "I have a few spare identities. One of them works there—" He motioned with his eyes at the splendid neoclassical portico of the Main Post Office across the road. "When I needed access to other people's information, this is one of the places I come."

Harris smiled slightly. "Your post office still runs the telephone company, then."

Falera nodded. "There are three PTT phone centers that handle most of the legal phone taps in this country," he said, "one in Zurich, the other in Geneva—"

"The financial and diplomatic connections, respectively."

"And the third here. Simply because it's out of the way—and convenient to one of the Army's major emergency command centers. Satellite signals intelligence feeds in too, from the SIGINT centers near the Jungfrau and Mont Blanc. But there is so much legal tapping going in and out of these centers—and this one even more than the others—that a bit of, shall we say, work on the side, is hardly noticed. So. I have the convenience of working from home, untraceably—for calls routed in and out of the three 'tap' exchanges have the identifying code headers stripped off to them—"

"Surely, though, they would notice someone using such a number from outside, without authorization—"

Falera shook his head. "There's always a 'back door'," he said, "a way for the government or the police to slip through the programming if they think their own system is being compromised. It was built in when the software was first commissioned. That's the way we're going in: through their own 'back door,' which of necessity can't be monitored or blocked."

Falera fell silent, typing again. Harris looked around at the screen as his beer came. Right now it was showing nothing more than a string of letters and numbers at the top of the screen. The cursor flashed but did not move, the typed characters not echoing to the display. Falera sat back for a moment and waited, reaching out to his own beer. "There are two pieces of work we have to do today," he said. "One of them is to locate exactly the material you want—since the vaults extend for almost half a mile. This will be the most difficult business, since while the banks share access to the databases containing the information, the bases themselves are encrypted. I have been trying to get today's encrypted key, which may take me a while, but not too much longer: the technicians doing the encryption have become careless and tend to use one of a recurring cycle of passwords as encryption keys. Once I have managed that, you will need to look quickly at the lists of available material—I dare not make copies, the choices must be made on the fly—and tell me which objects you desire; they will be classified by the original registration numbers. I believe you have a list—"

Harris tapped his head.

Falera raised his eyebrows. "For numbers so long?"

"A misspent youth," Harris said. "Train spotting was my great hobby."

Falera smiled. "A pity you will not be able to spend more time here. You would find our train system interesting. At any rate, the other matter to be dealt with is simpler: I must suborn the vaults' master alarm and access systems in preparation for our entrance, since they cannot be forced physically. Fortunately, or perhaps unfortunately for the security firms involved, the computers and routines controlling entry schedules and protocols can be reached by dial-up access—this being how the banks schedule their deliveries to the secure areas. The system developed a fault some months ago, and a phone repairman had to come to see to it." Falera smiled gently. "He repaired the fault . . . but also left a 'drop-in" bug attached to the circuit board which the security system uses to call out for assistance. The system can therefore be reprogrammed remotely to allow us in; and since records will show that the Kantonalpolizei in Zurich authorized the bug, seemingly at the request of the banks, there will be no danger of detection. In any case, I will now need from you your exact intended times of entry and exit. There can be no change of these times after this access: I am intending to coincide my computer access with a normal UBS-scheduled one, and to cut it off when we are done in such a manner that the system will mistake it for a 'failed connect' and raise no alarms when the UBS themselves call in."

"We don't intend to linger," Harris said. "We'll be at the entry you designated at one thirty-eight A.M. on the fourteenth of the month. Leaving at one-fifty."

"The doors will seal again at that point," Falera said. "Be sure you have left yourself ample time, as they cannot be forced from inside or outside once they shut. It would be embarrassing for you to have to greet the bank officials at the next scheduled opening in the morning."

"You would be there too," Harris said softly.

"Yes," Falera said, "of course. Now then, let us slip into the Telepac system and do what we must." He tapped at the keyboard again, then drank a sip of his beer and waited a moment, while the modem's speaker sang a soft hurried tone sequence. There followed the long soft beep of the Swiss ringing signal.

"Are you quite sure they won't notice such an odd entry and exit time?" Harris said.

Falera laughed. "There's nothing unusual about it. Entrances and exits are purposely kept as random as possible, to prevent them being noticed by people like you, and are staggered through all hours of the day and night. Indeed there's a slight preference toward nighttime entries: they're less noticed—there's not much nightlife in Zurich. Ah—"

The phone on the other end picked up. The model shrieked briefly, then fell silent as it fell into synch with its partner at the other end, and data began to flow. Falera typed a period, then sat back: The screen said CONNECT 9600, and then TELEPAC: 4 792 0723. Harris expected Falera to start typing again, but he simply sat back and began drinking his beer again, and the screen said R 17911303, and was answered a line or so down with "TELEPAC: call connected to 1 791 1393 . . . ."

"It's all batch-file automated from here," Falera said after another sip, "the less time I spend online, the better—the banks' own connects are all automated so, and a long connect would attract attention." He sat back, looking over the dome of the post office to where another huge white cloud, dark-bottomed, was sailing over the Calanda mountain, tailing a veil of rain behind it. "So," he said, "when did you stop transporting and go on to jotting down British Army jeep numbers for your masters, Mr. Harris?"

Harris frowned. "I might as well ask you when you started working as a double agent for the Kantonalpolizei and the Army here," he said, "except that it would be none of my damned business."

Falera lifted his eyebrows, a faintly satisfied look, and Harris bridled again, stung by the superiority of the expression. "At least we have a cause we're working for," he said. "Unlike some people, who simply do it for money."

Falera glanced at the screen and laughed. "As if the Wild Geese of old Ireland didn't fight on half the battlefields of Europe for five hundred years," he said, "and send their pay home to their families all the while. No, Mr. Harris, you won't find any chink in my armor there: money's no less good a cause, always depending on what you do with it. Preserve a way of life, perhaps . . . rather than destroy one, as you're trying to. My conscience is intact. But is yours, I wonder?"

Harris frowned harder, but there was no use, the man just didn't seem to care, and his tone of casual scorn only made it plainer to him that they really were going to have to kill Falera when this was all over. "Really," Falera said, "it's no wonder that you're having to pull heists like this, now, and having to enlist outside help for them: your people were never much good at thinking things through, at taking the long view. Didn't it occur to them that the Americans would catch on at last, that the 'armed struggle' they were contributing to in the little Irish bars in Boston and New York, was killing their relatives by accident as often as it was killing the Brits? And some of them were actually finding out, now, what you intend for Ireland after you get the 'Brits Out.' A tidy little Marxist-socialist government it's supposed to be, after you overthrow the clownish little democracy that runs the place now. Hasn't it occurred to you what the UN will do, if you manage that? Do you think sanctions apply only to the Serbians and the South Africans? What happens when your poor little island is blockaded, and trade sanctions go into place, and your access to British ports is closed down, and Europe leaves you to your own devices? It'll be another famine you'll have then, and 1848 will be nothing to it."

"At least our people will die free," Harris muttered, able to think of nothing else to say.

"You might ask them whether they want to die at all," Falera said, "but they've been telling you what they wanted for a long time now, and you haven't listened to that either . . . ."

A silence fell, angry and uneasy on Harris's side, and infuriatingly, a calm and untroubled one on Falera's. "Here we go," he said, "we're into the UBS system. Let's see if I'm right about the cryptography keys."

"And if you're not?" Harris said.

"Then I give you your money back," Falera said.

And we kill you anyway, Harris thought. You smell like a turncoat, Mr. smartarse Falera. You sound like you're going to sell us to the police here as soon as you get a chance. But he kept his face still, for this work was more important than his personal feelings . . . for the moment. Later, he would hope he was the one who got to watch this insolent face go terrified before he pulled the trigger.

"It was the third set," Falera said, "as I thought. Programmers everywhere get lazy after they've been working in a given job for a while: they really ought to change these people more often . . . ."

He leaned back. "And as for my double agentry, if that's the word we're looking for," Falera said, "you know enough about it to have come to me in the first place, having heard that I was very, very good at it. Not that you were able to find anything much about my life before World War II, but that's as I prefer it. I have been here a long, long while, using one weapon or another for my pay, and being well paid, and using the money to preserve what matters to me. And none of your damned business what that might be, indeed."

Harris blinked, for there again had come out that oddly Irish phrasing, very strange in this accent. Could he be working for the Brits after all, came the thought. But no, their own sources inside the British camp, which they trusted, had been very sure about that.

"The cryptography's handled now," Falera said. "Output will be in the clear; we're sitting just 'outside' the inventory database for the specialist gold reserves. Are you ready?"

"Yes," Harris said. "We're looking for registration numbers beginning with DB14."

"A few moments yet," He hit the carriage return.

The screen went dark for a moment, then began to fill up with figures which scrolled rapidly past. Harris stared at the screen, watching them go by, then said, "Stop!"

Falera paused the display instantly. Harris pointed. "That one," he said, pointing. "And that one—four numbers down."

Falera nodded and noted down the numbers on his pad. "All right," Harris said. "Next—"

The numbers scrolled again. For several minutes Harris watched the display, then said "Stop!" again, and pointed at the screen. Falera noted down a third number, said, "No more from there?"

"No, let it go again—"

One more the figures scrolled by at high speed. Then Harris said "Stop!" one more time, pointed. Falera nodded, noted the number. "Any more?"

Harris shook his head.

"Right. Now for locations." Falera typed in the four registration numbers and added a few characters, hit the carriage return.

The screen said, PALETTE 254, 266. 266, 268

"There are the pallet numbers where the bars in question are to be found," Falera said with satisfaction. "It's not a caged area; we won't need the wirecutters. Here—" He noted the pallet numbers down and handed the whole pad to Harris. "Now we can get out of here and make the call that will take care of the entry proper." He tapped at the keyboard again.

NO CARRIER, the screen said, and then another phone number appeared on it, and the computer began dialing again. "You're sure you're allowing yourself enough time?"

"If the vault map you sent us is accurate, yes," Harris said.

Falera nodded. The computer made another modem connection, shrieked briefly, fell silent again. "This should take less time," he said. "Can I interest you in another beer? The weissbier is really quite good."

Harris shook his head. He watched the computer screen fill up again with query and response, query and response, and finally, after several screenfuls of security queries and passwords, a menu labeled ZUGANG ZUM TRESOR, with blanks for time and date input. Falera touched a key, and his computer went automated again, filling in the necessary data. GERETTET, the screen said after a moment.

"There," Falera said. "It's saved the new access and exit times. That's our work done, Mr. Harris."

A few more messages fleeted across the screen, followed at last by the NO CARRIER herald. Falera sat back and pulled the cellphone's connector lead out of the back of the computer, tucking the phone into his jacket pocket.

"That's it," he said. "Now all you need to do, Mr. Harris, is meet me at Linth-Escher-Gasse 16, by the delivery entrance, fifteen minutes before the time appointed for entry into the vaults. There should be no problem with passing security, but for the sake of outward appearances, in case anyone should pass and see us in the street, I'll be sending you PTT coveralls to wear: the understanding will be that we're there to do something about the phones. You won't be changing addresses between now and then?"

"No, we're at the same rental apartment in Zug."

"Very good. Until then—" And Falera turned his attention back to his computer.

Harris got up and walked slowly away down the winding cobbled street, heading for the train station. He was absolutely determined that this should be the last time that the man would dismiss him like a schoolboy.

Behind him, Falera slipped his cellphone out of his pocket and began dialing.

Their third and last meeting took place at one twenty-three in the morning, on the fourteenth of the month, outside a dark doorway in Linth-Escher-Gasse in Zurich. The doorway was set in a bland-looking limestone-faced building; it was a silvery aluminum accordion-folding doorway, big enough to admit trucks, with PARKEN VERBOTEN painted across it. A small door in its side was open, and inside a man-shaped shadow waited for them: Falera, in another of the yellow PTT coveralls, carrying a toolbox.

Silently they slipped through the door, and Falera closed it behind them. "To the back of the loading ramp, if you please," he said, "the door on your right. Turn right as you go through it and proceed down the hallway."

"You first," Smyth said.

"With pleasure," Falera said, as if totally uncaring of the tone of menace in Smyth's voice. He led them up the steps of the concrete loading ramp where trucks would normally park, through the doorway he had indicated, and down the hall. It was a perfectly ordinary-looking hallway, painted in the kind of industrial beige-yellow that typifies office building basements. He pulled open a door on his left: it squeaked loudly as it opened, and they went through it, following him down the fluorescent-lighted stairwell.

They went several floors down, Harris judged, before coming to the bottom of the stairs and another door. Falera opened it and went ahead of them into a long bare hallway—beige-painted walls, beige linoleum floor. It sloped very gently downwards, and stretched ahead of them for what must have been about a city block. It was about halfway down it that Harris realized how completely all noises of the city had now faded away. The silence was total, except for their footsteps.

At the end of the long corridor was a bare steel wall. The three stopped, and Smyth stared at it. "Now what?"

"Now we wait," Falera said softly. "A few extra minutes were budgeted into the timing to allow for delays."

They waited. Smyth was quite calm about it: Harris was more excited—both by the prospect of what they were about to pull off, and by the prospect of what Headquarters had told him he would be allowed to do to Falera in a week and a half. Falera, for his part, stood there as calmly as if he were waiting for a bus. Enjoy it while you can, you arrogant son of a bitch. Harris thought.

There was a clicking noise, loud as a revolver being cocked. Both men's heads snapped around to stare at Falera, but he only smiled slightly at them, and looked back at the steel wall.

The wall swung outward toward them. Harris and Smyth hurried backed away from it as it swung out, and Falera immediately slipped in through the widening opening. They went in after him.

At first there was nothing to be seen but another hallway, identical to the first, about a hundred yards long. They hurried down it, toward the unmarked door at its far end. Falera reached it first, pulled it open: darkness lay on the other side. They followed him.

Inside the door, as it closed behind them, they stopped. It was not truly dark; the lighting was simply dimmer than the hallway outside, and it took a moment for their eyes to get used to it. Harris and Smyth looked around them. They were standing in a long, long room, surprisingly high-ceilinged, that reached far off to the right and left of them, and was about fifty feet wide where they stood. They had little time to tell anything more about it, for piled up on row after row of pallets, stretching away to right and left, lay something which mellowly reflected the lights in the ceiling in many soft bright patches of sheen and glimmer.

Gold. Gold. Gold by the acre . . . .

"This way," Falera said, heading off to the right. It was a moment before either Harris or Smyth could react, for the sheer presence of so much gold in this dimness made the place seem more like a church than a vault. There was a smell to it, a warm metallic scent, as if it were something alive. Slowly at first, then more swiftly, they made their way after Falera. The pallets had numbers stamped on them: they were only in the mid-100's. Falera was well ahead, and shortly they caught up with him. The warm smell of the gold seemed to get stronger as they went. They walked for what seemed a dreadfully long time, though by Harris's watch it was only three minutes.

"Pallet 254," Falera said. Harris looked down, there to their left, and saw it: gold in a single layer, the bars labeled 999 FINE, and there among them one that had more than the bare words, but the eagle gripping the laurel wreath that encircled the swastika, and the registration number starting with DB14 stamped on it. He reached into his coverall for the soft leather bag he had had stowed inside it, unfolded it and reached down to the gold bar.

It took both hands to lift it, and two tries: the first time he pinned his index finger under the thing and blacked the nail, and swore as he got it up at last. Behind him, Falera was already leading Smyth further down to pallet 266. Smyth bent over the pallet, found another of the Nazi-stamped bars, picked it up more carefully and put it in his bag, then started on the second. Harris went along to pallet 268, where the last bar lay: he huffed and puffed as he carried the bag with the first one, not being able to do it two-handed because of the injured finger. At pallet 268 he stopped, found another of the bars with the eagle and wreath, lifted it and slipped it into the bag. The sound of gold striking gold was soft and final, like the odor of an expensive car shutting.

Then he heard another sound: a long, slow, soft growl.

Harris saw the gleam of gold in the dimness, but the gold moved.

He fumbled inside his coverall for his gun, and looked around for Falera. Falera was nowhere to be seen.

"Come you, you bastard!" Harris shouted, as Smyth came up behind him. "Come out or we'll bloody waste you!"

"No," said Falera's voice softly, from somewhere deeper in the dimness, somewhere behind whatever it was that was golden, and moved: "No, whatever is wasted today, it will not be me."

The gold moved again, and abruptly, Harris saw the eyes looking at him and Smyth. They were golden too, and from the head in which they were set, that warm, metallic scent breathed thick. The eyes watched them, and they stood horrified as the slow shape clambered over pallet 270 and slipped toward them, deliberate-footed, heavy and huge.

Smyth pulled out his gun and shot the thing, most precisely, between the eyes.

The bullet whined away, making a dull clunk as it ricocheted into a gold bar somewhere else in the room. "Oh, no," Falera's voice said from behind the huge golden creature. "It takes a bit more than that to kill a *felddrache*. I should know."

The long, low, lizardy shape stepped toward them, gleaming dully in the dim light, and Harris and Smyth stepped back.

"You wouldn't have had much data about them, I suppose," Falera's soft, dry voice said. "They were all over Europe, once. Except Ireland, of course: the druids got rid of them, although Padraig took the credit, didn't he? He was never one to miss a propaganda opportunity . . . but never mind. They were everywhere, the drakes. A plague. It was a specialty of mine, killing them: I was much in demand. Of course I didn't know back then what I found out later, that the drakes weren't from here, originally, but from some other reality. That if you were exposed to their blood too often, there were side effects. A taste or so, and you might come to understand their tongue. More than that . . . wounds wouldn't take, the skin would harden, organs would regenerate. After that, if you still kept exposing yourself . . . long life. Surprisingly long."

Harris finally saw where Falera was standing, pulled his own gun and shot him, too, in the head. Falera staggered a bit with the impact, but immediately straightened and laughed. Harris emptied the clip, but the shots went wide, or else Falera simply shook himself and stood upright again, behind the huge golden dragon that still stepped slowly toward them.

"They could die, though," Falera said. "So many of them did. At first, when I started work, it was a blessing. But later, when there were almost none left . . . I realized they had to be preserved: they were part of our history, no matter how terrible a one. They were a deadly intelligence, but an intelligence nonetheless . . . and who knew whether there were any more of them left back where they came from? Who dares stamp out utterly a species that some god made? I found I couldn't do it. This last one, who lived down in the mountains south of Chur, I protected him as long as I could. It was always a problem: they crave gold as they crave blood. But finally, after many, many years, I found a way to turn that to our advantage. And the banks don't mind having one more secret to keep. External security, mechanical security, can always be beaten—but not instinct, not the *drache*'s chief urge. Gold to guard . . . blood to drink. They don't have to eat often . . . just every now and then. Often enough for the bank's purposes, and their own . . . for nothing satisfies them like a nice fresh thief. Fear," Falera added as if an afterthought, "improves the flavor for them. It's the sudden rush of hormones, I suspect."

Harris and Smyth cowered toward each other. Smyth emptied his own pistol at the dragon: Harris turned and fled desperately for the doorway through which they had entered the vaults.

"It's locked itself again, of course," Falera said calmly, as the dragon advanced. "I have my own way out: for security personnel, there's always a back door. But as for you—you didn't even watch the screen to make sure of the times I was inputting. So sure of yourself, and yet so easily distracted by a little criticism." There was humor in the voice now. "You just don't think things through, do you?"

Smyth screamed. Harris began hammering on the door. But there was no point in it. Shortly thereafter, having dealt with Smyth, a kind of gold which Harris had not sought came seeking him, and trod him under foot, and tore away at the choicest flesh, so that blood spattered its own golden hide and the gold piled up around.

Silence fell after a while. "You're going to have to clean those up," Falera said.

"Later, Gieri," said the slow, growling voice.

Harris was not quite gone yet, though it would be a matter of minutes, since the dragon had just bitten his leg off above the knee, and what shock had not yet managed, the hemorrhage from the femoral artery would shortly complete. "Gieri . . ." he whispered.

"It would have been George in English," Falera said.

And there was silence again. And nothing else but the gleam of gold.

THE ART OF REVOLUTION

by S.N. Lewitt

Czerny, the Dragon of Prague, awoke slowly in his place in the crypt of St. Vitus' cathedral. Voices filtered through to him before he had even opened his eyes.

"Here, comrades, we have yet another example of the waste of the aristocracy," a man said stuffily. "To keep and feed this dragon, the people of Prague had to pay additional taxes to the rulers here at the castle. Twelve percent of the bureaucracy was involved directly in keeping this beast in comfort! Now, however, he sleeps at the discretion of the people, so we are not burdened with extravagance and upkeep."

Czerny was confused. He was the Dragon of Prague. Whatever was the man saying about his "upkeep." All he needed was a cow, and that only every other day. In return he slept here in the castle and guarded the jewels. And the castle.

And then he felt deep shame. He remembered why

he went to sleep. He had tried, truly he had, to guard the castle. But he alone had been no match for the tanks that had rolled up the hill. Not the German tanks, nor the Russian ones either.

"In fact, there are stories about the Dragon of Prague trying to help defend the castle against the Nazis," the tour guide said. "However, he, along with the rest of the Czech military, was defeated. Had we not been rescued by our staunch Soviet allies, we would have suffered a terrible fate. Perhaps the city would even have been damaged, firebombed, burned to the ground and gutted like Budapest or Warsaw."

Czerny remembered. He had stood on the roof of the cathedral and spit flame at the invaders until he had choked. He had swooped out of the sky into the shooting invaders until his wings had been riddled with bullet holes and he couldn't hold his own weight in the sky.

He had tried, he had. He knew it. He had fought the invaders with every shred of his soul. And he had lost, and he was ashamed.

So he had gone to sleep, the long long sleep of recovery. The long sleep of dreams, where he remembered the good times. The fights against other invaders, fights he had won.

He only wished the golem were still around to help out. If the golem had still been working, Czerny was sure they would have defeated the tanks that roared up Castle Hill. They had repelled the French and the Germans at the Charles Bridge once before, the golem on one side and Czerny on the other. Between them they had cut off the bridge and thrown the would-be conquerors into the river. Those had been the good old days.

But Rabbi Loew had deactivated the mud monster and put it in the attic of the prayer house, and after all these years, it was probably only dust and mud again. And, to be quite honest, Czerny didn't like to fight quite as much as he had. The coffee houses and conversation before the last wars had intrigued him far more than breathing flame at enemies. And there hadn't been enemies for a very long time.

"However," the guide droned on, "several very fine works of art were found with this Dragon of Prague. As there was no adequate place here to display these works, they are now on loan to the Hermitage. A small deposit on the debt we owe our Soviet comrades who saved us from the Nazi scourge. Very fine paintings, they were. Adequate even for the Hermitage. The Czech people should be proud to have made such a contribution."

Even more than the music or the conversation, there had been the art. All the other dragons of Europe had envied him. Czerny had more beautiful, glittering things to hoard than three or four of them together. There were the jewel-like glass pieces in deep blues and greens and blood red edged in gold. There were doors in ironwork made to resemble the fluid undulating of flowers on a windy day. There were bright lights and silver tableware and chess sets of carved stone and precious metals. Only a small sampling of his personal chess sets would make Czerny's hoard one of the finest in all Europe.

Some of the dragons of Paris and London and Madrid had gold plate and crown jewels to compare, but Czerny's hoard of art was unsurpassed. Among dragons his taste was far more famous than his battles.

The older dragons of London and Paris, Brussels and Bonn might have more exciting war stories (though none of them had ever fought with a golem allied on the field, which Czerny always pointed to with pride to prove his lack of prejudice and how well the Jews of Prague were integrated into the life of the city). They might have smashed armadas or gone to the New World or met the Imperial Dragon of China in the Forbidden City in Beijing. But not one of them had Czerny's eye for fine art, and not even the collection of the Imperial Dragon

could match his for the elegance and sophistication of
choice.

Most dragons were fairly conservative in their prefer-
ences, and their hoards were depressingly similar. Basic
jewels (cabochon cut and rim beveled in the style of
the tenth century, usually) were the mainstay of most
collections. A few dragons had collected some icons and
gilded work. And one or two of the Italian dragons made
a serious investment in a Donatello bronze or a Chi-
mabue crucifix. Their taste was so conservative, though,
he had been able to negotiate on two graphite drawings
by Rafael.

Not one of the dragons had anything truly avant-garde
in their collections. Lovely, true, and rich indeed. But
not one dragon had such glittering service in Art Nouveau designs, bright ceramics in the most modern Deco,
paintings that reflected the cutting edge of the era in
art. They simply didn't have the eyes for it.

Czerny's collection was famous, even among dragons.
All the great wyrms of the earth prided themselves on
their riches and their exquisite taste. But only Czerny,
the official dragon of a city on the forefront of art, had
quite the instinct for the moderns.

Before he had gone to sleep, even the dragons of Paris
had consulted him on acquiring Cezanne, and he had
managed to trade some traditional but glittering stuff for
a rose period Picasso. That, along with the Rafael drawings, the glasswork, and a rather wonderful Matisse that
the French dragons just didn't understand, were the
prizes of his treasure. Not to say that he didn't have the
usual pearls and silver service and golden candlesticks as
well. But to Czerny, these were merely furnishings to
show off his true paragons.

He wondered where the Picasso had gone. He looked
around the bare stone that surrounded him and, with a
shock, realized that there was no hoard any more. The
most elegant collection in all Europe, it was all gone.

Czerny lumbered to his feet, stretched out his back, and let out a great roar of fury. His Picasso! His glass collection! His carved chess sets! All the things that were important for a dragon, that made life worthwhile. That gave him status among his peers.

Members of the tour group that had been staring at him in polite interest screamed and tried to run. A few braver souls struggled with their flashes in the dark crypt as the Dragon of Prague let out a bellow that could be heard across the river, all the way to Wenceslas Square.

"Comrades, comrades," the tour guide yelled ineffectively. "There is no reason to be afraid. Our resident dragon, while a tool of the former imperialist state, has never hurt a native of this city. He is merely . . . ." The tour guide fainted.

"My Picasso," Czerny yelled. Misery flooded him. He couldn't even take pleasure in the people screaming, running up the stairs as he stared at them with his vast, multifaceted eyes. The eyes, he remembered, that had inspired several of the glass artists for which his city was justly famous. He was not merely a dragon as a collector, he was one of the premiere models as well. And no other single dragon of Europe could say that!

Now, with his collection gone, he wondered if any of the brass street lamps with his likeness on them remained. Or had those, too, been taken by the enemy? Though which enemy was hard to say. Things were all so confused. He was confused.

A group of schoolchildren entered the crypt with their teacher. The children all had red scarves around their necks. Czerny wondered if it was some holiday, or a church sodality. He decided not to roar this time. Schoolchildren, when they were not afraid of him, often had treats. Czerny liked treats. Not so much as paintings, of course, but children couldn't be expected to understand that.

And he could have explained so much! He could have

shown them the difference between the Impressionists and the Academy. He could have explained cubism, shown how it had grown out of the industrial age. And they would have loved the Matisse. Children always liked Matisse, the brilliant colors and vitality of the figures.

These were, after all, the children of Prague. Some of them would grow up to become painters and potters and writers and musicians. One of them might even found a new style. The very thought made Czerny's eyes tinge rose with pleasure.

And then he realized that he couldn't show the children these things. He couldn't explain the philosophy of Dada or the evolution of Art Nouveau because he didn't have anything at all to show them. He felt sad and hoped that they would still give him peanuts anyway, the way children had in the last century when he was a fixture in the Third Courtyard of the Palace.

"This is the dragon, Czerny," the teacher said. "He once was one of the symbols of the city of Prague, along with the clock tower and the castle itself."

"Are we going to the square?" one of the children asked. "My big brother says that we should all go to the square today because something important is going to happen."

"Yeah, real history," a little girl with long dark braids added. "Not any of this old stuff."

The teacher held up her hand for silence. "You all know what happened before," she said softly. "There were . . . mistakes."

"A tank shot at the National Museum. Pow, pow!" one of the boys yelled.

A tank? Fired on the museum? Czerny didn't think he could possibly have heard correctly. "Who shot the museum?" he asked in his softest voice. He still made the heavy pillars shake.

The teacher looked around, panicked. "Who said that?" she asked. "I didn't say anything."

"Besides, we know it's true," said the girl who'd spoken before. "We know that you're all listening all the time and you don't want us to have our own government. My mother told me all about sixty-eight. She told me. She said you went out and killed people in Wenceslas Square. And she was there and she's my mother and she's right."

The girl looked over Czerny as if he were just one more element for Friday's history test. "Havel to the Castle," she said. "No more Russians in Prague. Havel for President. That's why my mother says." Then she turned and walked out.

The teacher was white with terror. "Don't say things like that here," she hissed. But the children were already leaving, singing. Singing a song Czerny found familiar.

Czerny looked around, wondering who they were talking to. Who had killed people? What was sixty-eight? He had been asleep for a very long time. He knew the year he had fallen asleep. It had been nineteen forty-five. He just realized that he had no idea of the date, no measure of how long he had slept. Only that he had been unconscious from the day the tanks had rolled up the hill and into the First Courtyard of the castle until today.

Except for the time he had woken up for some water. But that had been in the middle of the night. He had gone down to drink at the river and the water had tasted bad. Though if he thought of it, he couldn't remember his paintings being properly hung in the crypt then, either.

No, he had not been properly awake that time. His memory was hazy. The last thing he remembered was curling up on the stone floor of the unfinished cathedral and slipping into a deep, healing sleep.

He had heard of the long sleeps of dragons. The Imperial Dragon of China slept deep and often. The Great Dragon of England had once slept over a hundred years. Czerny was younger than those venerable ancients, and he had not fallen into the great sleep before. Though he remembered the Dragon of England saying something about it.

"The terror is that you wake up and nothing is the same," the old resident of Camelot had told a group of youngsters when they had come to celebrate the coronation of some queen named—Victoria, Czerny thought it was. Foreign royalty was so hard to keep straight.

"The cave isn't the same, the landmarks have all changed, and the people don't even know you exist any more," the ancient dragon had told them. "And nothing makes any sense. Once I went to sleep and it was a lovely little Anglo-Saxon village and I woke up next to a great heap of a fortress and they didn't even speak English. If you can imagine that."

Czerny couldn't imagine that. At least, so far, all the people he had heard spoke Czech. That was reassuring. And the walls were familiar. This was the crypt at St. Vitus. He recognized the stairway, the doors, the little door to the small underground chapel where the crown jewels were stored.

He turned and put an eye to the opening into the chapel. Something was wrong. It was all as he remembered it, the white cloth and the locked cases with the crown and the rest of the things that were not his to own but surely his to guard. But there were no candles burning on the altar. There were no fresh flowers in front of the statues. The place felt unused.

Slowly he stretched out his neck. Then he went to the stairs and came up out of his dark hole into the world. He left the cathedral and lumbered into the courtyard where he had perched at guard for so very long. He looked up. The cathedral, three quarters finished for hundreds of years, was complete. The second tower was done.

He wondered how much else had changed. He unfurled his wings and gave a few warm-up flaps. The hideous rents in his lovely scales were now healed. Only scars of pale iridescent blue showed how deeply he had been wounded. As he spread his wings across the sky there was more scar color than the deep shimmering aquamarine that was his true and proper color.

"My wings," he whimpered. "My Picasso and my wings." His shook his great head from side to side as if searching out the next thing that would be wrong. And then beat his wings against the breeze and rose effortless to the sky.

There was joy in him. He had not been fully awake until he soared, claimed his right to the air over his city. But he wasn't alone in the air. There were things there, heaving metal things that made him think of tanks, made him think of the Fokker running him down, shooting the tip of his ear so that steaming ichor ran into his left eye.

This time the things were far away and did not come close. He was ready if they came near him. He could feel the fire churning in his belly, begging for release. But the great metal birds stayed far away. They did not swoop down over the river as he did, gliding the length of the Charles Bridge, counting the saints against the orange-pink twilight sky. Over the river, out of the Mala Strana and toward the "new" city, Czerny inspected his demesne.

Prague had always been beautiful. The most beautiful city in the world, even the other dragons agreed. "The Light of Europe" the people called it. Its amazing clock and gilded and painted buildings had never been destroyed by any enemy. Even the basest invaders could not remain unmoved by this place. No wonder such art came from here, such love of elegance, such avant-garde arrogance. Czerny's oversized dragon heart was full of the glory of his home, full even beyond his capacity with awe at his city.

Yes, it was beautiful. But it was also different. When he looked carefully he could see the grim faces on the people, the digging in the streets. There was no music on the bridge any more, no twinkling in the coffeehouses where he had once heard Kafka converse with intellectuals and anarchists.

Czerny had been asleep. But, as the shadows of night deepened against the glowing streets, he thought Prague looked to be asleep now too. As if his own sleep had been part of the slumber of the city, that its pulse had slowed. Prague was now a place of ghosts and memories, where the past haunted the present. Where there was no present that mattered.

No one was in the streets that he could see. No neighbors tossing sticks for their dogs on the public green, no children playing ball in the streets, ignoring the calls of their mothers to dinner. There were no old men outside the study house in the Josefov, the Jewish Quarter, discussing some point of law. No one lingered on the bench where Rabbi Loew had once told jokes to his students and wondered what was for dinner.

Czerny saw all of this. He wondered where the people were, or if without his conscious presence the city had simply ceased to be. Then he saw a flicker of light down by Wenceslas Square. From the clock-tower square below it was only a short way to the great boulevard where the elegant hotels and chic shops had once rivaled Paris.

As Czerny came lower he realized that the darkness of the square was not empty pavement and plantings, but the packed bodies of a hundred thousand people. All kinds of people, working men and women in the uniforms of hotel maids, students in black hanging on street lights waving the Czech flag, whole families holding hands as if on a Sunday afternoon outing.

Czerny landed on the ornate facade of the Hotel Europa. He always thought that the elegant architecture set him off to advantage. It had been his favorite perch ever since it had been built as a hotel to match anything in Paris.

"Remember the martyrs," people screamed. And "Havel to the Castle," and "Russians go home."

So was it the revolution, then? Czerny had heard a lot about revolutions before he had gone to sleep. In the coffeehouses of the Mala Strana, university professors and artists and musicians talked about revolution all the time. Revolutions in art, revolutions against complacency, against the bureaucracy, revolutions against the concept of order itself.

Czerny had heard it all and it confused him. As a dragon he was somewhat conservative. But as the Dragon of Prague, he was proud of his stance on the cutting edge. He was the one dragon with true taste in the moderns, who understood the point of deconstructionism.

He was part of his city. Its being was his breath, its will was his mind, its will was his soul. And he had slept while Prague had slept the deepest dream, had rolled over once for water and was thwarted while martyrs burned themselves to death in Wenceslas Square. Now he had awakened again, he and his city together.

"They took my Picasso," he screeched to the crowd below. "They took it away to someplace called the Hermitage. My Picasso and the Cezanne and Matisses and the Renoirs. Even the Braque cubist pieces, and those were not the best."

"They took everything else, too," a man yelled up at him. "They took our best students, our industry. Everything."

"Not the Skoda!" another man screamed into the conversation. "We still have our cars."

Czerny blinked his oversized insect eyes. Everyone had lost precious things. All of them. His hoard was gone, all except the crown jewels. Those even the Russians dared not take.

"Russians go home," the crowd started chanting.

Czerny joined in with the rest of them, his bellow rumbling like the whole mob together. "Russians go home." He was part of the mob, but his anger was swallowed by sorrow. All the beautiful things that had been stolen from him were gone. And he didn't know how to get anything back again.

The Museum of Art is sandwiched between the castle and the winding streets of the Mala Strana, about halfway up Castle Hill. The number 22 tram line runs up there where the hill is too sharp to walk comfortably. Czerny, of course, could never fit in a tram. But he followed the twenty-two dejectedly up toward his lair under the cathedral.

He didn't want to go back. He wasn't sleepy and he didn't want to be alone. Especially not with the blank walls and the memories of the art that should have hung there. That he now knew had gone, like all their dreams, into Russia. He barely had the desire to fly up the hill. If a dragon could trudge, he would have. The fire, the energy of the evening had died suddenly inside him. It was going to be sixty-eight again.

He had heard plenty that evening about sixty-eight. About how the people of Prague had gathered nightly in Wenceslas Square and the Soviet tanks had rolled in and fired into the crowd. How one commander had mistaken the National Museum for the Parliament and ordered his heavy armor to fire at the Baroque building that housed what paintings were left and scraps of the past. Fired on the museum. Czerny felt the rounds as if they had pierced his own scales.

And then there were the martyrs. Jan Palach, a student, who had immolated himself in front of the museum. His picture was set up in the carefully groomed circle and flowers smothered the spot. The next night, five more martyrs had repeated the action. The Soviets had not moved at all. They had crushed the nascent

Czech nationalism with heavy tanks that had ended up in a working-class district well away from the heart of the city.

Soviet Tank Drivers' Square it was called, in the area known as Smichov. It was a place where Czerny had never been, far from the castle and the bustle of downtown. And it bothered Czerny that there was an area of the city he did not know, though much of the outlying areas had changed.

As the rally died, Czerny took off from the roof of the Europa Hotel, circled Wenceslas Square twice, and flew down over the river to Smichov. He had heard of the district, he knew where it was supposed to be. And it unfolded to his right, though his eyes were on the castle overlooking the water.

Even in the dark there were lights focused on the cathedral. The twin spires glowed against the indigo sky, brooding on the city. Seeing home so proud against the night, Czerny felt a surge of power so strong it made his eyes sting.

Home. There had been invaders. He had fought them off. He remembered the troops threatening the Charles Bridge, fighting over the cobblestones to cross the river and take the castle. Rabbi Loew's golem stood under the bridge tower while Czerny had attacked from overhead. They had stopped the invaders cold, and won the banner and perpetual protection for the Josefov. And Czerny had won a special commendation, too, with a glittering decoration set with blood dark garnets to add to his hoard.

Remembering this made Czerny happy. For a moment he was able to forget this disgrace, his defeat, and the pillage of his treasure.

"And all because of those Russians," he thought, furious. He remembered the tanks rolling up the hill, great metal monsters belching fire as hot as his own. As if they could not enlist their own dragons in their fight and so had created machine replicas of what a guardian dragon could do.

Just the thought of the tanks shot a stream of flame from his nostrils that lit the Smichov streets like lightening. Two men wearing caps stared up at the fire-breathing dragon gliding over the drinking clubs and the silent tram tracks in the middle of the street. Czerny came lower. They had been drinking, he could see from the uneven way they walked, and he wondered if these would be good people to ask. Then he realized there was no one else around.

"Excuse me, could you direct me to Soviet Tank Drivers' Square?" he asked.

The two men blinked and looked at each other. They looked up at Czerny, who could not hover long and had perched on the top of an automobile. One of the men shook his head and started to walk away. The other blinked and pinched himself as if he thought Czerny might not be quite real. Then he mumbled something unintelligible and waved in the direction of tall buildings.

He really should make a point of getting away from the castle and the Mala Strana, Czerny thought. People didn't seem to expect him to show up any place in the city. He was supposed to be asleep in the cathedral so that teachers and tour guides could talk about waste in the past. No one seemed to expect him to *do* anything. No one expected him to be able to help.

Czerny blinked his great rolling eyes, trying to shield himself from the knowledge. He had become superfluous. He could no longer defend the city. He couldn't even keep his hoard. He was defeated, a failure.

Other dragons had never considered him quite their equal, either, he thought. For all his knowledge of art, for all his sophistication, he had only rarely repelled invaders, and that with the help of golem. He had never wrestled with knights or fought off pretenders as had other dragons. He had never been hunted, had never been the object of a quest. Indeed, everything in Prague had always known precisely where to find him. Children in the royal family grew up sliding down his tail and pulling on his ears.

He was a failure. The only thing he knew, the only thing he understood, was art. Which was not his fault. He lived in a city that was better known for art than for war, and Czerny was proud of that. Just as he had been proud of his own collection, the finest in Prague.

No young artists would come to him any more, the way they had before his long sleep. How he remembered them trudging up the hill from the cafes to see his paintings. They sometimes brought wine down into the crypt and talked with him about art, about what was happening in Paris and New York and in their own studios in Prague.

Czerny must have been the only creature who didn't mind the sharp vinegar wine and the day-old bread the art students brought. He had enjoyed listening to them talk, argue with passion about expression, nature and the mechanization of humanity. He had even contributed his own opinions, and more than once he had seen one of his ideas expressed in some gallery show that he could see only dimly through the windows, even when he had received an engraved invitation to the opening and they were serving champagne inside. He as too large to fit through the doors of any gallery in Prague.

Lost in his thoughts, Czerny flew over all of Smichov. He wheeled over a great open square filled with hulking sculptures that threw crazy shadows over the pavement. Then he suddenly realized where he was. Soviet Tank Drivers' Square. He flew lower to get a good look.

Indeed, there were tanks lined up in the square. A single one in the center was mounted on a concrete stand like a monument. Czerny thought it was a terrible monument, and that some poor sculptor who didn't get a commission had gone hungry so that an ugly pile of metal could sit in the middle of the park.

Tank Number 23, read a plaque on the cement mounting. The first tank to break the Nazi occupation of Prague. the first tank through the gates to liberate the Czech people. Their friendly Slavic neighbors in Russia had come to Czech aid, and this tank was their pledge to do so again, whenever needed.

The plaque made Czerny want to spit fire and melt the whole thing down right then. He wanted to do to Tank Number 23 what he couldn't do to the Nazi tanks that had come up the hill. He wanted to flame down all the Russians he had seen, all the soldiers standing in the shadows in Wenceslas Square while the people had held their rally, all the Russians to whom people yelled, "Go home."

Everyone go home. Prague for the Czechs, Czerny thought. Prague for *us*.

But he didn't know what to do, what one dragon against the forces of history and technology could do. What one dragon whose true love was art could accomplish. Though, he remembered, he had often told the other dragons that art was more important than war. That art was eternal and victory was brief, that art could turn the world around.

He had said all those things in Paris, when the Grand Dragon of Paris had invited them all to see the fireworks and feast for the hundredth anniversary of the storming of the Bastille. Paris had done a great deal in a mere hundred years. But even the Grand Dragon of Paris had listened and agreed with Czerny on that evening while the fireworks over the Champs de Mars had glittered around them.

He had believed it then. Now the words seemed so naive, so hollow. So self-seeking. Czerny had been the only dragon there who had never killed a human in single combat. He couldn't explain to the others that, where he was from, it simply wasn't done. No one had come to kill him, he was simply an integrated part of the life of the castle, of the eternal bureaucracy of government. Like all the others, he did his job.

So, in the silent dark he flew back to his home. But he did not crawl into crypt and he did not go to sleep. Instead he perched on one of the tall spires and looked down at the city, watching over its sleep and watching it rise.

In the courtyard of the Museum of Art, Czerny saw them gather. Even from his distant perch he could see quite clearly the group that assembled between the fountains behind the high concrete walls that already were covered with graffiti. They were young and many of them dressed in black, just as they had before he had gone to sleep. Many of the young men had long hair tied back, the young women all carried their portfolios under their arms.

The young artists, the avant-garde, were meeting in their accustomed place. Czerny could not help it, he had to be with them. He unfurled his wings and launched off the cathedral tower to glide lazily halfway down the hill. The high courtyard wall was a perfect perch. He could hear everything. He could look at each portfolio as the students showed their best work and decide which of the aspiring painters he should watch.

And, of course, he was quite visible on the wall. When he had come down to the Art Institute regularly, collectors came to consult with him and students would shyly open the large black folders and show him a drawing, a study, and ask his opinion on composition.

That was a long time ago, Czerny reminded himself. He had slept for a very long time. He had at least managed to sneak a look at the newspaper someone read while sitting on a bench in the sculpture garden and he knew it was 1989. He had slept for forty-four years.

Suddenly he wished he could talk to the Great Dragon of Britain about coming back to the world after sleeping so long. No doubt that archdean of dragons would say something cryptic and profound that would take Czerny another forty years to decipher.

"We should do something about the tanks," one of the long haired young men in black was saying. "The Russians might say they're there to celebrate the liberation of Prague, but they're also there to remind us that they can roll in any time. Like they did in sixty-eight."

Czerny's ears perked up.

"Be careful, Vasclav," said one of the young women with a large folder. "You don't know who's listening."

"I don't care who's listening," Vasclav said in a very loud voice. "I'm sick of worrying about what I say and who's listening." He raised his volume to a full yell. "I hope you are listening, because I have a message for you. Go home. Leave us, go home. Take your tanks somewhere else!"

Hesitant applause punctuated the speech. Czerny found himself nodding in agreement. He had seen enough of what the Russians had done. They had taken his hoard, and that was more than any dragon could bear.

A dragon without a hoard was like, was like anyone here, he realized, amazed. He had been treated exactly like the humans. For a second he was furious. And then he was proud. Maybe they didn't see him so much as human as Czech. Czerny sat a little straighter on the wall.

The girl who had spoken before smiled now. "There's more than tanks," she said cheerfully. "Its just because you live down the street from them and have to look at them every day. The rest of us can just ignore it."

Vasclav turned back to the crowd, his mouth tight with fury. "No, we cannot just ignore it," he said. There was menace in the low rumble of his voice. "We've just ignored too much for too long. The Wall is down, the

Germans are free. Are we anything less than the Germans? But every day in our city we have those damned reminders of how easy it is for them to crush us. I say we should go there now and turn them all over. Tear Tank 23 to pieces!"

"I wonder if we tore it to pieces and painted it, if it would make a good mobile?" the girl said.

The group in the courtyard of the Art Institute turned to her in silence. She looked over their faces and shrugged. "Well, it's one thing to act on the symbol. It's another thing to change the symbol, turn it into something that is ours. That's all."

Heads shook. Vasclav sneered. The girl faced him down. "If you react to what the monument means, then you are building up the symbolic value," she said firmly. "The only way to disarm it is to turn it around and make it ours."

"Sometimes I can't figure out if you're stupid or if you're just scared," one of the crowd yelled.

"Shove it, Peter," the girl replied. "If you ever bothered to study symbolism instead of your idiot color wheel all day, you might grow some brains."

Czerny had heard enough. He knew student distractions, knew how they wouldn't resolve anything. They were art students, after all. Just the fact that every night they went down to Wenceslas Square to join the rest of the population of Prague in demonstrating for their freedom was more than art students usually did.

Except make art, of course.

He opened his wings and the span of them shadowed the courtyard as he left. Eyes turned to the sky, as they always had. He was, after all, the Dragon of Prague.

He, too, was a symbol, Czerny realized. He had always known it in an abstract sense, the way he had known that the Impressionists were working with light and that the cubists were trying to discover the meaning of geometry and express a mechanized world. The girl was right, he thought as he gained altitude. Symbols were important, and if they were changed they were changed forever.

And then Czerny saw it and smiled, high in the sky where no one could see him. He dipped a wing, turned a cartwheel over the castle. The tanks. He couldn't defeat them with attack. But he could turn his own failure around. He could defeat tanks with art.

Pleasure flooded him. His scales sparkled dark turquoise-green flecked with gold in the sunlight. He belched fire overhead from sheer joy. He never noticed that below people watched his flight and saw one more symbol of Prague, unfettered and free.

The plan was so simple, but Czerny had never tried to get materials or do any art before. He had always collected and criticized. He had never tried to paint. And so when the woman behind the counter at the shop asked what size brushes he wanted, and if he wanted sable or horsehair or nylon, he was confused.

"A big brush," he said finally, looking at the claw that covered most of the counter. "The biggest one you have. And two gallons of paint."

The woman pushed her glasses up her nose. "Paint. What kind of paint? Wall paint? Oil or latex? Or do you want metal paint, or acrylics."

This at least was safer ground. "Metal," Czerny said firmly. "Can you mix up colors for that."

The woman sighed heavily. "What color do you want?" she asked.

Czerny hung his head. He had thought about it all day, from the moment he had returned to St. Vitus' to his resolve. He had looked around the castle, the fine blue-grey of the walls, the glowing hues of the paintings in the cathedral, and had decided that none of them would do.

Red, of course, was a bad color now. Czerny was sorry for that. He thought red very pretty. But now it just meant Russians, and so that was not possible. All the bright jewel colors were too rich, too important, he thought. The idea was to make the tank silly, laughable, manageable. Light blue maybe? That would be like the sky. Or orange? Orange was a silly color sometimes. But it made Czerny think of fire.

A boy in a school uniform with a red scarf around his neck came into the store and inspected the selection of watercolor papers. The boy was chewing loudly, blowing large bubbles and then popping them with a loud crack.

The gum was pink. Hot blinding pink, a color no one could mistake. A color no one could ever take seriously. Czerny smiled and whistled to himself. "That color," he told the woman. "Like his candy."

The saleswoman cleared her throat. She did not approve of the choice. Czerny didn't care. He shifted his weight from one foot to the other. After a lifetime of loving art he was going to make art. He was very excited and a little scared.

He took the paint cans and the brush the woman set out. "Wait a minute, you have to pay for those," she yelled as Czerny squeezed himself through the door. "Stop, thief," she yelled as he jumped into the darkening sky. Didn't she know the tradition, that the castle would cover his expenses? Except for art work, of course. That was his alone.

It was hard to paint in the dark, Czerny thought. In fact, it was hard to paint at all. The brush did not fit comfortably in his claw. The paint spattered everywhere, some of it speckling his belly scales and toes. The paint did not go on evenly. It ran over the vertical planes and pooled at the base.

Czerny nearly gave up more than once. But then he remembered the tanks coming up the hill. This time he was going to defeat this one, this time he would win. He was going to erase his old shame and overcome his fear.

This was HIS tank, in HIS city. He had slept far too long.

Besides, he told himself, it gave him a better appreciation for the artists. He had always loved the paintings. Now he could understand a little of the effort it took to make them. His arms became sore from the unaccustomed back-and-forth strokes. The paint smelled bad, and he could feel it coating the inside of his nostrils. It made him want to belch fire and burn it out very badly, and once or twice in the course of his work he did just that. But he was very careful to turn away from the partially painted tank and the empty buckets around it. "Very flammable," the labels on the cans had said.

In the dark he couldn't tell if he was getting the color even, or if it was streaked. He was worried that the dark green and the red star underneath would show through. But there was no way for him to tell.

When the sky lightened enough for him to make out the outline of the castle across the river, he knew he was finished. He stretched his wings and his neck from the night's labor, picked up the paint cans, and flew back home. He threw the empty paint cans into one of the worksheds before taking his place on top of the cathedral and tucking his head under his wing for a well-deserved nap.

Czerny awoke to a furor. Russian soldiers were marching down the streets at double time. People were tittering behind their hands, laughing behind the Soviet backs. Czerny took a lazy loop overhead to see where they were all going.

They were headed to Soviet Tank Drivers' Square. Already Tank 23 was half repainted olive green. It didn't quite match the other tanks in the square.

"You will pay for this," said a Soviet officer. "You can't do this to us."

Around him the crowd just laughed. And Czerny

laughed too. He was terribly sorry to see the tank painted green again. It was very nice in pink, a kind of postmodernist statement, he had thought.

"If we ever catch who did this, he's going to jail," the officer growled.

Czerny folded his wings over the pink spots on his belly. He had tried to wash them off, but they stuck firmly to his scales. He didn't want to go to jail, not that he thought the Soviets could hold him anyway. He just didn't want to find out.

By the time evening fell and the people gathered in front of the National Museum, the tank was completely green again. But through the throng in Wenceslas Square, dancing to the rock music that broke though when no one was making speeches, everyone was talking about the pink tank.

"I don't know what it is to them," someone in the crowd said. "What's the big deal?"

Czerny whistled through his teeth. It was a big deal indeed. There were Soviet troops cordoned around the whole of Wenceslas Square tonight that hadn't been there before.

"The big deal is that they take us seriously," someone else answered. "We're not afraid any more. They know that. And if we're not afraid of them they can't win."

Czerny thought about that. Maybe it was true. He still wished the tank was pink, that the Russians were gone. He wished he had his Picasso back. He wondered what Pablo would have said about the tank. Maybe even Picasso would have thought it was art. Or had been art. It was only a green tank now.

And Czerny thought he had lost again. He had made people proud, but he had also made the enemy angry. And he hadn't destroyed even a one of them. They were all going to take Prague back and his city would never be the glorious center of art it had always been before.

It would just be one more satellite state without a soul. Czerny looked down at the crowd and began to weep.

And then, as his great tears fell splashing onto the pavement, he saw a group of men in overalls with paint cans. They were grey-haired, most of them, and dignified. They looked like they should be wearing uniforms or suits. They walked very straight and the overalls were crisply pressed.

Each one carried a can of bright pink paint and a brush. They marched in line as if they were a military band. Out of Wenceslas Square they led the crowd, down into the Metro.

Czerny followed them. He had never been in the Metro before. Great long caverns, the dragon thought this was a better place than the cathedral vault. The sides of the station were decorated with metallic colored hands.

But he didn't have long to admire tunnels as fine as any dragon could desire. The men in overalls led the crowd briskly. They took the line to Andel Station, where everything was faced in pink marble, and they were only a few blocks from Soviet Tank Drivers' Square.

Russian troops ringed the monument now. Czerny was surprised as he looked at their faces. They were tight, afraid. Czerny thought that some of the boys in uniforms with the red star cap pins looked like they might cry. He felt sorry for them.

The men in overalls began painting Tank 23 bright bubblegum pink as the crowd cheered.

"Stop that," a Russian officer came over to challenge the painters.

But the men in overalls weren't at all perturbed. The man closest to the officer stopped painting and pulled an identity card out of his back pocket. "People's Congress," the man said, smiling. "We have immunity, I believe." And then the congressman turned back, dabbing bright pink paint on the turret.

Czerny felt a giant lump in his chest, like balefire only bigger and harder like it was going to burst out of him. Pride. He had done it. Just like the dragons of Paris and Britain, who had always thought he was too lost in art to be any real use. But he was just like them. He could save his city, too. But he could save it by being exactly what he was, the Dragon of Prague. The one dragon protector who understood art better than war. After all, sometimes art won.

MERCEDES LACKEY

The Hottest Fantasy Writer Today!

URBAN FANTASY

Knight of Ghosts and Shadows with Ellen Guon
Elves in L.A.? It would explain a lot, wouldn't it? Eric Banyon really needed a good cause to get his life in gear—now he's got one. With an elven prince he must raise an army to fight against the evil elf lord who seeks to conquer all of California.

Summoned to Tourney with Ellen Guon
Elves in San Francisco? Where else would an elf go when L.A. got too hot? All is well there with our elf-lord, his human companion and the mage who brought them all together—until it turns out that San Francisco is doomed to fall off the face of the continent.

Born to Run with Larry Dixon
There are elves out there. And more are coming. But even elves need money to survive in the "real" world. The good elves in South Carolina, intrigued by the thrills of stock car racing, are manufacturing new, light-weight engines (with, incidentally, very little "cold" iron); the bad elves run a kiddie-porn and snuff-film ring, with occasional forays into drugs. *Children in Peril—Elves to the Rescue*. (Book I of the SERRAted Edge series.)

Wheels of Fire with Mark Shepherd
Book II of the SERRAted Edge series.

When the Bough Breaks with Holly Lisle
Book III of the SERRAted Edge series.

HIGH FANTASY
Bardic Voices: The Lark & The Wren
Rune could be one of the greatest bards of her world, but the daughter of a tavern wench can't get much in the way of formal training. So one night she goes up to play for the Ghost of Skull Hill. She'll either fiddle till dawn to prove her skill as a bard—or die trying....

The Robin and the Kestrel: Bardic Voices II
After the affairs recounted in *The Lark and The Wren*, Robin, a gypsy lass and bard, and Kestrel, semi-fugitive heir to a throne he does not want, have married their fortunes together and travel the open road, seeking their happiness where they may find it. This is their story. It is also the story of the Ghost of Skull Hill. Together, the Robin, the Kestrel, and the Ghost will foil a plot to drive all music forever from the land....

Bardic Choices: A Cast of Corbies with Josepha Sherman

If I Pay Thee Not in Gold with Piers Anthony
A new hardcover quest fantasy, co-written by the creator of the "Xanth" series. A marvelous adult fantasy that examines the war between the sexes and the ethics of desire! Watch out for bad puns!

BARD'S TALE
Based on the bestselling computer game, *The Bard's Tale.*™

Castle of Deception with Josepha Sherman

Fortress of Frost and Fire with Ru Emerson

Prison of Souls with Mark Shepherd

Also by Mercedes Lackey:

Reap the Whirlwind with C.J. Cherryh
Part of the Sword of Knowledge series.

The Ship Who Searched with Anne McCaffrey
The Ship Who Sang is not alone!

Wing Commander: Freedom Flight with Ellen Guon
Based on the bestselling computer game, *Wing Commander.*℠

Join the Mercedes Lackey national fan club! For information send an SASE (business-size) to Queen's Own, P.O. Box 43143, Upper Montclair, NJ 07043.